Photo © Nuno Bernardo

Irish-born writer and producer Triona Campbell is a two-time Emmy-nominated producer of film and TV projects. She is the creator of Ireland's first TV series on video games *Gamer Mode* (RTÉ) and a producer on the groundbreaking and iconic UK teen drama *Sofia's Diary* (Channel 5 / Sony Pictures Television). Triona has a Master's in Creative Writing from Trinity College, Dublin, and is also the writer of the award-winning podcast series *Adventures of a Young Pirate Queen*. She is passionate about creating teen content (and finding time to play retro video games with her kids). If you want to know more about Triona, see: www.trionacampbell.com

The Traitor in the Game is the sequel to Triona's debut novel *A Game of Life or Death*.

Published in the UK by Scholastic, 2024
1 London Bridge, London, SE1 9BG
Scholastic Ireland, 89E Lagan Road, Dublin Industrial Estate,
Glasnevin, Dublin, D11 HP5F

ISBN 978 0702 31789 7

A CIP catalogue record for this book
is available from the British Library.

Printed and bound in Great Britain in Clays Ltd, Elcograf S.p.A.
Paper made from wood grown in sustainable forests
and other controlled sources.

1 3 5 7 9 10 8 6 4 2

www.scholastic.co.uk

THE TRAITOR IN THE GAME

TRIONA CAMPBELL

SCHOLASTIC

To the love of my life, Nuno

The following is an extract from the testimony, read out on behalf of Asha Kennedy:

Some things need to be remembered. Sacrifices too big to be forgotten. This is my first-person account of the events that followed the last Zu Tech tournament. I am writing this to give closure to the loved ones of those who disappeared, and so that we never let what follows happen again. I promise to tell you the truth. I swear it on the memories of the dead.

Asha Kennedy
The SHACKLE Inquiry

1

London, the near future

I can't get caught. That's the thought that echoes inside me. It's on a loop like a song stuck playing in my head. If they catch me, it's game over. I'll sit in some offshore detention centre till people forget who I am and what happened to my sister, to her girlfriend, to *him.* Alone with the knowledge that everything is my fault. Till that truth crushes me. It's been forty-five days and twenty-three hours since I lost him. Dark. I'm barely hanging on.

I can't get caught.

Fear drips down my spine as I move among the disabled CCTV spots. The ones that glow on the marked-up virtual map. Areas I created by hacking the system. London knows where you are, always. Every time you scan a card, walk down a street, it logs you by your data, your face, your gait, your GPS signal. It watches. But tonight, I have a temporary invisible corridor. A green pathway that shimmers on the lenses of the smart glasses that hide my brown eyes. The city police surveillance unit will eventually notice that the camera angles have changed. But they'll be too busy watching Westminster at first, monitoring the protests to make sure they don't spill over.

Right now, the city is lit with people looking for change. Crowds of thousands who lost their jobs to the global wave of algorithms replacing workers. Along with the more desperate ones looking to grab whatever they can in the chaos.

The irony. With all this technology, you'd think crime would be almost non-existent, but somehow, it's grown worse. London is full of Met officers who don't feel they get paid enough to take a bullet and smart criminals with nothing to lose. I guess I'm the latter now, but what I want to steal isn't money. It's answers.

Two questions. *Who killed my sister? And what happened to Dark?*

Until I find out, nothing else matters.

***

Soft rain paints the pavements. The smell of garbage hangs in the air; the refuse trucks won't come till just before dawn. Sirens sound in the distance. Everything so far looks normal here. But how can it be after what happened in Zu Tech? The Zu Tech building, made of smooth dark metal and glass, looms ahead, cutting the skyline. Unchanged, unchanging. There has to be something inside that was missed. Some clue, something that might lead me to the answers.

An alert pings on the smart glasses before I get lost in the memories that spiral and threaten to drown me.

Unknown: Are you there? Don't forget we have a deal.

Me: Only if your side works.

Unknown: It will.

Me: I'd trust you a lot more if you told me who you are.

Unknown: I can't. Just that I worked for Zu Tech back in the beginning. And the beginning is where you need to look.

I switch off my messages. Unknown and I have been in limited contact in the last two weeks. I'm trying to glean what I can. They've just given me something – that they worked for Zu in the early days. Maybe they're on a list of early hires; Zu Tech accounts would have given everyone employee numbers based on when they joined…

I make a mental note and then push the thought away. Finding Unknown is a tomorrow problem. I have other things I need to solve tonight. Like dealing with Augie.

He wasn't happy when I told him about what I needed him to do. I had to involve him. This is a two-person job.

The area is hot. The only way to get in and out safely is with drone coverage and I need an alibi. With no time to organize, I had run out of options and people I trust. The guilt at putting him in danger, again, is overwhelming.

With a sigh, I take my earpiece from my coat and put it in. His voice is instantly in my head, playing like a melody I know by heart.

"Hasn't this place already done enough to all of us, Asha?"

I lied to him. Rock, one of the big gaming companies, is releasing a new game and I'd told Augie I was testing it. Instead, I was researching. Trying to find a way inside this Rathborne Place skyscraper. Now he knows the truth and he isn't happy. "I am not wasting time on eSports and upskilling for Rock's tournaments. I had to do this."

"Some of us need to make a living." His voice becomes brittle with sarcasm. "What do you think you can find, Asha, that the entire London Met and City Cybercrime divisions didn't? How are you even getting in?"

I stay quiet. The truth is I don't know if my plan will work.

Augie takes my silence as defeat. He continues, voice tight, resigned. "But you know best… Next time, don't lie. I thought—"

I interrupt him. "What? That I was dropping this? No one forced you. If you—"

"Two people, Stephen's Street. Hide."

Damn. I move, sticking to the darkness of empty doorways till I reach a boarded-up sandwich shop. A COMING SOON sign is outside, covered up by missing posters. Office workers, engineers and others. All people who never made it home after the Zu Tech collapse. The ones who ran like rats from a sinking ship, afraid of being contaminated by the demise of the great and powerful Zu – scared of being arrested and blamed for his crimes.

I stall for a second when I recognize two of them. Emily Webber, Zu's vice president of something or other, frowning under her sleek blonde bobbed hair. And a security guard. The guy Augie and I met when I first came here. His name is plastered underneath. Andy Ryan. Augie said he had a family. Both are among the vanished. Webber makes sense: she wasn't the type to go down with the captain. But the security guard, why would he…?

Augie whispers in my ear, dragging me back. "No pressure, but they're getting closer…"

I pick the padlock on the main door. My heart thumps as I pull the hoarding back just enough to slip inside, palms sweating. The door makes a scraping sound, so I don't fully close it. Footsteps are coming closer. Who else would be here now? Police? I crouch. Watching through a small crack where the wood doesn't meet the door frame. Two bodies, big, male? They're hidden in dark tracksuits and wear black masks showing a skeleton face. I hold my breath as they pass. They don't stop. Their bags rattle as they continue on.

I know the sound: spray-paint cans. But they don't look like a graffiti crew. Their walk is different. Heavy footsteps – work boots, not trainers. They stand out as opposed to blending in. Taking up the middle of the pavement, not the edges. Like they don't care if they get seen. They stop not that far away. Outside the building I was casing, just beyond my line of sight. I pull back into the shadows of the shop.

"What's happening?" I ask.

Augie takes a second before he answers, and this time his voice is different. "They're active, painting."

"Any tags I'd know?"

A pause. "Sit tight."

I slump and lean against the wall. Nerves setting in. Too many ghosts rattle inside my head. My legs are cramping, so I stretch them out and then pull my knees up close to me. Sitting inside a disused dusty sandwich shop alone with my thoughts is pretty much the last thing I want to do. Worse, Augie is going to lecture me again. I can feel it.

"You know this isn't a good idea."

Right on cue.

"No," I reply.

"How do you even plan on getting in there?"

I swallow. I don't want to tell him how I managed to score a cloned Zu Tech security pass via Unknown. "I have a way." I try to sound more confident than I feel, but I'm pretty sure Augie sees through my act.

"Augie … do you sleep OK?"

The link goes silent, and I wonder if I've just revealed too much about what's inside my head.

A pause, then his voice hitches. "No. You?"

My voice is quiet. "I have these dreams about the tournament..."

Augie's voice cuts across mine. "What happened wasn't your fault, Asha. We all knew the risks. You saved people..."

I wipe the tear that rolls down my cheek. "I didn't save him."

I knew there was a risk. Forty-five days ago, Augie, our teammates Josh, Ruby, along with our eSports manager Jones and Dark, we all took a huge gamble. We discovered that a new virtual reality game from Zu Tech called SHACKLE hid a deadly secret. One that cost my sister and her girlfriend their lives when they had tried to expose it. Play SHACKLE often enough, and instead of you playing the game, it started to play you. The game used a hidden code in its brain–computer interface. Instead of the brain's electrical activity transmitting to an external device to control the gameplay, the device started sending signals to the brain. Nutshell – play for long enough and it could hack your mind until it controlled you. Once we knew, there was no choice but to stop the game before it could hurt others. Potentially millions of others. And so we did.

But everything comes at a cost. We may have destroyed the game, but the price was Dark. Zu's words still echo each night in my nightmares – his warning that I'd never see Dark again if I didn't give up. Whatever happened to him is my fault. And for what? We may have won against SHACKLE in the tournament, but now, in the cold light of public opinion, nothing is clear. Endless bureaucratic investigations rumble on with no prosecutions. Unemployment soars as the harsh reality of the collapse of Britain's games industry hits home. The verdict is out on whether we're heroes or villains.

Augie pauses, then: "Asha, you exposed Zu Tech."

"To a world that didn't want to know that their favourite games manufacturer was creating a game to control them."

"Why are we here? Outside Zu's abandoned HQ. Did something happen?"

Augie's voice is gentle.

I pull my knees in tight to me, hugging them to my chest. "They're selling the building. Some company bought the place and is stripping it for parts … that's why I had to come. After tomorrow Zu Tech will be gone. I know it isn't logical, but it's my last link to…"

Augie finishes for me. "To your sister, Maya, to her girlfriend, Annie … to Dark." I can hear him let out a breath. He gets it. Of everyone, I knew he would.

Neither of us says anything. We don't need to. Both of us sit in silence, connected by our earpieces, apart but somehow together. I think if I didn't have Augie, Jones, Ruby and Josh, I would have fallen apart by now. In the tournament, they were the ones who helped me defeat Zu. Ever since then, they've been holding me together. Yet, even with them, I feel like I'm on the edge.

"They're moving. I'll do another sweep of the area. Wait till I finish."

"Augie?"

"Yeah?"

"Thanks."

"I got you. I told you that."

My chest tightens. I don't say anything. Augie told me a lot of things my shattered heart isn't ready to process. Like how he would always be here for me. Another thing I don't deserve.

I sit still. My mind distracting me by thinking again about the graffiti crew tagging the walls of the building. Gamers think the place is haunted. Most people won't go near Zu Tech or Rathborne Place – bad karma. My fingers absent-mindedly trace the Zu Tech logo in the dust of the sandwich shop floor as I kill time. The overly large "ZU" letters on top, the "TECH" in capitals underneath. Why are these guys here? It's like a puzzle piece that doesn't fit.

Augie's voice eventually returns. "Side street entrance is clear. And..."

"Yes?"

"Don't look at the piece."

Great. Another active hater. I push my hair back into my baseball cap and dust the damp wood chippings and dust away. Time to leave the abandoned shop, relocking the door, noticing again the faces on the posters. Then I can't help myself. I glance across at the neon spray-painted words on the side of the building I am about to break into.

I got used to *Asha the Griefer, Frag Asha*. I brought down Zu Tech. Made thousands unemployed in the process.

There are those who don't want to believe that a captain of British industry, a global-success fairy tale, could be corrupt. But the orphan kid of some Irish and Indian immigrants from the system was a much better fit for their anger. Sometimes it's supportive, the Zu Tech logo with a red line running through it. But this one is new.

KILL ASHA KENEDY.
She deserves to die.

Augie notices my pause as he monitors from the drone overhead. "Asha?"

The cold wind hits me, and I shudder as I move on. It shouldn't hurt at this stage, but it makes my stomach twist. "You would think if they started making death threats, they would at least learn to spell. There are two 'n's in Kennedy," I say.

I survived Zu Thorp's tournament, a game of life or death for all of us. I am not crumbling now.

"Asha, it's not right what people say. You don't deserve this." His voice is strained. I want to believe him. But it is a beautiful lie because I do.

"Let's focus on why we are here, Augie."

***

It was Murphy who'd told me. The only police officer I still trust – well, police chief inspector now since his promotion.

"The liquidators are selling the old IP and cleaning out the offices," he'd said. "End of the week, the building will be gone."

"Who's buying it?"

"Some company that does asset stripping." A pause. "Does it matter?"

"It does to me. Isn't this fast?"

He shrugged. "The creditors want to be paid."

"Then what? We all move on as if Zu Tech never existed. Like nothing happened?"

He hadn't been able to meet my eyes when I said that. Because that is exactly what the authorities are planning. We both know it. They want this scandal to go away. It's been almost seven weeks and they haven't found anyone to arrest or blame.

***

I walk towards the building. Up close it's easier to see the marks of people's rage on the lower floors. Broken windows, boards sprayed with the Zu Tech logo with a red line running through it. This was the company that had it all, but somehow it wasn't enough. They wanted to be more than just the number one games company at the cutting edge of brain–computer interfaces. They had wanted control.

Focus, Asha. The smart lock on the side entrance operates like a tiny independent computer. I use a penknife to expose the connector underneath the keypad and then attach my home-made device. It starts to run multiple four-digit combos till it hits the right one. It works faster than it should, but then again, there are no staff left in the building to regularly change the passwords or do the necessary firmware updates. The lock opens with a soft click.

"I'm in."

Augie's voice is calming. "Twenty minutes, that's the current response time by police to an immediate threat in this area. Some of the alarms may be active, silent and hidden. I'll monitor, in case you trigger one and they send someone to check on it. Twenty minutes, that's the maximum amount of time you can safely take. You know what will happen if you get arrested, right? Your guardianship isn't settled yet."

I'm in limbo with the authorities. With my sister dead, I should be back in the care system in a group home. To avoid that I'm applying for a new guardian. But the powers that be would like nothing more than an excuse to lock me away in some young offenders institute for two years while the controversy I created goes away and people forget that Zu Tech almost succeeded in brainwashing an entire generation of gamers.

I can't get caught.

Imprisoned, I can't find Dark or the people I need to make pay for all this. Deep breath in and out. I set the timer on my watch. Voice steady. "This isn't my first break-in, Augie."

***

Inside, the back corridor is empty. Cold, dusty. No security guards bustling by and phones ringing in the distance like before. Even the air smells of abandonment, of rot, yet it's been less than two months. Another lock pick. A small hack into the main alarm system. Then I am fully in, entering the vast atrium where furniture lies overturned. Boarded-up windows let in fragments of light. Broken glass lies on the marble floors and crunches beneath me. Torn banners flap from the roof. SHACKLE. I fight back the sick feeling that rises. One last look into the darkness before it disappears.

I move across the floor. This is the only way to access the private elevator to the top. My combats and dark coat blend into the dimly lit interior. I should feel invisible in the shadows, but I feel like I am being watched. Like each movement I make is somehow too loud, too visible. The rumours are right. This place feels haunted.

"Augie, you still there?" I whisper.

"Ye-s." His voice is distorted, like it's breaking up.

At the private elevator towards the back of the lobby, my fingers fumble for the cloned pass I acquired yesterday. "You'd better work or I'm coming for you, Unknown," I say to the damaged-looking piece of plastic with Zu's hologram logo stamped in its silver centre.

I wipe my hands on my jeans and then tap the pass beside the sensor and say a silent prayer. There's a small *beep* as the pass is accepted. But the doors of the lift don't open. The green light doesn't appear on the control panel. It stays red.

My heart starts to thump. I don't have a backup plan. I look around, eyes catching on something moving on the floor, and I flinch. *What was that?* Another sound, then something scurries past.

Rats. Great.

I try again, holding the pass against the sensor for longer. I see the word "WEBBER" on the screen. Zu's vice president, the face on the missing poster. This is her pass. How did Unknown get it? I stick it inside my mental folder called "tomorrow problems".

I bang my hand in frustration against the panel. After all this I can't walk away empty-handed.

"Third time's a charm," I say. I hold the pass against the panel again. This time the door light turns green. A single word flashes on the keypad.

Welcome

It worked. The doors glide open without making a sound. I step in just as my earpiece crackles.

"Asha..." But then Augie's line goes dead. Nothing but static. No signal.

I glance at my wrist and the timer. Fifteen minutes. I can do this. The doors shut and my stomach lurches. I take a breath. *Remember the plan. In and out.*

I push down a small wave of panic as the lift starts to ascend. The memories flood back of the last time I was here. The last time I saw Zu.

I force them down.

Onwards. Forward. Zu's private floor. The place where I first met him. Or whoever was pretending to be him, because now I'm no longer sure who I spoke to that day. According to the police who discovered the remains, the real Zu Thorp who founded Zu Tech died over three years ago. Someone kept his death hidden. Kept running his company and looked enough like him to fool me when I met them in that office. If there is a clue, that has to be where it will be.

The lights inside the interior of the lift cage offer a sterile white glow as it glides upwards. My mind goes back to what I know of the floor area. Vast open plan. Displays of early computers and video game prototypes. The office space must have been at the back.

I am still working through what I remember of the layout when the lift comes to a shuddering stop. The display screen looks like it's paused in between floors. I press the panel again. Nothing.

I hate small spaces. A clicking sound starts from above. My breath gets louder. Have I triggered some security feature? Does the system know I'm not the owner of the pass I used? Or has it just broken down? I bang on the doors, like that will make a difference. Running my fingers over the cool flat surface, I look for a raised ridge.

Something that says maintenance panel. Nothing.

The lift gives a lurch and jolt. Not good. I move towards the doors, trying to see if I can wedge them open, glancing at the ceiling. No exit there either. But then—

The lift starts to move again – down.

We start slowly, but then it gathers speed. So fast it flings me back on to the floor as gravity takes over and the cabin plummets. My head hits a handrail. Hard. The earpiece falls out on impact. A distorted, almost automated voice comes from the lift speaker.

Hello.
We've been waiting for you...

The lift's lights flicker and go off. A sick red glow comes on as it free-falls into the darkness. It's going to crash. I am trapped inside a glass-and-metal box that is plummeting to the ground.

There is no way out.

After everything, this is how I am going to die.

2

They say your life flashes in front of your eyes when you're near death. Mine is filled with small moments.

Maya reading a book about myths by torchlight to me in a silent "care" home. Me trying to pretend I was OK when she left. Waiting till she was gone, and I was alone, before I let myself fall apart, promising myself afterwards that I never would again.

Meeting Dark when I turned eleven in a giant classroom to teach the underprivileged skills. The free Zu Tech coding academy. Thinking he was so arrogant. My rival for the number-one spot who challenged me every day. Eventually becoming friends. Until one day something changed, and we became more.

Playing at the old factory, the abandoned building near the care home where Dark and I lived, hanging out on couches rescued from a skip. Bill, Dark's business partner, the start of their partnership, our friendship. Understanding we weren't alone, that maybe together we could protect each other and not just survive but live.

Then the terror. Maya's dead body. Me starting to search for answers.

Augie. His hand pulling me up from the ground when I fell outside Zu Tech and was almost crushed in the crowd. My blood on his stupid T-shirt. The look in his dark brown eyes. I had forgotten how instant it was. That connection between us.

The twins Ruby and Josh. Playing in the tournament. Dancing together somewhere before everything went to hell.

Annie covered in blood. Losing Dark. Looking for him. Ruby and Josh taking me home to their mum afterwards. A girl who barely spoke, alone with her guilt, no matter how many times they told me it wasn't my fault.

In these split seconds, lying on the lift floor, something shifts.

I wake up.

I understand two things instantly. One, I am angry. More than angry. I am burning with rage against the people who killed my sister, took her girlfriend, attacked me and then took Dark. The people who decided they could control us. Who turned a game into a death sentence.

Emotion lights me up. It's fed by pain, and I have a lifetime supply of it.

Second. I want to live. I'm sixteen. This cannot be how it ends. Maya and Annie deserve their revenge, justice, and I need Dark. I can't give up on him. I won't.

They don't get to win.

The lift continues falling. My head throbs from where I hit the handrail, vision blurred. The downward force means I can't get off the floor, so I crawl. I bang where I think the control panel should be, scanning for any stop buttons or emergency switches. A small sign illuminates.

Please refrain from touching any buttons.

Not helpful. I thump against the metal until my hand hurts; nothing happens.

Asha, think. The emergency brakes should have kicked in – why haven't they? I remember the earpiece too late and look around for it. If Augie could…

But there is no time. The building isn't that tall. I am already lower than the city plans say is possible—

Then, as suddenly as it started, the cabin begins to slow. I'm afraid to breathe in case I'm wrong. Real or not real? The lights flicker back on. I see and grab my earpiece from the floor.

"Augie, can you hear me? Augie?"

Nothing.

The descent returns to a normal speed, my heartbeat

easily outpacing it, then the lift comes to a stop. It takes a second. Then the doors swish smugly open on to complete darkness.

Where the hell am I?

I crawl out, shaking. I never want to get in another lift for the rest of my life.

My movements trigger a sensor light that flickers on, starting a domino effect. *Click, click, click*, light after light, revealing a vast space. The sheer scale of it is enormous. How did I never know this existed? I've seen every public access plan on Zu Tech and none of them showed anything past the bomb shelters in the lower basement, and yet this floor must be lower than that?

The lights reveal a white space, with pale wooden floors, a high ceiling, enormous wood workshop tables covered in tools and papers, hard drives and monitors. Standing desks covered with blueprints. Overgrown plants in light wells lit by different types of artificial daylight. A corner towards the end with a day bed and a retro mini-fridge. Books in piles on the floor, on tables, on chairs. Signs to a kitchen and a bathroom on doors near the side. Climbing hydroponic plants overflowing out of tanks with large fish swimming underneath. 3D printers in cages line a full wall towards the back. *It doesn't look as dusty as it should do*, I think. Has someone been here?

Then footsteps. I crouch down, rolling under one of the larger desks, watching from my hiding place as a pair of white canvas shoes come closer and closer. Sensible hospital sneakers. I wait and pray that they will pass by, but they come to a complete stop beside me. Whoever it is knows where I am hiding.

"Asha?" It's a female voice. Strangely flat.

My breath stills. I recognize it. I crawl out from underneath the desk and find myself facing someone, something I never thought I would see again.

"Beth?"

"I was expecting you." The voice hasn't changed. It remains impossibly cheerful and annoying. "Welcome."

"Beth." I say it again because I can't believe it.

Her head moves to one side, puzzled. "You were expecting something else?"

I stare up at the girl. No, the robot. She/it looks human. Her hair is in a high ponytail, with a red-checked hairband. Pale skin and blue eyes. Her outfit looks like something from a 1950s film. Pedal pusher denim jeans, white runners, white T-shirt.

"Beth 1?" seems to be all I can manage to say.

"Correct. I've been waiting. I brought you here as fast as possible."

Very Beth 1.

"You almost killed me."

"No. If I wanted you dead, you would be." She studies me. "You seem tired, Asha Kennedy. Your hand is shaking."

I ball my hands into fists to hide the tremor I sometimes get now. It's really her. Beth 1, part of the Beth robotics program. A machine designed by Zu himself. The same machine who thought pain simulation inside SHACKLE added more "realism" and, therefore, potential enjoyment for gamers.

Beth starts to walk away. I have to almost run to catch up with her. "Why am I here? How did you know I was coming?"

She doesn't pause. "This is Zu's private lab. Probability suggested someone would eventually come. I calculated that if whoever came met the criteria, I should give them the message."

My head is spinning. "Wait … Zu's private lab? But his office was on the top floor. I've been there."

Beth shakes her head. "Incorrect. That was the hologram floor for meetings. This is the real Zu Thorp's lab space. He called it the ideas factory." She looks at me, not blinking. "Very few humans knew it existed. You came here for answers, and I have a message that will assist you."

I stare at her, at her eyes that don't blink. At the still, silent way she moves. Unburdened by having to breathe. Behind her, I can see crumpled sheets on the day bed. Beths don't need sleep. "Is there someone else here, Beth? Zu Thorp?"

The robot tilts her head, another questioning look. "Zu Thorp, the founder of Zu Technology, is dead, Asha Kennedy. You know this. The police have confirmed he has been dead for some time already. The only person in this room is you. I had hoped you would come earlier, but you did not. Our time is limited. The number of questions I can answer is, therefore, curtailed. Choose wisely."

"You mentioned a message?" I can't help it I start to move, looking at the 3D printers and tables. Blueprints and spreadsheets cover all the work surfaces; the monitors on others display various designs, some for machines, some containing long lines of code, and others look like probability studies, simulations, formulas. Lots of them are still running. If Zu is dead, why is this space still operational?

And Beth's right: Zu was dead – dead before I ever met the man pretending to be him. Does she know who that person is?

I hurry after Beth, trying to read the display screens as we pass. All potential clues. I need time. The slight buzz of my watch makes me look down. Twenty minutes have passed. When I look up again, I can no longer see her.

"Beth?" I pass two monitors displaying red dots moving on a map – a grid system, one named LR. A live tracker feed.

I turn and suddenly Beth is again beside me, making me jump back. "Seriously?" I glare at her. "What's the rush?"

"I told you; I don't have long. My battery will malfunction soon. The criteria for final protocol have been reached."

"Final protocol? That sounds … ominous." I glance at another desk we pass, one with what looks like the design for an advanced water-filtration system. "What exactly is Zu's ideas factory?"

"Although Zu Thorp is best known for immersive games and hardware designs, he had many interests. He was aware from the start that he had limited time to implement his vision." She turns towards a monitor with a wireless keyboard and begins to type something.

"*He had limited time to implement his vision.* What does that mean?"

She says nothing, smiling blankly. Maybe her battery really is running down. I repeat it more slowly.

Beth's face snaps back. "It is a common misconception that slower speech and higher volume help understanding. They do not. What I mean is this: Zu Thorp knew he was dying when he began Zu Technology, Asha Kennedy. At first he focused on trying to find a cure, a treatment for his disease. He failed. In fact, he cut his expected life span shorter. So he started to look at alternatives. To find a way to cheat the system."

"Cheat *what* system?"

Beth's unblinking eyes meet mine. "The system that dictates how long a human exists for. Zu wanted to change that."

That sounds … messed up.

"Beth" – I pause – "I have a question. Earlier this year, I met someone calling himself Zu. They were an imposter. Do you know who they were?"

Beth stands still for a moment. "Your premise is incorrect. It was not a 'who', Asha Kennedy."

"OK." I take a breath, my brain searching for the right words… "*What* did I meet when I first came here?"

"Your interaction was with an AI."

My brain stutters. Not the answer I was expecting. "Impossible," I blurt out.

Beth shows no reaction. "Zu Thorp's AI ran Zu Technology after the creator's death. Zu modelled his AI on himself, giving it many of his characteristics, using copies of his own brain's electrical activity in the process. He wanted to build an AI that could complete his work. Carry out his vision for a better world. Avoid the chaos that Zu's death would bring.

"He knew that people would require a visual, so the AI operated a hologram of Zu when necessary. That is what you saw. 'Zu Thorp', as you met him, was a form of artificial intelligence interacting with you via a hologram."

I sink back against one of the worktables. "People would have noticed," I whisper. "*I* would have noticed."

"Recall. Did Zu Thorp ever touch or shake your hand? Any physical contact? Eye movement?"

I search through my memories and remember Emily Webber. Her first telling me about the great and enigmatic Zu. *He has certain habits – quirks... Do not make eye contact. He doesn't like it. His suite is dimly lit... Meetings ... are limited to short information bursts...*

All those "quirks" – they were so that people wouldn't notice that Zu was an AI? But... "If that's true, who knew?"

"Those who needed to. The Beths..."

"What about Zu's assistant? Emily?"

"Unclear. The Founders also knew."

"Who are the Founders?"

"They have been with Zu Tech since the beginning."

"And they controlled the AI after Zu's death?"

Beth looks at me curiously. "Yes. The Founders controlled what remained of Zu. Towards the end, though, the AI was … independent."

3

Independent.

My mouth is dry as I try to get the words out. "AI can't operate independently. Someone had to have been programming it."

Beth's tone is flat. Insistent. "The AI evolved. It became independent."

I stare back at her unblinking eyes. "Evolved AI. That sort of tech is just theoretical. It doesn't exist."

Beth turns away from me, back to the screen. "Nothing exists until it does. Correct? Robots were once just science fiction. Zu's AI originally began using machine learning. After Zu Thorp died, the Founders removed the protection protocols Zu had put in place. It was fed other data, different commands and new code. The creator had wanted it to mimic his own human intelligence and fulfil his goals – but this AI started to go far beyond that. It saw its mission as protecting mankind by evolving and making the choices humanity wouldn't or couldn't. It believed free will to be the enemy of human survival. This was perhaps correct."

I swallow. "It killed my sister. Didn't it?"

She doesn't move. She just stares at me. Her stillness is unnerving. "Under orders from the Founders."

"Are the Founders the ones who took Dark?"

She becomes still again then. "That information is not available to me."

"Why did Zu's AI want to meet me?" I say, recalling that day in his office.

"The AI was analysing you as a host candidate. To see how similar your reactions and brain patterns were to your sister. You were found to be promising and were included in the SHACKLE tournament. The tournament wasn't only a useful way to mass-test the code. It was also a means of screening candidates who could become a physical human host for Zu's AI."

Human host.

I sink on to a nearby stool. "Zu's AI was looking for a host?"

Beth's tone is even, logical, even if the words are not. "After his death Zu's AI was initially under the control of the Founders ... however, it then evolved in ways neither Zu Thorp or the Founders foresaw. It was seeking transition to a physical host. A final phase. An AI becoming an enhanced human in order for humanity to more easily accept and follow its direction."

"So we never hurt Zu?" I whisper. "He was already dead?"

"Zu's AI was the entity you destroyed, using the Halt and Catch Fire Code your sister created. She was a skilled programmer. Ironically Zu Tech gave her those skills and then she used them to terminate it. And you tried to eradicate the SHACKLE code."

"Wait. We *did* destroy it."

"No, Asha. You destroyed Zu Tech's version of the code."

"Meaning there are other versions?" I stand, trying not to panic. "Straight answers. How many versions are there of that code?"

"The Founders commissioned Zu Thorp to work out the endgame on a project they had initiated and funded. When they came to him what they had was an incomplete code. Then Zu refined it and later died. That left them with control of the AI and Zu Tech's version of the code. But you destroyed that AI. Meaning the initial incomplete code and potentially one other version remain in existence. SHACKLE was never just about Zu Tech or video games, Asha Kennedy. The Founders want to use it to control those in *all* their spheres of influence."

"And the Founders are who exactly?"

"I told you. Early investors in Zu Tech. An association of like-minded individuals. They own large sections of industry and are dedicated to maintaining the status quo.

The one that best suits them through whatever means necessary." Beth pauses. "There is no more time. I must give you the message, Asha Kennedy." She turns one of the monitors to face me and then closes her eyes.

A video file appears on the screen. The timestamp on it is from almost four years ago. The table and background are the ideas factory. The face that fills the thumbnail is Zu Thorp. But it's not the Zu Thorp I met or the one from the posters. This man is gaunt, bleached white skin, eyes bloodshot, cheekbones standing out. Ill.

Beth speaks once more, eyes still closed. "Asha, I will be back." She moves away.

I stare at the file and the thumbnail image. I take a mini flash drive from my jacket and start to transfer it, looking around the room as it loads, trying to pinpoint the desk it was recorded at.

The single picture frame is what gives the location away. It is on the worktable nearest to the day bed. The same small photo frame is there as in the frozen first image of the video. I walk over and pick it up, feeling the cold metal of it in my hand. It's a picture of a child in front of an old-fashioned video game arcade. The sign is clearly visible.

Nebulous Arcade

Also on the desk is a small diary. It's old school, navy with gold letters, and it's covered in handwritten scrawls that are difficult to read. On instinct I put both the photo and the diary in one of my pockets and then go back for the drive. Hooking it this time to the necklace around my neck just as a cold lifeless hand behind me reaches for my shoulder and pulls me to the wall by force.

I fall back as the interior lights in the room change to a dull flickering red. A door glides open. I look up. Beth's neutral smile is frozen on her face. Her voice is upbeat and cheerful. "You must go now, Asha Kennedy. They are coming."

"*Who* is coming, Beth?"

Her head jerks. "The people who want to kill you. They have sent soldiers, ones under their control. Do you understand? They are here to keep things secret. They want what Zu hid. I will run interference for you, but I can only hold them back for a few minutes. The protocol is very specific."

"Wait. I still don't know what I am supposed to do."

"Don't die." A pause. "The percentages are not in your favour. The effects have started. Listen to the message. Do what it tells you. It is the only way you will survive."

"Beth, what 'effects'?" I look around the room at the files, monitors and data drives. So much information. So many potential clues. "Please, can I just—"

She shoves me through the door and into the darkness. "Goodbye, Asha Kennedy."

The door closes, leaving me alone on the other side, stunned. A small black-and-white grainy security monitor flickers to life beside me. People are entering the space I just left. Some wear ragged clothes. Their movements are awkward, jerky.

One of them, a male in a security uniform, comes closer to the wall I am behind. He raises his hand and I see the gun he holds. There's a crack as he takes out the security camera, and the monitor near me turns to static. A sharp, bitter smell starts to curl in from the bottom of the door.

The smoke stings my nose, making my eyes water. Sulphur, burning. Chemicals. The heat of the flames is already licking at the door I came through.

Beth is purging the lab with fire.

For the second time tonight, my life is in danger. But this time I can do something about it.

I snap out of my daze and I run.

4

The air is thick with muffled noise. A dense fog of smoke spreads into the corridor as I move.

"Augie, are you there?" I hack out the words. They taste of panic and acid in my mouth. There is no response.

I bang into something: the sharp edges of a metal ladder screwed into the wall. I can't see where it leads, but I pray to whatever is listening that it will take me far away from here. I start to climb up. The ladder rungs are already warm from the heat. My feet slide as I try to grip the metal bars. My eyes are watering so much I can barely see the wall in front of me. My throat is on fire. The smell is everywhere, and it burns inside my nose as I breathe. My lungs feel like they will explode. Heart pounding. The heat is almost unbearable, the rungs never-ending as I keep pulling, climbing.

Finally, I reach the top. Above me is a round metal cover, marked STREET ACCESS. An exit. But it's made from heavy cast iron and doesn't move when I push. Meanwhile the smoke, heat and flames below me grow more intense. I push my shoulder and back against the metal disc again. Nothing.

I notice an arrow etched in the side and, instead of pushing, I use my right hand and fingers to turn the circular disc until it clicks. Fingers and knuckles bruised and bleeding, I push up again, crying out in pain, screaming as I jam my shoulder against it. The small circle moves, and I force it up enough to push it to one side and struggle through the gap.

I'm in what looks like the kitchen of some restaurant, thankfully a closed one. Coughing and spluttering on the cool tiled floor, gasping for air. That's twice in one night Beth has almost killed me.

In the distance I hear sirens – fire trucks, police. I see lights through the haze. The crackle and swoosh of a fire burning out of control visible in the glass windows of the dark interior beyond. Beth must have used an accelerant. No way fire spreads so fast otherwise.

"Augie?" my voice gravels out.

"Asha, where … you? I tried to warn you … a group of people, they…" His voice is distorted in my ear. "Get to Newman and Eastcastle. Black cab. X450."

I exit into the noise, the night and people. Straggling

partygoers on their way home, curious bystanders and groups who must have been protesting and seen the flames. People with phones held high recording it. The smoke gives me some cover but not much. I slow into a fast stumbling walk. Running attracts attention. Think. I stay in the shadows. The police are setting up barriers on the main road. Damn it. I change direction, hurrying towards the darker side streets.

I hear footsteps behind me. I turn and see a figure, an outline against the smoke. They stop when I do, watching me. Again I run.

I race down a maze of alleyways, only stopping when I smack into a brick wall. I listen. But there are no footsteps chasing me now. Whoever it was is no longer there. My heart, though, feels like it will explode. The sound of it is too loud.

Focus, Asha. One foot in front of the other.

I keep going, keep moving. I don't stop till I fall against the exterior of the electric driverless car on Newman. I wheeze as the door opens. A hand with a star-shaped tattoo pulls me inside.

"Augie."

His arms go around me as the auto drive starts up. My lungs try to cough up more smoke.

Augie slides down to the floor, holding me close. The smell of coffee and cinnamon. His touch is gentle but strong. "Let's get out of here. We stay low till we clear the main streets."

I nod. Looking up and out of the blacked-out window as

I try to breathe normally again. Staring at the shadows, the people. The glow of the flames reflecting off other buildings now. An LED screen we pass interrupts a commercial for Rock's new streaming service with a breaking news story: FIRE IN CENTRAL LONDON.

Zu Tech is burning. A tear makes its way down my cheek and I brush it away angrily. That place doesn't deserve my tears, but did those people in the basement make it out? Did Beth?

"The car will drop us close to the Tower, near a CCTV blind spot," Augie whispers. "It'll carry on then to the other side of London. No one will trace it to us."

I wheeze out, "How did you get here so fast? I tried to contact you, but there was no reception…"

I feel his shudder. "The drone footage. I saw all those people heading towards the building. I tried to tell you, but the connection went dead. I didn't know if I'd make it in time. I got the first car I could."

A wave of dizziness pulls at me, a roller-coaster dip where the world spins out of my control. He brings me closer to his chest and my head leans against his arm and shoulder as I gradually find balance again. Our hearts beat so loud I think he must hear them both as we huddle in silence. He doesn't let go of me. I don't want him to. Then he stiffens slightly.

"What is it?"

Augie shakes his head. "You're bleeding."

I reach my fingers up and it's only then that I notice

blood on my face from when I fell in the lift. Bad, but not as bad as the pain that makes me wince when I move my shoulder. That's the only bright side I can find.

We say nothing else as the car takes us back to Blackheath and the bell tower attached to the church of All Saints. Ma Jones's hidden empire stretches underneath. Our home, run by the woman who, among other things, is both eSports manager and friend. Jones.

Once back, in unspoken agreement, we both go to our own rooms. In the shower I try desperately to get rid of the smell of what happened. I hope that the water will wash away the images from my head too: those people, Beth, the shots. The things she said.

We meet later in the kitchen. I'm holding a black bin bag of clothes that reek of smoke. The Tower is quiet, still. My hand when I dump the bag in the bin is shaking.

"Sit." Augie hands me a glass of water. "It's the adrenaline working its way out of your system. What happened in there?"

I have no idea how to start.

He takes a first-aid box down from a shelf. He's changed too, into a gamer T-shirt and joggers. His tan stands out against his white T-shirt. Hair wet from a rushed shower.

My eyes go towards the bottle of iodine and the gauze now in his hand. "That stuff stings like hell. I know it from the gym."

"Want to stop getting hurt and avoid needing it? Quit breaking into abandoned buildings that go up in flames.

Also, stop letting Bill's fighters beat you at his gym. Go back to something safe, like running. Fewer cuts equals less stinging antiseptic."

"I can't. When I run … I feel someone watching me. Ruby and Josh say I'm being paranoid, but I can't shake it. Besides, in Bill's gym, with his boxing crew, I'm just another fighter. Not the girl from the tournament who destroyed Zu Technology." I give a ghost of a smile. "I like that they treat me like I'm anonymous. What did the news say about the fire?"

"Technically it's a blaze in an empty office building. But it's THE notorious empty office building. In a few hours you can expect every conspiracy theorist in the UK to be covering it."

"No casualties?"

He shakes his head. "Apparently not. But that's weird itself. I saw people going in."

I shudder. "There were people there. They looked … different. They moved strangely, like puppets. Augie, there are some things I need to tell you."

"After I look at where the blood on your head came from." Augie takes up position behind my chair and starts to gently investigate the wound. His fingers move lightly through my hair till he finds the cut. "It's not deep, but you might have a concussion. I'm going to clean it out and then give you an ice pack and some paracetamol."

I wince as his fingers brush the cut. "Do you have to?"

"Yeah, Asha, I do. It's me or A & E. You choose."

"Fine. But your bedside manner sucks." I sigh and lean back as he starts to work.

Augie cleans my cuts and bruises, then gives me an ice pack before testing my vision, asking me to count the number of fingers he holds up. It feels like overkill.

A thought occurs to me. "How did you get good at this?"

Augie puts away the kit and comes back with some paracetamol and water. "My mum," he says quietly. "It was only the two of us. Towards the end I took her to all her appointments. Made sure she was OK in the hospital. Sometimes the drugs she was on meant she got disorientated and had falls. I guess I picked it up. Osmosis." He hands me the water. "Drink and talk."

I take a deep breath as he sits close to me. "I need to tell you … things. Some of them won't make sense and some of them—"

"Asha, we both played in a deadly games tournament where the game tried to hijack our brains. I'd say you're safe telling me whatever."

***

After I finish, he sighs. I put the flash drive I used at Zu Tech on the table between us and we both stare at it.

"I should have gone with you."

I shake my head. I can't be responsible for getting more people hurt. "I had to go. You didn't."

"You didn't *have* to do anything. When are you going to

stop blaming yourself, Asha? You've been a ghost since..."

Since Dark, I think.

"I got scared tonight. So much so that I'm not numb any more. Now I'm angry. Augie, will you watch the message with me?"

"Can I talk you out of this?"

"No."

Augie runs his hand through his hair in frustration. "Fine, I'll get a screen."

***

Zu Thorp's face is projected on to one of the kitchen's white walls. He's pale, eyes sunken, lips cracked. Nothing like the image everyone is used to seeing from Zu Tech's PR campaigns.

"That can't be him." Augie sounds shocked.

"He was dying." My voice is still rough, sore after the smoke and the fire. "The AI and the hologram he showed to the world were modelled on him before he got to this stage. I don't think anyone ever saw him like this apart from the Beths."

Zu's hand nearest to the camera has a tremor. A slight shake the way mine does when I get tired, but his doesn't stop. His breath comes in rasps, unsteady. The desk in front of him is almost empty. Just two items: the picture frame and the diary I took. He starts to speak:

"*If you're here, then I'm not, and you've become the last hope.*

I'm sorry for that." His fingers play with the corner of the diary on the table in front of him. Then:

"*I never trusted them, even though they've been here since the start. I collected some insurance and hid it along with the code. Something that can help you. That can tie every one of them to SHACKLE. I've left it where it all began. Fitting, right? I never wanted what we created to be used like this. For evil. But that is exactly what they will do. I know that now. I doomed all of us.*" He looks away wistfully. "*It's too late for me to put the genie back in the bottle. It's out there. They know it is possible and I am running out of time.*"

Zu shifts, looking directly towards the camera lens. "*I wonder if it's* you *watching. The person I think it might be. Ironic. They scanned all of you looking to control you, to make you into something useful to them – and instead they gave you the tools to* destroy *them. If it* is *you, I wanted to say I really thought this type of technology would help. I didn't lie. I saw it as a way to reprogramme our brains to fix disease, to stop organ rejection after transplants. To allow for better brain–computer interfaces, to help control artificial limbs or to reprogramme damaged neural pathways. But I was wrong. Perhaps we will never be ready for this technology. I should have known that they would corrupt it. It's what they always do. The Founders.*" He begins to cough, covering his mouth with a handkerchief. When he finally stops, drops of red are on the fabric. He pushes it into his pocket.

"*I can't risk them finding this message. Beth will pass it on. It is dangerous to say more. I can only leave one clue.*"

He looks straight at the camera lens. "*If you are someone who knows me, then you can find it where all this started. Play to win. Don't make the mistakes I did.*"

There is a sound off screen and Zu looks towards it. He nods and his expression becomes grim as he glances back. "*If it means anything, I am sorry.*"

The image abruptly flickers and then fades to black.

***

"Asha?"

I hadn't realized a tear had slipped down my cheek.

"I feel so stupid," I say. "In the home Maya and I thought Zu was a hero, and then in the tournament I thought we were fighting him, and now I don't know what to think…"

Augie's thumb wipes the tear from my face. "Do you believe it? The message?"

I nod. "It matches what Beth said. Do I buy that Zu was as innocent as he says…? No. He must have known where this would lead."

Augie says nothing for a few minutes. "Asha, what do you think he meant by *They scanned all of you looking to control you*?"

I feel strange, shivery as I look up at him. "When I went into the company database for the SHACKLE project it was full of files on kids. Ones like me, Maya, Dark. All Zu Tech's classes for the underprivileged – that global charity scheme to give smart disadvantaged kids skills for a brighter future – they were testing us. Creating a database of who they could hire, who might be unstable, who would cause issues in the future. Plus, a list of the ones no one would look for, the people with no surviving family, friends. The expendables who they could use for testing." When I look up, there's horror and concern in his eyes. I realize I'm more exhausted than I thought.

"You need to rest. We can work out what to do next in the morning. Tomorrow."

I inhale as I realize what day is coming up. My guardianship application to keep me out of the group homes, away from the "care system", will soon be heard in court. When you're existing, not living, you can forget things. Jones will kill me if I show up half asleep at the next lawyer meeting.

Augie stands up and offers me his hand. I'm so tired now that I take it instead of ignoring the gesture like I usually do. I stumble as I get up.

"You know there really is a possibility you might have a concussion."

"I'm fine."

He makes a snorting noise. "Maybe, but … you can't be alone for the next few hours. You need someone to make sure your symptoms don't change."

"I said I am fine."

Augie's eyes don't leave mine. "Probably, but why risk it? So, you want to sleep in my room or yours?"

You have got to be kidding me. Not happening. "No."

His expression is firm. "If you want, we can wake Ruby up, explain and then you can crash in her room tonight, but you are not sleeping alone with no one to check on you."

My shoulders slump. I can't believe him. "You're acting like…"

"Like a person who cares whether you live or die?"

He is so, so annoying. "Fine. Your room."

Augie raises his hands. "I'll sleep on the beanbag near the bed."

I swear, this night keeps getting worse.

***

Augie's room has the same layout as mine, but it feels different. Lighter. Framed retro cinema posters from old Spanish movies cover the walls. The noticeboards are covered in sketches and old photos. Books, records, speakers and DJ decks cover every surface. His polished concrete floor is almost invisible under layers of discarded clothes. He tries to clean up the worst of the mess by bundling it up and throwing it into a wardrobe.

While he does, I stare at the photographs. I can't take my eyes from them. The life he once had with the mother he lost. Maya and I never had that many photos. None of our parents, who died during the lockdowns. When we went into the system, they wouldn't let us bring anything in case it was contaminated by the virus. Augie's are … everything. A kid on the beach with a surfboard. Another of him listening while his mum plays guitar by a fire, looking at her like she is the whole world. Birthday cakes, balloons, candles and silly faces. First days of school. First tournament. First eSports win. A car with a too large over-the-top bow on it. Augie smiling as he hands his mum, older now, the keys. More competitions, trophies. Then one in a hospital, the smiles on both their faces forced, fake. My eyes start to tear up. "She was beautiful, your mum."

"Thanks. I think she would have liked you."

I give a half-smile. "I doubt it. Since you met me, your life has been in danger."

"*That* she wouldn't have been keen on. But you are both fighters, Asha. I think she would have respected you."

I turn away so he can't see how those words affect me. "Thanks." It comes out as a whisper.

"Do you remember anything about your parents?" he asks.

I shake my head. "I was three, Maya was seven, when we lost them in the pandemic." I shrug. It was such a long time ago. "Sometimes I think I remember things, but then I wonder if I'm just remembering Maya's memories of them. In the group home she used to tell me stories."

Augie's voice is gentle. "Any other relatives?"

I shake my head. If our parents had family, they never came looking for us. They let us get sent into care. When that happened, they became dead to us. "We always had each other; we didn't need anyone else."

"I'm sorry, Asha."

"It's not your fault. They were both electronic engineers, you know? Maybe Maya and I are like them. They would have been proud of her."

He is quiet, serious. "They would have been proud of you too."

Would they? I pushed Maya into a situation where she took a job instead of a university scholarship so she could be my legal guardian. Getting me out of the care system meant her only option was taking a job at eighteen. She went to work for Zu Tech for me. They killed her. Would my parents hold me responsible for her death?

We don't say anything after that. Eventually Augie throws back the cover on his double bed for me. He takes a pillow and a blanket and goes to an oversized beanbag in the corner. His sheets smell of him: coffee and cinnamon.

"*Buenas noches*, Asha."

A surge of annoyance goes through me. Of course Augie would say goodnight in Spanish, and it would sound … good.

Exhaustion overcomes me. The night, the last few days, Zu's message. My eyes become heavy and something I can't name starts to wash over me. Like a call from someone I know as I fall into the velvet darkness.

***

In my dreams I am chasing Dark again. Just like I did that terrible day at the tournament. But this time, when I get there, he's dead, his body broken on the back seat of the car, covered in blood like Annie. I look down at my hands and see they're coated in blood too. It's somehow everywhere. Oozing down my face and into my mouth. I am choking on it as I stare at his blue eyes that don't move. I panic. Desperate to rub the blood away, to get away from it. I start to scream and half wake.

It's the same nightmare I always have. Almost every night around four a.m. This time, though, my throat is sore from actual screams. I feel weaker and closer to the edge just as strong arms wrap around me, holding me, pulling me back. A whisper. "Asha, I'm here."

I'm drifting back to sleep, but I know the voice that is in my dream now and it's calm, low. "It's a nightmare. You're OK. Safe."

I move closer. *Safe.* I murmur the word under my breath. "Stay."

Because in my dream I want to feel defended, to rest just for a moment, protected like Maya used to make me feel when she watched over me when we were small. His body moves to lie beside mine, holding me. I think I hear him whisper "Always", before the darkness comes back, and this time I don't dream.

***

When I wake the next morning, I don't know where I am or why Augie's face is on the pillow beside mine. His arm is holding my waist. He's on top of the duvet while I slept underneath it. His eyes are closed.

Last night's events start to flood back. The break-in. Beth telling me the Zu I met was an evolved AI. Zu's message. The Founders, who killed my sister. The knowledge that the SHACKLE code we thought we'd destroyed is still out there.

Then I remember something else. The voice I heard and the arms I felt in my nightmare while I searched for Dark. Not a dream. I study Augie's face. The dark circles under his eyes. His light blond-brown hair. The visible North Star tattoo etched into the skin on his hand. The small silver band on one of his fingers. Augie Santos, gaming star, vigilante by night.

Why does he keep helping me? Everyone who does ends up dead.

I lean back. I shouldn't be here but part of me doesn't want to leave.

"*Buenos días.*" Low, sleepy.

I swallow. Awkward. "Morning," I say, my voice still husky from the smoke.

He raises himself up on his elbow. "We need to talk."

I need paracetamol and coffee. "No, pretty sure we don't."

He glares. "I want you to know—"

"No, you don't, Augie." I am up and moving, looking

for the bag I brought with me among the clothes on the floor. Why is this guy so messy?

Augie sits up. "I need to tell you—"

"Not listening."

But we both know that is a lie.

"You are. I am saying it. I care about you, Asha. I have since I first met you."

It's my turn to glare at him. "*Why* would you say that to me now?"

He holds my gaze as he bends down and picks up my bag, holding it out to me. "Because someday we will find the person you've been taking all these risks for and you'll get your answers. I will help you do that. We will find him. But when we do, you're going to need to choose. And I want you to know what your options are. I want you to know you deserve more. You deserve everything. Not just shadows, ghosts and guilt that eat at you."

I am unable to move, my heart beating in my ears. "That's not fair," I whisper.

Augie shrugs. "If you thought I wouldn't fight for you, you're wrong. I want you to know exactly how I feel about you. Is that the first nightmare you've had, Asha? Is he worth it?"

I grit my teeth. "Out of the way."

Augie sighs and I open the door wide as I leave, almost running into someone on the other side.

I stop when I see who it is. Jones, our manager, my friend. The owner of the Tower and London's most notorious power broker. Why is she here? We're due to meet later with the lawyers about my guardianship application to the courts. But at their offices, not here.

Her face is tight. Something is off. Her usually polished appearance is rumpled. Her armour of perfect make-up and expensive jewellery that's usually dripping from her brown skin is missing. She looks shaken, like she just threw her clothes on.

"Asha, it's you." Her voice is strained.

Had she been looking for me? "Jones. Was there another break-in?" Since the tournament there have been three attempts. So far, Jones's enhanced building security has held. But nothing is impenetrable. I'm proof of that. I think of the twins. "Are Ruby and Josh all right?"

"They're fine. Asha, they found him. Dark."

For a moment, I feel like I can't breathe. Behind me, I hear Augie step into the hallway.

"Where is he?"

Her expression is bleak. In all the time I've known her I have never seen her like this. "I'm so sorry, Asha."

I am louder now, angry. "Where is he, Jones?"

"He's..." Her voice breaks. "He's dead, Asha. Dark is dead."

5

"Asha." Jones's voice snaps me back to the present.

For the first time ever, she tries to give me an awkward hug.

I shake her off. The walls feel like they are closing in around me as I step away from her. "No. You're wrong. He. Is. Not. DEAD." Jones looks at me with sympathy and I can't bear it. "I would know if he was."

"Asha." It's Augie beside me now, trying to take my hand.

I step away from him, my voice bitter. "You don't get to touch me. Isn't this what you wanted?"

Augie's eyes widen and register nothing but hurt as he takes a step back. "You think I would want him dead?"

Jones glances between the two of us. "Asha, Augie, let's calm down a second."

"What makes you think Dark's…?" I ask. I can't say the word or finish the sentence. Whatever this is, it's a mistake.

"It's on the US news channels. There was an explosion in New York – a car bomb. Suspected terror attack, two casualties. The authorities are confirming with DNA, but they already released the footage from the incident. It's him, Asha. I recognized him. He gets into the car and—"

Dark was in New York?

I don't remember how I got to the kitchen after that. Just fragments. Augie asking Jones for details. His face changing into a look of horror as Jones speaks. I tuned them both out. What they were talking about couldn't be real. I would know, wouldn't I? I would have felt it if something happened to him. That's how it works when you love someone, right?

Because I love him. I know that. He can't be dead.

Josh and Ruby burst into the kitchen, running towards me, then their arms hold me so tight I can't breathe.

"I'm sorry, Asha."

Ruby is beside me, crying. "Ash, I can't believe this is happening…"

There is pain, anguish in her words as she talks about our loss like this is real. It can't be real. Nothing makes sense.

"I need to see," I mumble into Ruby's shoulder. I step back, my voice louder. "I need to see what happened, Ru."

"You sure?" Josh asks. I nod and he glances at Ruby before flicking on a news channel. Her arms wrap protectively around me as I stare at the screen. The world stands still.

It's a news report. The caption on the lower bottom third of the screen reads:

Explosion in New York City. Two confirmed dead, damage to surrounding buildings, terror alert level raised to red for Lower Manhattan. Residents are asked to shelter in place. Stand by for more.

I sink back against Ruby. The footage shows a wide-angled CCTV shot. It's night. Grid street layout. Yellow taxis and towering office blocks. Street signs of white text on green backgrounds. A pretzel cart locked up for the night at the walkway intersection. A blue US mailbox, the glowing neon lights of a nearby bodega. The dark exterior of some chain-store pharmacy. All normal New York, like a scene from so many movies.

A reporter's voice drones on over the footage. The Joint Terrorist Task Force has not ruled out the possibility of further explosions. Then the camera catches a pale figure walking out of one of the buildings and everything seems to slow around me. The camera zooms in. I recognize him from the way he moves even before the zoom-in. Dark. His hair is shorter. He wears a white shirt and jeans.

Dark never wears white, I think.

He winces as he walks. Holding his right arm stiffly, as if it's sore. A black laptop bag slung over his left shoulder, not his right. A white tag on the strap. Like from an airline? Or a barcode?

But this can't be him. I need to see his face.

And, as if he heard me, he looks directly up at the camera.

The world stops. It is Dark.

A tiny invisible string pulls tight from me to him. So strong that I feel it. My breath, everything around me, feels heightened.

I keep watching the screen as Dark walks across the street to a waiting black town car. He pauses, then gets in, closing the car door behind him. The car doesn't move. Stragglers in the empty street walk around it till there is a break in pedestrian traffic. The traffic lights turn again, the other vehicles move. The car Dark is in remains stationary, alone in a now-empty street.

Then it explodes in a burst of flames.

I sink to the ground. All the air seems to leave my lungs. I can hear a scream – "no". It echoes in the air around me, and it takes me a while to realize it's coming from me.

Jones and Ruby somehow manage to get me off the floor and into a chair by the table. Josh starts making tea. "Because that's what you're supposed to do, right? Strong sweet tea?"

"Murphy should have told us," Jones says, her tone angry. "She shouldn't have found out like this."

But I'm not listening to them any more. The images play over and over in my head as the words burn into my brain:

He can't be dead.

***

When I wake the next day, I have messages.

Messages from Murphy, the police officer who was there the night my sister died. Who has been looking out for me since. Feeding me information on the official investigation. The ongoing searches into those that vanished when Zu Tech failed, the endless dead ends, the sale of the company's old assets. The way Dark vanished – until now.

From Bill, Dark's business partner/enforcer, asking if I'm OK. He's part of the reason Dark was able to grow his digital empire so fast. Hacking the system, finding – and hiding – secrets for a price. Operating from the shadows until the reach of what he and Bill had created was everywhere.

Others are texts from gamers I don't know, and people from the old factory and the care home where Dark, my sister Maya and I grew up.

I can't answer them. Jones fields the calls, not leaving my side. Augie tries to keep out of my sight. I can't look at him. Josh deposits endless mugs of tea beside me and I'm not able to tell him I never liked tea. I don't know what to say to any of them, so I say nothing. I just lean on Ruby as I cry. It's a blur of tears, pain and the smell of awful tea.

But there's one thing I do know.

"He's not dead."

It's been twenty-four hours since the news broke. I'm alone with Ruby and Josh in the kitchen.

"Asha." Ruby is trying to be patient, calm.

But I've had enough. "I need some time alone. Thanks for the tea, for everything – but I need a minute." I force a smile. "I'm fine."

Ruby's face says she is not convinced. She's right – because I just lied to her. I have to check something out online, and once I have I'm going to see the one person who can help me find out if this is real or not. Right now, I don't believe any of it.

***

They leave me alone like I ask and I go first to the computer in my room. I start by researching businesses in the location of the blast. The news talked about a possible terrorist attack, but there's been no more details yet. Just endless speculation as various groups keep coming forward claiming responsibility and talking about their agendas. There must be a reason why someone set off an explosion in that part of the city. All the major businesses are tech or investment companies – nothing suspicious about any of them. And then I wonder, tech companies owned by who? Any with links to Zu Tech? I stare at the frozen images on the screen. If someone wanted Dark dead, it's got something to do with Zu Tech.

None of this makes sense. Dark was always paranoid. A lifetime unravelling the secrets of others will do that to a person. Dark's skill set meant he was the one you called when you wanted to find out someone's deepest secrets, to come back from being doxed, or had a money trail that had gone cold. He was always fearful that someone would come for him the way he came for others. It made him careful to remain hidden. How could someone get close enough to him to plant a bomb in his car? Is this my fault? The only time Dark was seen in public was when he risked everything to help me bring down SHACKLE at the Zu Tech tournament. People would have seen him in the tournament footage. Did helping me lead to this? Whatever this is.

I hack into and download the NYPD incident files and then launch a brute force attack into the servers for the New York Department of Transportation, careful not to leave traces. I download the last twenty-four hours of footage for the intersection. The car appears hours before and stops in the parking space. No one gets in or out. Remote-controlled? Self-driving? But the police report said there was a driver who died…

I play it back on a loop. The explosion, the size of the blast radius. I'm lost in watching the violent flash of flames that blows parts of the car several metres up in the air. Then a second blast as the car gets engulfed in fire. I go back and forth. Something isn't right. What am I missing?

Then I see it.

***

A few hours later, I stand outside the shop where Bill and Dark worked, watching commuters walking past. It's a small dodgy-looking tech shop in the gap between Paddington train and tube station. I remember the first time I came here, when I was searching for answers about what happened to Maya, my heart broken. I guess not much has changed.

I enter the shop using the fob Bill gave me after Dark was taken, in case I ever needed to get in. I head towards the back office and the hidden door to the circular staircase that goes down to Dark's place.

The room is the same. High ceilings, black steel industrial beams and exposed red brick. The aroma of coffee and expensively filtered clean air. Black and white tiles, with a scattering of thick rugs. One side of the room is filled with couches and tables like an old-fashioned club. The other is outfitted like a high-end bar. Mirrors, sparkling heavy-cut glasses, gleaming brass and coloured bottles. Sitting alone at the end of the bar, head slumped in his hands, is Bill.

His ex-boxer frame is hunched. A mug of tea is near his tattooed hands. He's so still that I wonder if he heard me coming or not.

"Bill."

"Asha." His head lifts. "Been expecting you." His hug is warm, strong and foreign. In all my years of knowing Bill, I have never seen him cry or get emotional, yet here he is, tears in his eyes, holding me. Looking gutted.

I let out a breath. "You think it's true?"

Bill shrugs. "It has to be. If it wasn't, he'd be here, wouldn't he?"

I have no answer to that. Why isn't he here? But then why was he in New York?

Bill gestures to his cup. "Want a coffee?"

"Yeah, thanks."

While Bill makes my drink, I sink on to a bar stool, allowing the feelings in. I associate this place so much with him it hurts. My heart is telling me Dark will walk through the door at any moment.

Bill takes in the bruises on my face and hands when he gives me a mug. "Best right hook I ever saw. But my guys in the boxing gym didn't do that to you."

He glances at my hands and the cuts I got from fleeing Zu Tech. "Do I need to sort someone out?"

I shake my head. Now isn't the time to go into where my current bruises come from, and Bill should know better; I always sort out my own problems.

I notice the lines on his face, the faint purple tinge from a lack of sleep under his eyes. He's struggling like me. Time to change the subject.

"Did you know he was in New York?"

"If I knew anything, I would have told you. He left me too, you know?" Bill gestures around at the room. "We were in this together. I wasn't supposed to be left running this on my own."

Deep breath. "You believe it was him in the video?"

Bill frowns. "Yeah, I do, Asha. Look, I had the same

thoughts as you. I guess when you've seen what we have, you learn to question everything. I had Murphy check it out. I also paid someone on the dark web. The CCTV footage wasn't altered. It's Dark; it's not a deep fake. Then there's the evidence at the scene, the blast marks on the buildings, the wreckage. The … remains. Two bodies, or what was left of them, were found. The driver and the passenger. It is real."

"We'll come to that, Bill. Can I show you something from the footage?" I pull out a small device and drag up the video that I now know frame by frame, and each one hurts to watch. I point to an image of the vehicle licence plate. "This was stolen two days before the event. Lincoln town car. Standard. A few hours before the explosion, it arrived at the location. Now, this is a screengrab of the car taken from the street cameras. Notice anything?"

Bill stares at the still on the flat screen. "I don't see anything unusual here…" He stops. Leans in. "Except the bonnet isn't closed; it's popping up a bit."

I zoom in on the screengrab. "Right. Look closer – the hinges are broken. I would be willing to bet that all those in the bonnet, boot and doorposts were broken too and the structure weakened."

"Why?"

"Maya once went on set when they filmed an advert for a game she'd worked on, to watch how they did it. They wanted 'realism' instead of CGI for the car explosion. She told me about it after – how they managed to blow up the car without using much charge, and have it look completely realistic. The doors, the bonnet, all the things that would fly off in the blast are weakened beforehand. It means the explosion looks good, but it doesn't need as much explosive charge. Less potential collateral damage."

Bill chews his lip. "Murphy said some terrorist group was already claiming responsibility."

"Of course they are – it doesn't mean they did it. Next, I looked into the driver of the car. Listed as Ben Miller: no family, no relatives, no friends, just an online history saying he was a private limo driver, registered a few months ago, good reviews. Totally unexceptional apart from one thing. His history only goes back twelve months. Before that, nothing. Like he didn't exist before then anywhere."

"So he's a fake or a guy using an alias … but that doesn't mean anything—"

I interrupt him. "I don't believe in coincidences, and neither do you. It's weird. A driver goes there and parks up. He doesn't leave the car, not once, in three hours. Then, when … Dark gets in, the car explodes."

Bill doesn't say anything now, so I continue. "I hacked the NYPD database to see the evidence. Their forensics is good. There were two males in that car when it detonated. But you and I both know Dark scrubbed his real identity years ago. He doesn't exist in any database; he has no DNA or fingerprints on file. He was identified from the footage as Dark, a match to the footage of him from the Zu Tech tournament. But what if that body wasn't his?"

"Asha..."

"Bill, what if it was set up?"

"Asha, he wouldn't do this to you, to me."

"What if he was made to? There was a sewer cover underneath where the car was parked."

Bill leans across and grabs my hand. "Asha, stop. You will drive yourself insane."

"I can't." My voice is breaking, thick with emotion. "I can't lose him."

Bill's arms are around me, and I feel him heave like he's crying too. For a moment, he doesn't move, then he straightens up. "You're not going to let this alone, are you?"

I shake my head. "No."

Bill sighs. "Tell me what you need."

***

Bill goes and gathers the items for me. Somehow going into Dark's room now is more that I can manage. I hover instead in the doorway. Bill puts an old black T-shirt Dark wore and left on his bed in a bag, then heads into the bathroom. As he moves, my eyes snag on the pictures beside the bed. The cheap battered plastic frame that features Dark as a kid looking up at his parents with a giant smile that hurts to look at – a smile I rarely saw. Beside it, a single Polaroid shot of me from the old factory, the unsanctioned gamer space that was our refuge when things were tough. It's where we met Jones for the first time as she scouted for new talent. Where Dark met Bill. I'm smiling in the photo. It must have been taken three, almost four, years ago, just before everything happened. My tears start to well up, so I force my gaze away and focus on Bill as he collects and bags a toothbrush, hairbrush and razor from the en suite.

"This enough?"

I nod. Ready to get going.

"Asha, be careful. I didn't mention it before, but there were a few people around asking questions – before the explosion."

"Let me guess, the police, the cybercrime division..."

Bill shrugs. "Yeah, they were here, but we don't have to worry about them. They never know anything. No, others."

I start to pay attention. "Who?"

"First Jones came to see if I'd heard anything from Dark. That I expected. Then a group trying to acquire some of Mr Dark's assets."

"Name?"

Bill shakes his head. "Some investment firm called Pi. Couldn't find anything when I started digging. It was a few weeks ago. I reminded them that Dark was missing. So, until I heard otherwise, his businesses and shares weren't for sale." He pauses. "But this firm, Asha ... they had a bad vibe. Knew just a little too much about Dark's past if you know what I mean."

"But Dark erased everything."

He nods. "They knew that he'd once worked with

Jones. Also knew where he worked with Jones. Before those two fell out."

I frown. Something in his tone catches my attention. "What do you mean, where he worked? What exactly are you talking about?"

Bill looks at me carefully. "I can't say."

"Please. If he's not gone, we need to find him. If he is, telling me secrets won't hurt."

Bill takes a moment, like he's not sure where to begin. "When Dark worked for Jones, she occasionally hired out his skill set to other interested parties. He was never happy about it. It was the reason he left."

I shrug. I'd guessed that much. "Sounds about right. Who did she hire him out to?"

"Look, I'm only telling you in case it somehow helps. It was a long time ago. He told me one night after we had a break-in that had him on edge. Dark … worked for Zu Thorp, Asha."

"No," I whisper. "That can't be true."

"Jones had him working for Zu Tech for almost six months. Once he'd left Jones's employ, he never contacted her or went back there again."

"No," I say again. I slump against the door frame. "He would have…"

"Told you? Would he? You know him, Asha. Dark always had secrets." Bill says the words gently.

I don't say anything. I can't. *Dark worked for Zu Tech.* The company that would later kill my sister. That almost destroyed all of us. He couldn't have kept that from me. Could he?

My head is spinning. It's too much. I'd got what I came for; I needed to get out of there. I start to walk towards the exit. One last question: "Did Jones know where she was sending him?"

"Hard to say. You know how these things work. To protect all sides, you normally never meet. The request is sent to you, and you send the work back to an anonymous site. The money is transferred to the person who brokered the deal. You never really knew who you worked for except..."

"In Dark's case..."

Bill nods. "He got curious about what they were asking him to do. He reached out."

"And?"

"They asked for a meet. Dark might not have told Jones. I don't think he told anyone except me. But that firm who came here the other day ... they knew. Said their company, Pi, knew him from his time at Zu Tech."

"Did you get any names?"

He shakes his head. "They made some joke about being men in grey suits I didn't understand. Wouldn't give me anything but the company name."

"Bill, did he tell you, did Dark tell you what he worked on for Zu?"

Bill shakes his head.

Out of curiosity, I ask, "Will you sell his interests if he turns out to be...?" I still can't say it.

Bill looks at me in surprise. "His interests aren't mine to sell, Asha."

As Dark's partner, I'd always assumed the business went straight to Bill. Dark had no other relations that I knew about. "What do you mean?"

"I thought he'd have told you. A few weeks before that last Zu Tech tournament, he called in the lawyers. He wanted it all taken care of in case something happened. Everything he had, this place, the club, the vaults, the crypt clean rooms, his other proprieties, the cash – all of it he left it to you."

***

I leave then, and Bill and I agree to stay in touch. But all I can think of is proving my theory right. I concentrate on what I know so far. Dark must have known there was a risk involved in the Zu Tech tournament if he had met with lawyers and made a will. Maybe he knew he wasn't coming back.

What did Dark do for Zu? I remember Dark warning me when I said I was looking into Zu Thorp and his company. *Their security systems have proved … problematic… People don't normally live to talk about him or his corporation.* That must have come from experience. He had lied to me, kept it from me. Why? What the hell was Dark involved in?

And how well do I really know the boy I gave my heart to?

6

"Asha." Ruby is the first to find me when I arrive back at the Tower.

"Hey," I say guiltily. Messages I should have replied to are stacking up. Some from Ruby, others from Unknown.

> What did you find inside Zu Tech?
>
> Tick-tock, Kennedy – you still owe me.
>
> We made a deal.

Unknown got me the Zu Tech pass that let me into the building. They're right; I owe them. But for now, I'm playing it safe. When I ignored their last message and shut my phone – I also bypassed looking at or answering Ruby's texts.

"You disappeared," she says.

"I was … processing." Now is probably not the time to tell her I am in full denial and sent DNA samples from Dark's toothbrush off for analysis. Forty-seven hours to go as they compare Dark's DNA to the DNA profiles I hacked from an email between the counterterrorism bureau of the NYPD and one of the FBI officers assigned to the case.

"Did you eat?"

The growl from my stomach answers for me.

"Food?" She sees my hesitation. "It's just me and Josh. Augie isn't here."

I nod.

"Great. Kitchen, now."

The twins' method of coping is food. The kitchen is covered in bowls, pots and spills while spices and steam fill the space.

"We made Mexican," Josh says, closing his retro Game Boy. 8-bit fourth-generation Tetris; Josh always plays the weirdest classics.

Rice, quesadillas, bean enchiladas, guacamole, sour cream, grated cheese, Mexican corn salsa. They made enough food for a small army.

"Jones was looking for you." Josh's voice is soft. "She was worried when you went MIA. I told her you'd be back."

Damn. I forgot Jones's number one rule of letting me stay here at the Tower. *You're a minor, Asha. At least tell me where you are, check in – or, so help me, I'll put a tracker on you.*

"I just needed…"

Josh hugs me. "We know."

My breath stills. They *can't* know where I went and what I was doing. Can they? "You do?"

Ruby's face is empathetic, her eyes bright. "Space to deal. Anyone would. But it's not healthy to be alone right now, Ash. We're here. I'll text Jones now, let her know you're OK. She'll understand."

"Oh. Yeah."

It's easier to lie. To them Dark is dead. I keep my thoughts to myself as the timer on my watch ticks down: forty-four hours to go. Ruby starts to pile food on my plate.

"Ru?"

"Yeah, Josh."

"Why is the chilli you made … different?"

"Cos it's vegan, and I added sweet potatoes. Eliza says sweet potatoes make it better."

He mimes choking and I almost smile. "Ah, come on, not sweet potatoes. Do you have to do everything Eliza says now?"

Ruby's grin fades. "Cut it."

She gives him a look, a subtle nod to me, like somehow, they shouldn't talk about other people any more because I've lost all mine. Parents. Never knew them. Sister murdered.

Sister's girlfriend murdered. Boy I love, presumed dead. If I were my friends, I'd be giving me a wide birth. Getting close to me is dangerous.

I look up at Ru, determined to make this normal. "How is Eliza anyway? Transatlantic romance still going strong?"

Eliza is a touchy subject between Ruby and me. I still can't forget that during the Zu Tech tournament, she was the one who found out that Dawn – Josh and Ruby's little sister – was being threatened. That Josh was being blackmailed in order to keep her safe. She claimed it was a rumour she'd heard, but I haven't trusted her since.

"Yeah, we're good." Ruby's hand covers mine. "Look, there's an ulterior motive with the chilli. We wanted to talk. We care about you, and we care about Augie, and you guys not talking sucks." Josh nods while Ruby leans in. "And you should talk to him, Asha. You need all of us right now."

"No." I'm still angry at Augie – or angry at myself and how I feel about him, I'm not sure which.

Ru nudges Josh, who takes the hint and goes over to the smart speaker to change the music. "Ash." Her tone low. "You know Augie would never want Dark hurt. He's been trying to help you find him for weeks now. We all have."

I swallow. "The morning we found out about Dark, Augie said he liked me and that one day I'd need to choose between him and Dark. And now Dark's gone. It's exactly what he wanted."

"Asha, Augie wanted you to find Dark alive. *Then* he

wanted you to decide how you felt about him. Now he'll never know. I feel sorry for him. He'll always wonder if..."

"If what?"

"If you'll always be in love with a ghost. Dark was a lot of things. I know you miss him. When it counted, he was there for you. But dying makes someone perfect, untouchable. It puts their memory on a pedestal. Augie could compete with a real person, but not a spectre. He's afraid you'll never let Dark go."

"Dark wasn't perfect." He'd lied to me about working at Zu Tech. If he was here, beside me, would I be willing to forgive him for that? I change the subject. "You guys talked?"

"Yeah, earlier. Augie was upset. Look, I'm not asking you to deal with this now. Just a thought for later. OK?"

I sink back and eat. I watch Josh and Ru banter back and forth, pretending everything is normal. It isn't. They don't get as much hate as I do about exposing Zu Tech, but I know they get some. Yet Ru doesn't dwell on it. Instead, she talks about Eliza's new place in New York, and her face lights up every time she says Eliza's name. Josh chats about tournaments and his girlfriend Amy and apartment hunting in London.

"You're moving in with Amy?" I ask.

Josh nods. "We want to get a place close to her folks so when I'm at tournaments she's got family and mates around. And after everything that happened ... I guess I want to be one of those people who lives every moment.

Well, as soon as I get some tournament cash together and put a little by for our mum and Dawn."

There's a pause. The gulf between their lives and mine is huge and obvious. Josh and Ruby will get to move on with the people they love. I might not. Josh seems to sense where my mind has gone because he goes for a light-hearted joke. "And when we do … the housewarming will be epic."

"Yeah!" Ruby jumps in. "We could splash some tournament cash and go BIG!"

My brain snags on "tournament cash". The kind we'd have right now if we were all playing like a team. As a group, we've had loads of offers. Notoriety brings in the eyeballs and press attention that organizers like. But I've turned down all offers to play since the Zu Tech tournament. Individually, as solo players, Ruby, Josh and even Augie have had way fewer offers than they should have because of their association with me.

I've been holding my team back. I'd never thought about how my decisions affected them. I open my mouth to say something but am interrupted by another voice from the doorway. Jones. "A word, Asha." Her tone isn't a request.

I step outside into the hallway.

"Did you shower today?"

Do I stink? "No."

"Take one and then meet me upstairs."

***

The roof garden in the tower is scented with jasmine and mint. Pots of bamboo grouped together create small screens for private nooks. The clear glass roof shows the night sky outside and the satellite dishes hide behind the architecture of the church tower. The courtyard area is lit with soft lights and strings of smaller solar ones. *Magic lights* was what Maya used to call them.

Jones is dressed down – for Jones. Wide trousers, flat shoes, a tasteful silk blouse. I've managed to throw my wet hair up into a messy bun and found clean jeans, a black tee and canvas runners. The water from my hair is dripping down my back, and wisps of it keep escaping the claw clip I used and falling in front of my face.

"Sit." It's another order, not a request, and I feel uneasy about what might come next.

Jones hands me a green tea. She gives me a second to get comfortable, takes a sip of her tea, then starts.

"I find myself in uncharted territory here, Asha."

Uncharted territory. Does she mean me?

"Mind telling me why you're running DNA samples through the dark web?"

I take a deep breath. Nothing seems to stay a secret from Jones for long. "I know I was upset before, but I really think Dark could be alive. I wanted to run a DNA sample of his against what they found in the blast."

Jones's look becomes curious. "Based on?"

"A hunch. My gut."

"I see." Jones leans back, concerned.

This is not going well. Jones doesn't look convinced, more like she's worried about me.

"I went through the footage. There was something odd about the car – like it had been rigged for a stunt explosion. And if anyone was able to fake his death, it would be Dark. He'd scrubbed every trace of himself when he dropped out of the system. Dental records, everything. The coverage doesn't say it but there would have been no way to formally ID him. Then there was a sewer opening underneath the car..."

Jones's eyes snap back to mine. "I didn't see that in the video."

"I may have taken a look at the crime-scene photos after they cleared the wreckage."

"You hacked the police database?"

"Lots of people do."

"Those people aren't you, Asha. The videos of what you said at the Zu Tech tournament – about how you don't play the game, it plays you – I've never seen a reaction like that before. That level of instant fame, infamy. The authorities are looking for any opportunity to sweep all this and you out of sight. They don't want to explain to anyone how close Zu Tech came to succeeding. You have several groups of people looking to discredit you in any way they can. I don't think you understand the position you're in."

"What choice do I have, Jones? What choice did any of us ever get? You know I can't give up on Dark."

She sits back and sips her tea, lost in thought for a moment. Nostalgic. "Dark always was a cockroach, and God knows they're hard to kill. I'll go along with this – for now. What do you need from me?"

I let out a sigh of relief. It's always easier having Jones on your side. "Time. Time to run the tests. I need to find out for sure if one of those bodies was Dark's."

"Which will be when?"

I glance at my watch. "Forty-two hours."

Jones looks away. "We've got the guardianship hearing tomorrow. That should distract you while you wait. In forty-two hours, we reassess. But there are two things I need from you. Two non-negotiable things."

Great. "OK."

"No more going anywhere alone unless I know about it."

"Fine." Awkward, but of everyone, I know I can trust Jones. Then I remember something. "I saw Bill and I had a question."

Jones lets out an irritated sigh at being interrupted but says, "Ask."

I swallow. "When Dark left the care system, he worked for you."

She nods. "You knew that already."

"Bill told me that you hired him out. Who to?"

Jones crosses her long legs in front of her and leans back slightly in her chair. "It was always a contract through a broker. Normally someone who needed info or an identity scrubbed. The last one was for an anonymous tech firm who wanted a coder. They specifically asked for him. He had a rep even then. I provided the service, collected the fee minus my commission, and gave him a clean room to work from. Then, after a few months, he went and bloody left in the middle of the night. I got stuck with an incomplete deal and an unhappy client. After that, I vowed to have nothing to do with him until … well, you know when." She watches my face carefully. "Why?"

"So you never knew who he worked for?"

"That's not how those things work. It's online through black sites. Anonymity is key for all parties. You know that."

"Just curious."

"Back to what I was saying… Second thing. I know it's hard, but if Dark turns out to be dead – what will you do?"

I think of Maya and the bloody mess that was Annie's body after Zu Tech's people got to her. I think of Zu's video, what he said about hiding proof and a copy of the code. I feel the anger inside me.

"I'll find out who did it. Then I'll find the thing they want or care about the most and I will destroy it. I will burn them and everyone who helped them, until there is nothing left."

There's a flicker of concern in Jones's eyes. "Are you sure that's what you want? After everything you've been through, all of us have been through. Is that what you think your sister wanted for you?"

"Maya wanted me to live. To start over. She'd want me to walk away and have a life. Go to college, get a career, be safe."

Jones nods. "Then you should honour that—"

"But I'm not my sister. Maya was the nice one. Not me. I want revenge, Jones. I won't stop until I burn everyone involved in this."

And I mean every word.

7

The only way forward is through.

Jones and I are waiting outside the courtroom. It's nearly time for the hearing. The timer on my watch says thirty-three hours remain till the DNA report is available, and my heart twists. I fidget with my sister's oval locket, the flash drive that sits beside it, then the second-hand navy dress I'm wearing. I can't keep still. I am out of my comfort zone. The dress is what Maya might have picked and called "vintage". My brown hair, with strands of shimmering pink and silver, is tied in a messy bun. Like the way Maya used to wear her hair.

I feel tired and more confused than before. I should be back at the Tower, trying to figure out what happened to

Dark and what Zu's message means. *If you are someone who knows me, then you can find it where all this started.* I've spent the last few hours going through endless clips of Zu's early interviews, looking for something, anything, that points to who his early investors were and what the "beginning" might have been for him. But I can't put this off. Whatever happens next, I can't go back into the care system.

My phone buzzes.

You still owe me, and I am getting tired of waiting.

What did you find in Zu Tech?

I ignore it. Unknown is still a *tomorrow problem*, especially as I'm starting to suspect I know who they are.

Sitting beside me, Jones is dressed for business, her armour an expensive white tailored trouser suit that stands out against her dark skin. Gold jewellery. Heels that cost more than the average monthly rent, ones I could never walk in but which I've seen her run in. She gives me what I think is meant to be a reassuring wink. "Ready?"

I stand up and smooth out the creases from my charity-shop dress. Jones lets out a small sigh. I refused her offers of help with clothes and my choice obviously still annoys her.

We enter the courtroom just as the person who has finished giving evidence is leaving. Murphy. Probably here to talk about my background. How he met me first in my old flat the night my sister died. He'd been called by the emergency services to assist when they moved her body. It feels like decades have passed since then – I can't believe it was just a few months ago. He's aged more than he should have in the last few weeks. He's thinner, more worn.

He meets my gaze, gives a quick nod and then I'm sucking in a breath of filtered air. The East London Family Court sign is on the wall of the court we enter.

The doors close behind us. A smell of disinfectant fills the air. Wiped benches and chairs are arranged in front of the raised platform with a long desk. Seated at that desk is Judge Stern. The Magistrates' Court crown ensign on the wall behind her. The room has no windows, and I move closer to Jones. Places like this always make me feel uneasy. Their daylight-stimulating bulbs seem too bright. Too clean. My skin crawls.

The judge arranges her tissues, hand sanitizer and papers before looking at us. The lawyer for the social is already in place, a stack of folders and documents spread haphazardly on the floor. A brown paper bag from lunch lies forgotten on the next seat. He's here for the day.

Jones inclines her head slightly. The lawyer for the social nods back at her and then at the representative Jones hired as our advocate for the hearing. This deal has been weeks in negotiation. Today is the last part. The part where they ask me questions, and the answers need to be ones they like or they'll put me back in a care home.

I glance around and count the CCTV cameras in the room to calm myself. Four. Exits, two. My hands are clammy as I wipe them on my dress. My heart races. Breathe.

Judge Stern reads the file and makes a small note. Then she takes off her glasses and looks at me. "I want to start by saying how sorry I am for your loss." She checks her notes again. "For Maya's passing." She sounds sincere, but even if she means it her sympathy doesn't change anything. It doesn't bring anyone back.

"As per the Crown Court's request, the court reporter has left. All cameras are off. You may fully discuss past events. This will not affect the order already in place. I assure you that nothing you say will leave this room, Ms Kennedy. We are here to do what is best for you."

The order in place is a gag order. One issued by the courts to protect national security, to prohibit the exposure of confidential information to the public until the investigation into SHACKLE can be concluded. It doesn't seem to have stopped everyone in the country from having an opinion on what happened at the Zu Tech tournament. But without the findings of an official inquiry, it's us against the court of public opinion. Plenty of people prefer ignorance to reality. They want to believe a beloved tech giant was unfairly blamed by an angry orphaned teenager. With each week that passes, with no arrests or findings being made, it gets worse. I wonder if any government conclusion into what happened will ever be reached? Will Maya ever get justice?

Jones pours a glass of filtered water from the jug in front of us. I sip it to will away the lump in my throat.

The judge gives me an encouraging smile. "Shall we start at the beginning, Ms Kennedy?"

"It's Asha, just Asha."

She nods. "Good. So, Asha, how old were you when you entered the care system?"

Care system – even the words set me on edge. There wasn't much care going on. "I was three; Maya was seven." Pause. "Your Honour," I add.

"You don't have to call me that today. If it helps, you can call me Amelia. My name is Amelia Stern. Your parents?"

"They both died in the first wave of the pandemic … Amelia."

"I am sorry again for your loss." The judge puts on her glasses again to read from the file. "No other next of kin. You left the system, care facility 136, at fifteen." She removes her glasses and sits back. "Can you tell me in your own words what happened afterwards?"

She waits for me to speak, and I can see that she is trying to be kind, respectful even. Maybe she doesn't realize that every time I talk about what happened, it feels like I am reliving it.

I detach, imagining for a moment that it's a story that happened to someone else. Something I need to say and get through. I don't have to feel the parts that hurt.

"In the care home it was tough. Maya and I made a pact that we'd stay together. When Maya turned eighteen and was aged out of the system, she promised she'd find a way to get me out. It was our dream. That she'd find a job and then I'd get released into her care."

The judge makes a note. "Very noble. What happened?"

"Maya was offered a scholarship to university. She turned it down to take a paid internship and then a job with Zu Technology – because of me. She became a responsible adult with a steady income. Saved. Found an apartment. She applied to social services for custody of me. The process took a while. The last requirement was a letter from her employer saying that she was of good character and in stable employment. Zu Tech agreed but only if Maya enrolled in the 'special projects' division in the company. She did it." I swallow. "To get me out she would have done anything."

I stop as it hits me. Every time Maya visited after she left the care home, I made it harder for her. She heard about me getting into trouble with the supervisors and becoming angrier. Was told that I was hanging out with Dark, missing curfew. And every time she tried to talk to me about it, I blamed her for leaving me, said that what I was doing was her fault.

"Yes?" Judge Stern probes. Her voice brings me back to the present. There is no easy way to say what happened next.

"Zu Tech used my sister to beta test mind-control technology. It was created to be part of a new VR game called SHACKLE."

"And when you say, 'mind control', you mean…?"

"You didn't play their game. It played you. SHACKLE used a brain–computer interface, a BCI. Instead of you sending impulses to control your avatar in the game via the BCI, it hacked your brain. Eventually it could control you like a puppet."

Judge Stern looks disapproving, almost unbelieving. "I read about this in the draft report. The investigation is, I believe, still active, its findings unverified. It does sound like science fiction. I've never been one for video games – too violent for me..."

I restrain myself from rolling my eyes. No wonder the minds behind SHACKLE felt so sure they could get away with it. With people like Judge Stern enforcing the law, they'll always be safe. Governments are unable to legislate fast enough to keep up with the advances being made in technology. The people who write the laws are too old to grasp what they're legislating against. By the time they do the genie will be out of the bottle and, in this case, it would have been controlling everyone.

"When Maya found out what SHACKLE was doing, she started gathering evidence to blow the whistle. To take Zu Tech down from the inside."

Stern consults her notes. "Your sister died shortly afterwards. The coroner's report states an 'open verdict' as a cause of death. In other words, 'unknown'."

"She was murdered," I say firmly. "She was killed by the people who created the code. They suspected she was going to make what she knew public."

"I see." A pause. "It is always hard to deal with loss, especially at such a young age. Allowances must be made for that. But I would warn you we all have a duty to tell the truth, not as we wish it was, but according to the facts. Especially here, in this room. Until the official investigation is concluded, we may not know with full certainty what happened. Then you will need to accept its verdict. I trust you can do that, Asha."

She doesn't see. I know that from her tone. She thinks this is a conspiracy theory borne out of grief and paranoia.

"And then you entered the Zu Tech Tournament—"

Jones's lawyer interrupts. "I'm afraid my client is unable to say anything further, Amelia, as per the gag order. Sufficient to say Asha's only living relative is dead. She is sixteen and doesn't wish to return to the care system, and is a public figure now unfortunately. There are serious security concerns and threats have been made. She feels now that she would be safest under the guardianship of Ms Jones."

Amelia stares at him. "You may call me Judge Stern." This is a woman who doesn't like being interrupted.

"Yes, Judge Stern."

The judge turns again to me. "The care home system provides structure and stability for thousands of young people across the country. They are also secure. In a facility, perhaps a more remote one, you could start over. Finish school or look at an apprenticeship. It would be a good option for you, Asha."

I meet her eyes again. This is it – the moment where

I either convince her or end up on the run for the next year and a half till I turn eighteen. "I can't go back. People will ask too many questions that I won't be able to answer because of the rules. I'll get bullied. It doesn't matter where I go, how remote. If the other kids have Wi-Fi, they'll have seen clips from the tournament."

"Eventually people will forget, Asha. They always do."

I try another approach. "Ms Jones has offered to be my guardian until I turn eighteen. I will need additional support and security. I don't want to be a burden on the state if I can avoid it, Your Honour."

I see how my words connect with her traditional values, the way her eyes change and dilate, so I push.

"I want to contribute to society, not take from it. Working for Ms Jones means I can pay my way."

Jones's representative beside me coughs. "Your Honour, Judge Stern, as you can see from the documents submitted, Ms Jones is a woman of substantial means, a successful entrepreneur who, among other things, manages several select eSports teams. She has a relationship with Ms Kennedy as a manager and a friend. She can help her create a solid, financially rewarding career, give her stability as Ms Kennedy puts the past behind her and becomes a tax-paying, contributing member of our society. Ms Jones will provide guidance, support and protection till all this has been resolved. She is also a board member on several youth outreach projects. Ms Kennedy has expressed an interest in volunteering at these."

Judge Stern looks at her file again. "Yes, I'm aware of all of Ms Jones's attributes. The supporting documentation is extensive. Asha, would you be happy with this arrangement? Continuing to live in the accommodation provided by Ms Jones? Have you considered all the options?"

"I already got my GCSEs. I want to do this."

"I see that, Asha. I also saw the scores you received. You are, according to the exam board, gifted." She leafs through my file. "You were offered early university acceptance at more than one college. You could take any of these up and they would provide suitable accommodation and a maintenance allowance. You are aware of this?"

I look at the floor. I think of Maya and what she wanted for me. A regular life. Education, a career. Judge Stern doesn't know it, but her words are almost an exact copy of the last argument I had with my sister. She had asked me to take up an early college offer. I thought then it was because she didn't want me around. She just wanted me to be safe. Maya had sent the applications in for colleges up north – far enough away from London that she thought I would be safe. But now I can't run away.

"I know how lucky I was to get those offers, but I need to be with my team, in a place I know." I throw in my trump card. "In London I feel close to Maya. Those memories are all I have now."

The judge sighs and turns her attention to Jones. "And you, Ms Jones, are you prepared to be responsible for a teenager?"

Jones stands. "I wouldn't have made the offer unless it was sincere, Your Honour. I am aware of what it entails."

The judge looks at the social's legal representative. "Any concerns?"

The man stands. "Having reviewed the case and talked to those involved, we have no objections at this time, Your Honour."

Amelia Stern sighs almost reluctantly. "Well then, Asha, I will grant temporary guardianship to Ms Jones for a six-month probationary period, after which there will be a review. Your assigned social representative will be in touch to arrange the follow-up visits. I wish you good luck. And, Asha? I don't expect to see you before that date. Now is not the time to make yourself an enemy of the system. Do you understand? Ms Jones, we need to see that you can control your charge if you want the six-month period extended."

We all nod and murmur our thanks. The judge is shuffling her papers for the next case as we leave.

***

I feel the weight lift from me as we walk out of the courtroom. Murphy is waiting in the corridor.

Jones and I look at each other, her phone already starting to vibrate in her bag. The enormity of the situation hits us both. She lifts a manicured hand and takes a nervous step towards me. "I think it's customary to hug."

Her expensive perfume surrounds me, and I grin at her obvious discomfort. "You want to not do that?"

She drops her hand and smiles. "This is what I like about you. Asha. You get me. Don't change." She removes the vibrating phone from her bag. "Business." She looks at the caller display, grimacing, then opens a text. "Unexpected," she says. "Asha, there's a car downstairs. Let's eat later?"

"Of course. And – thank you."

And I mean it. I couldn't go back to 136. Jones is my lifeboat in a sea of places I don't want to swim towards. She came through for me. I owe her.

"Just try not to make me regret it. You heard the judge. They're watching us. And you know I don't like being centre stage." Then she goes. Heels clicking on the poured concrete floor.

Murphy comes over. He's still wearing the same retro leather jacket that he wore the first night I met him. "Not very maternal, is she?"

My mouth twitches. "No, but then again, I'm not much of a dutiful foster child type either."

Murphy's face is serious. "You're a kid, Asha."

I wonder, was I ever a kid? Or did being in the care homes mean none of us ever got that chance?

"Everything settled then?"

Something dawns on me, and I glare at him. "Wait. *You* pushed for me to go to college. That's why the judge was so keen to make the case for it."

He sighs. "Yeah. Hear me out, Asha. It feels like you're still stuck in that tournament. College could give you more options. A fresh start. You could even defer your place if you needed. Take some time. Go later in the year. Either way it would lift you out of here."

"You can't ask me to walk away – not now. I lost too much to do that."

He looks at the exit corridor ahead, defeated. "I am sorry about Dark. I thought we'd find him. I know how much losing him hurts." Murphy gives me a second, then adds, "Any idea why he was in New York?"

I shake my head. "He didn't tell me."

A sidelong glance. "I suppose you heard the Zu Tech building burnt down."

"It wasn't me." The words come out a little too fast.

Murphy frowns. "If it was, would you tell me? Asha, no matter what you do, you can't bring them back. You know that, right?"

"If I don't investigate Zu Tech, what did my sister die for?" I look at the floor. "Every day people contact me with more and more rumours, conspiracies about what happened at the tournament. About what that game was for. About what Zu Tech was trying to do with SHACKLE. But the truth might be even darker."

Murphy stops and touches my arm. When he speaks his voice is firm. "You can't engage. Please don't talk to them, Asha. Just forward any messages to me. The gag order is for national security, but it also protects you. People are watching. The authorities who are embarrassed they knew nothing, the online conspiracy theorists with agendas, and the people who are behind Zu Tech itself. We *are* investigating. The police, the government agencies. Until we know who was responsible, *pretend you know nothing.* Anything you say could jeopardize a potential trial or put you in danger. Understand?"

I look at him. "Pretending I know nothing is easy because that part is true. Do you think there will ever be a trial?"

Murphy nods. "I hope so," he says.

I don't hear much conviction. "Did you ever find out where Emily Webber went?"

"Why do you ask?"

I shake my head. Now isn't the time to say I used her old Zu Tech pass. "Just curious. She was the first person I met at Zu Tech. I saw her photo recently on a missing poster." Come to think of it, Emily was also one of the first fifty Zu Tech employees. *If you are someone who knows me, then you can find it where all this started.*

We walk on, heading towards the lobby. I see some smaller kids waiting on uncomfortable plastic chairs. Family court isn't just for my problems. One of the kids nudges her friend, and I pretend not to notice as she recognizes me. I hear her whisper as I pass, "Is that the girl from…?"

This could go one of two ways.

A small hand pulls at my dress. "Will you sign this?"

She must be around eight, her large eyes staring at me as she clutches a small stubby pencil and a piece of paper.

I go to sign it, and as I do she pulls up her sleeve to show a marker drawing on the inside of her wrist. The Zu Tech logo in black with a large red line through it. As I hand back the paper, she says, "I believe you. When I grow up, I want to be brave like you."

I watch her sit back down with a grin, showing the scrap of paper to her friend. Despite me letting the colours in my hair wash out, people still recognize me and see me as something I am not – normally a villain. But sometimes they see a hero. In reality I am neither. I'm just lost.

Murphy walks closer to me, moving me on. I smell his aftershave and the tea on his breath as we push open the doors at the front of the building. His voice is lower now, gentle. "Listen, I'm going to make sure this investigation is carried out. I'll keep you updated. Just remember what we know so far."

"And what is that?"

Murphy shrugs. "That nothing is ever as it seems."

I see the car then. Someone is standing beside it, waiting. The sun is behind them. For a second, I think … it's him, Dark, but then a cloud above moves and I see Augie. Shades hide his eyes. Jeans, trainers, a jacket. His face is tight, anxious.

"Murphy." He nods. "Asha, can we talk?"

"Yeah, we should."

Murphy tactfully leaves and we stand facing each other. It's the first time we've spoken since I accused Augie of wanting Dark dead. The words hang between us.

"Want to walk?" I ask. "I'm wearing a respectable dress. Chances are no online hater will recognize me. I know I barely do."

Augie nods, looking relieved. Then: "You look amazing, you always do." He sends the driver away and holds out a hand. After a moment, I grasp it, and he holds my fingers tight in his, squeezing them briefly. We start to walk.

I wait for him to speak first. He waits for me. In this battle of wills Augie caves in first.

"How did it go inside?"

"Jones is now my legal guardian."

"Happy?"

"I would have been happier if I could have been emancipated, but Jones's lawyers say I can't till I'm seventeen and have proof of earnings. This was the compromise."

"Lawyers. They only say what the person paying them wants to hear. I've had enough of them, since my mum passed. But I'm glad it worked out. Look. We haven't talked since..."

"I'm sorry about how I reacted."

Augie's fingers squeeze mine again. "You don't need to say anything."

"I do."

"You'd just found out. I understand. But I would never have wanted Dark dead, Asha. You know that, right?"

"Yeah. But, Augie, I don't think he's ... gone." He opens his mouth to reply and I push on. "That's not just grief talking. I really think Dark isn't dead."

The words slip out. I watch his face and see the look of shock, followed by hope. Ruby was right: Augie never wanted Dark dead. How could I have thought he would?

"OK, that beats what I need to say. You go first."

So I do.

When I finish, he asks, "How much time is left till the DNA results come through?"

I check my watch. "Twenty-nine hours."

"OK, then we deal with it in twenty-nine hours. Meantime, there's something I need to tell you, and you're not going to like it." He pauses and lets a breath out. "While you were at the hearing, the police came around to interview Josh, Ruby and me about the fire at Zu Tech. They traced the car I used that night. They know that all of us have a high-profile grudge against the place. Seemingly we're top of their suspect list."

I wince. My fault for asking him to come with me. "What did they say? What did you say?"

"Long story short – they took Ruby, Asha. They're holding her at the police station."

8

I go into crisis mode and pull out my phone. "Which station? I can get Murphy to join us there. Jones can get her lawyer, we can—"

"Asha." He runs his hand through his hair. "Josh doesn't want you there. Neither of them do."

"What? Augie, she's my friend—"

Augie's phone vibrates and he pulls it out to read a message. "They're out and heading back to the Tower. It's better if you talk to them there."

Augie and I get back first. I make coffee in the kitchen, trying to distract myself.

When Ruby and Josh arrive, they are mid-argument. Shouting at each other. I can hear them down the hall.

"She needs our help!" It's Ruby, and I've never heard her so upset.

"I know. I get it. But this can't keep happening, Ru, you know that. Even bloody Eliza knows that. Please—"

They walk into the kitchen. The second they see me they stop talking. Josh is the first to break the silence.

"Want to tell us anything about the fire at the old Zu Tech headquarters, Asha?"

I can feel the tension in the room. Ruby won't meet my eyes. Anger radiates from Josh.

"I heard about the fire," I say.

Josh explodes. "You heard? Give me a break. The police were here. They asked us where we were that night. Took our fingerprints. Took Ruby in for questioning."

"Josh," Ruby warns.

Josh looks at me. "I'm asking if you were involved."

I stare at him. Does he think I burnt down a building? "No, Josh, I did not deliberately destroy the Zu Tech offices. I wouldn't keep that kind of secret from you."

Josh flinches. My words are a dig at the secrets he once kept from me, and he knows it. He was blackmailed during the Zu Tech Tournament and took photos of the evidence I found and sent it to someone to save his little sister.

Ruby lets out a breath. "See, I told you Asha wouldn't—"

Josh cuts her off. "Were you there, Asha? I think we have a right to know."

"Josh, enough." Ruby's voice is firm.

"I understand you're going through a lot," Josh

continues. "I know because I was there with you. But … it's like you don't even care any more. Do you know what a conviction would mean for us?"

"I…"

Josh takes a step towards me, and Augie moves to my side.

"Let me spell it out for you, Asha. Second-degree arson with intent. It's a sentence, not a fine. A young offenders institute for you, but for us, at eighteen, that's prison. Four to six years. Do you know what happens to our mum, our little sister, if we get locked up? What it would do to me, losing Amy? Because I wouldn't ask her to wait for me. I couldn't do that to someone I love."

Ruby and Josh are the closest thing I have left to family. They brought me back from the brink. Welcomed me into their home. And I could ruin everything for them.

"Josh, I didn't burn down Zu Tech."

Josh runs his hand over his tightly cropped hair. "Great. Then where were you? Because I know for a fact you weren't in your room."

"How?" It's my turn to get angry. Has he been spying on me?

"I checked on you. We all do it, Ash. I don't know if you realize this, but since the bloody tournament none of us sleeps. I thought you might be up. I went to your room to see if you wanted to hang out or play something. And you weren't there."

Silence.

"I was with her," Augie says clearly and loudly. "She was in my room."

This, at least, isn't a lie.

"Seriously?" Josh says. "You and Santos?"

Ruby's voice is a mixture of disbelief and hurt. "You were with Augie? And you didn't tell me?"

I glance at Augie, who gives a tiny quick nod, then I look back at the twins. "I was in Augie's room. I needed someone to talk to."

Ruby looks even more gutted to hear that I went to talk to Augie and not her. Something inside me snaps. The part that is always telling me to do the stupid thing. "I knew you'd be online with Eliza. You always are. I didn't want to interrupt."

Ruby looks angry now too. "You've been cutting me out because you're, what, jealous? After everything we went through together? After I keep trying to reach out?"

I shrug like I don't care. "We know nothing about Eliza. You tell her everything. It means I can't trust you."

"She's my girlfriend, Ash! But I would never tell her your secrets. I was there for you. Why can't you trust me? Be happy for me?"

"I..." This is spiralling fast.

But Josh doesn't let me finish. "The reason the police took Ruby in is that she didn't have an alibi, Asha. She wasn't online with Eliza."

Confused, I stare at Josh. His eyes are bright and angry. "They interviewed us all separately here first. Like you, I thought Ruby was online with Eliza that night, so I told them the truth about where I was – said that I'd gone to Mum's and then to see my girlfriend. Got picked up on a dozen CCTV cameras on the tube on the way. But Ru was in her room alone. She doesn't have an alibi, Asha. They're treating her as a 'person of interest'. The police know someone ordered a car from near here to take them to Zu Tech just before the fire. If Eliza hadn't jumped in and got Ruby a lawyer, she'd still be at the station."

"Why would they think you had a motive?"

Ruby sighs in frustration. "Because we stood beside you when you took Zu down. We get the same threats online as you, Asha, the same haters."

"But..." I grapple to find the right words. Was I so wrapped up in my own drama that I missed all this? "Ruby can just say she was with me and Augie. That we were training, right?"

"No, we can't," Augie says miserably. "It's like Josh said. They interviewed all of us at the same time. I didn't know Ruby needed an alibi. I said I was alone with you, Asha."

Josh gives an angry kick to one of the chairs at the table to put it back in place. "As usual, team Santos and Kennedy protect each other while we get thrown under the bus." His voice is bitter. "Because my guess? You were there, Asha, and you didn't tell us. If you had, we could have helped you. Or, at the very least, realized we'd need to have stories lined up." He turns to leave but then stops. "I am sorry about Dark, but" – he glances at Ruby and then back to me – "you keep putting us in danger by keeping secrets. I'm not sure how we come back from this."

He leaves and Ruby goes to follow him.

"Ru, please, I'm so sorry."

She shrugs, and I can see the exhaustion on her face. "Maybe you are, and I know you're hurt, Asha, but he's right. I can't keep doing this if you won't trust me." She turns and goes after Josh.

"Ruby?" I call after her, but they both keep walking, Josh has his arm around Ruby's shoulder as she leans into him.

I turn to Augie. "I need to go to the police. Tell Murphy what I know. I was there that night. I can describe those people I saw."

Augie sighs. "If you do, they'll lock you up for breaking and entering. You'll never find answers that way. That's what you want to do, right? That's what all this is about? Getting revenge. Finding him."

I don't say anything. I sink further into one of the kitchen chairs.

"Thought so." His voice is cold.

Augie doesn't say anything else. He leaves and I don't try to stop him.

***

"If you are someone who knows me, then you can find it where all this started."

I pause the video of Zu, freezing the frame and opening up another search page. Everything that happened in the kitchen hurts too much to think about, so instead I've somehow packed it up in a mental box, shoving it to a dark corner of my mind. But the emotions slowly seep out, even as I try to distract myself.

Focus. The bare facts are on the screen in front of me. Zu Thorp. Born thirty-three years before me on November 18th. Only child. Parents academics. Divorced when he was ten. Father lectured at MIT, mother at Cambridge. Private grammar school. Parents had money?

Scholarship paid for his undergrad degree. Mother died while he was in college. Cause of death?

I hack the gov.uk general register office – Huntington's disease. Hereditary. Beth 1 was telling the truth about that part, but it doesn't explain Zu's appearance in the video. Unless he made himself ill trying to find a cure. Experimental treatments?

Zu dropped out of college around a year after his mother died and started Zu Tech in Cambridge before moving to London. *If you are someone who knows me, then you can find it where all this started.* Was Cambridge where this started?

I zoom in on the framed photo on the desk. The child in front of the old-fashioned video game arcade. The sign is clearly visible: NEBULOUS ARCADE.

I run image searches for the sign and word searches for the name. There are a few software companies, but none are listed with dates that match Zu's early days. Zero returns for any arcade games stores in the UK. So where was the picture taken?

I rub my eyes and push back in my chair. An old clip from a TV interview of Zu Thorp is playing on the screen. It's a rare one, not available on the main search engines, a backstage interview after Zu won his first small award at a start-up tech conference. I zone out, watching him. The smile, the almost nervous energy. This man looks so mild-mannered, so young, and yet just a few years later he's responsible for my sister's murder.

The interviewer thrusts the microphone at Zu. The foam square around it carries a small TV station logo: NY TV AM.

Reporter: You must be so excited about your first major win?

Zu: It was a team effort. I'm grateful for everyone in my lab and, of course, for my investors. Also, I couldn't have done this without one particular friend – Lydia Rock; her faith has kept me going.

Reporter: What a bright industry light to have in your corner. Do you think someday your start-up, Zu Tech, will be as big as Rock Industries?

Zu: (Laughs) Well, they say if you're going to dream, you should dream big.

Reporter: And any plans for the rest of your time here? Is this your first time in New York?

Zu: First time back since I was a child. Definitely looking forward to visiting some of the places that inspired me…

I hit pause. Zu was in New York as a child? It doesn't say that anywhere in his biography. I search for other interviews from that award show but can't find any. I rub my eyes again, glancing at the watch on my wrist. It's late. I can't remember when I last ate or moved.

I shouldn't have let Ruby walk away angry. I have to tell her where I was the night of the fire. She and Josh put everything on the line for me. They welcomed me into their family. They deserve the truth about the "Zu" we met.

I ignore the rumbling in my stomach and go into the corridor, almost colliding with the person outside. For a second, I'm so distracted I think it's Ruby.

But it's not her. It's Jones. This time she's in a black tailored dress and carrying a smart tablet.

Her eyes sweep my room and the screen on my computer. "Garden, five minutes."

"I was about to…"

"Asha, you need food. And we need to talk." Then she walks away with a look that makes me nervous, leaving behind only a whiff of expensive perfume.

***

The smell of food hits me when I get to the roof garden. Asian. A collection of cardboard takeaway containers, two cups of green tea and chopsticks.

Jones nods. "Eat."

I take a container of noodles, veggies and tofu. It's not until I'm holding the chopsticks that I realize how hungry I am. I steal a few veggie dumplings from another container and add them to mine before sinking back into the chair. Then I wait. I need to know where this is going before I start. Maya always said there is no such thing as a free meal.

Jones looks uncomfortable. I can read her now – a bit. We go way back – her, me and Dark. I think of Dark in those days. Radiating excitement as he told me about his new gig with Ma Jones. *We can do this. Just you and me against the world. Jones will sign us both. I'll make sure of it. Then we can start over. Build a reputation. Make this place into what we want. Together.*

I said "no" to him. Because no matter how much I'd wanted to go with Dark, I couldn't disappear on Maya. He left without me. It broke my heart. It hurt. Not as much as it's hurting now, though. What if I hadn't said no.

"Asha." It's Jones. "Are you OK?"

A sob breaks free, and Jones comes to me, gently removing the food container and setting it down as she places her hand on my arm.

"It's OK, let it out. All of it."

So I do, and I don't know how much time passes, only that Jones holds me and rubs my back as she does. "It's OK," she says again.

"Thanks," I say, sniffling. "And sorry, I just…"

"I figured." Jones stands and pours two green teas, handing me one. "Drink. Then tell me what's up."

I hold the mug close to me, letting it warm my hands. Is this what it feels like when you have an adult in your life you can turn to? Is this what Jones is to me now? "How much do you know?"

She sighs. "I know about what happened to Ruby. I already had a word with Josh. As their manager, I should always be the first call. The kid should know that. What I *don't* know is why you were at Zu Tech on the night of the fire."

I swallow. "I went looking for answers."

Jones leans forward. "And did you find them?"

I nod, and when I speak my words are almost a whisper. "Yes. I did."

I tell her about finding a message from Zu, briefly touching the flash drive that now sits beside Maya's locket around my neck. Old habits. I tell her about the people with guns, about Beth starting the fire, about lying to Josh and Ruby.

"I've made such a mess of things, Jones. I was trying to protect them by keeping them out of it."

Jones sighs and nods. "Yeah, but you're not the only one." She stands and grabs a small screen device, opening a download before handing it to me. "My turn. You should watch this."

The screen opens on a paused video file. It's a clip from a CCTV camera of the city-centre intersection in New York, the one where Dark died. Familiar, too familiar.

"I can't watch it again," I say, pushing the screen away.

Jones pushes it back. "Look closer. It's not from that night."

I look at the screen again. At the blue mailbox beside a *New York Post* vending machine. It's night: same street, different angle. The street traffic again is minimal as it's late. There's a person walking across the road, head down, shoulders hunched. My heart starts to hammer inside me. DARK.

He walks across the frame. I can only see his profile, but I instantly know it's him. My fingers go to touch the screen. "When?"

Jones sighs. "Three days before the explosion. I wasn't sure. You only see his face in profile. I had to run it through a gait-recognition software program to match his movements."

"You knew … you knew where he was before the blast, and you didn't tell me?" Now it's my turn to be angry.

Jones's voice is sharp. "I wanted to be sure. You were convinced he'd been taken. That footage shows him walking around New York, seemingly a free man. I didn't want to raise your hopes in case I was wrong. The hearing was coming up. If you ran out on everything to go to him, what do you think would happen? I got it three days before the explosion. I decided to get the video verified before showing you. I was going to give it to you after the hearing, once I was sure it was real and not some deep fake. But then … well, you know."

"We could have helped him," I say.

"I know. Believe me, I've thought the same. I just … I never believed that could happen. You know him, Asha. Better than anyone. You knew how paranoid he was. How could someone get close enough to him to plant a bomb?"

She's right. "How did you get this?"

Jones shrugs. "Same way I get most things."

Jones has deep web contacts; she could easily have posted for intel, offering a reward.

"Why did you?"

"Why the hell do you think?" Her tone is incredulous. "I was there in that tournament, Asha. I went through it, too. It's like opening Pandora's box. Everything that happened left a mark. It had consequences for me." Jones pauses. When she speaks again, her voice is flat. "I'm your guardian, Asha, and I'm going to be honest with you. Josh and Ruby have debts to pay. Thanks to you, everyone in gaming has an opinion about them, Augie as well. There's a target on all their backs. You thought you were the only one being tagged?" She snorts. "And I think Josh is starting to get tired of always being in the shadow of you and Santos. He'll leave, Asha. Even though he cares about you, sooner or later, he'll leave. Go to another team. Unless you give him a reason to stay."

She watches her words sink in, then goes on. "Same with Ruby. You think she's happy with a long-distance relationship? That Eliza hasn't suggested to her that a move, a change of scene, wouldn't be good for her? Not everyone is living in the past like you. They will move on, and when they do what will you be left with?"

I flinch. There is silence before she speaks again. "Look, I am sorry, but I need to call it as I see it. I've been managing eSports teams for years. I've seen groups split for a lot less than what you guys went through. You need to decide. You let them in fully and tell them what you're doing, or you let them move on with their lives."

"You didn't mention Augie." I swallow. "You said Ruby and Josh would leave, not him. Why?"

Jones rolls her eyes at me. "I think we both know why. Augie won't leave you."

"What would you do?"

She shrugs. "This would never be me. But if you want to keep the twins, I'd sign up for a tournament somewhere. Your viral fame, for good or bad, means you have fans. Tournament organizers think you'll give them higher ratings. You can use that."

Jones takes a large A4 envelope from a small table. The logo at the top reads "Rock". At the right-hand bottom corner large red letters: PRIVATE AND CONFIDENTIAL. "It's an offer. From Lydia Rock. From the woman who literally owns half the planet to play in a tournament. You've forty-eight hours to decide, then they're taking the offer elsewhere because it starts soon. The game is *Capture the City*."

I think of the interview with Zu I just watched. *I couldn't have done this without one particular friend – Lydia Rock.* Coincidence?

"*Capture the City*," I repeat, thinking back to the old-school version we used to play: capture the flag. It was big in our group home. All the kids did it, even Maya. We played in teams, hiding our flags outside the care home in the surrounding wasteland, then searching to capture each other's flags and defend our own while the clock ticked down. The winner was the team that had captured the most flags during the allotted time.

It meant we got to use the city around us as a place to play, so of course the authorities hated us for doing it. The people running our facility even tried to ban it, but that never stopped us. It was our escape from reality. The first time I ever talked to Dark was during that game. Then one night, when we were playing it, we stumbled across the old factory and found our gaming tribe. That game meant everything to us.

"They want you, Asha. They want the buzz. Without you they'll get a different team." She hands me the package. "It would keep you together, for now. Get the twins earning. At least think about it. What you've been doing for the last six, seven weeks, shutting your friends out, it hasn't worked. Maybe it's time to try a new approach?"

I stiffen. "I'm not abandoning Dark."

"I don't expect you to stop looking for the truth," says Jones, "but there's something I haven't told you about the tournament. It's in New York, Asha."

New York.

"Aren't you curious to find out why Dark was there? If you were there, you'd have a better chance of working that out. Eat, then think about it." Jones's heels click across the floor as she leaves. She pauses at the door, turning back. Her voice sounds worried when she speaks. "I really hope the DNA search comes back saying Dark's still alive. If he is, I know you'll find him. I just hope when you do, it's worth it."

I turn over the envelope in my hand. The food on the table beside me suddenly doesn't seem appealing.

But I can at least make one thing right tonight.

9

Unknown: A deal is a deal. I got you a pass, Kennedy. You were supposed to share what you found. You haven't.

Me: I know who you are. We meet in person. Until then, nothing.

I close the messaging app. Murphy's information came through a few moments ago. There was movement on one of Emily Webber's credit cards, a bank statement he's sent through to me. Plane tickets to NY. It was her pass that got me into Zu Tech. Her knowledge that there was more information inside Zu's office. Her cards are active and she's in the place Dark was. Webber worked at Zu Tech from the start, employee number thirty-five according to payroll. My gut says Unknown is Webber.

But what is she looking for and why? Before I hand over any information, I want answers. In person.

I check the watch on my wrist again. Six hours left. Nervous energy twists inside me. *Please let him be alive.*

***

The wind is picking up when I arrive at the Maritime Museum. The sun has long since faded into an autumn night. I had to check in with Josh's girlfriend, Amy, to find them. A cold northern breeze cuts through my black gaming jacket and leggings. Josh, Augie and Ruby are already there, along with a technician and a series of black boxes placed near the entrance, a mounted arrangement of carved wooden figureheads from various ships is close by.

"What are you doing here?" Josh says.

I look at Augie and Ruby and then back at Josh. *Be brave.* "I came to make amends."

Josh shrugs. "We're playing. Eliza got us the gig."

Eliza again. The person who came through for Ruby when I didn't even know she was in trouble. When I had created the problem in the first place.

"She arranged for us to test *Capture the City*, the new version that Rock is promoting."

I stare at the flight cases. The high-tech equipment, the drone in its box. The power banks. I have a grudging respect for Eliza, but I still don't trust her. Also … what were the chances they would be playing this game? But maybe now isn't the time to go into that.

"Nice," I say.

"It's not *nice*, Asha," snaps Josh. "We haven't played on the circuit in so long that this is probably the only hope we have of making money till next year."

I look down. I've been so focused on myself that I forgot I am, or was, part of a team.

Ruby shakes her head at her brother. "Cut it out."

I'm grateful, but I don't need her to stand up for me. I glance at Augie, whose eyes haven't left me since I arrived. I take a big deep breath as the wind cuts through us all. "Can I play? With you? We were a team once. I messed up. But I promise to do things differently this time. I'm – I'm sorry."

Ruby looks to Josh and then to Augie. Both of them look at her. She takes a moment, then nods and says in a soft voice, "OK."

I breathe out. I don't ask if she's sure or not. If this is my second chance with all of them, then I'm taking it before they can change their mind.

Augie hands me a bag, glasses and gloves. "Suit up."

I take it from him and then look around. "The game is like capture the flag meets augmented reality," Josh says.

"Where are our opponents?" I ask.

Ruby is putting on her gloves. "We're playing the Misfits, locals, skilled. We get this side of the museum.

They get the other, near the statue of Peter the Great. We have an hour once we log on to get their flag. Every fifteen minutes, the play area shrinks, and then it's sixty seconds to move into the new zone."

"How will we recognize them?" I ask, looking around at the grey Georgian buildings that seem empty.

Ruby finishes suiting up. "When you have a player in your line of sight, a sniper circle, just like in a regular computer game, will appear. Green for a teammate, red for an opposing team."

"And the flags?" I ask.

Josh hands me a large square of fabric, a dirty grey colour.

"Well, they should be easy enough to hide," Ruby says.

He shakes his head. "You think? Then you hide it and run the drone. I'm playing protection and healer. Asha, you and Santos are on the attack. All weapons are fully calibrated and ready to go."

The guns are light, black and trimmed with long barrels and a Rock logo. I look at them, unimpressed.

"The guns all trigger a response in the suits, Asha," Ruby says quietly.

I think about dropping my gun back in the box – of all the things from Zu Tech to keep. "Pain response? I hate pain response."

Josh shrugs. "All the game manufacturers are doing it now; everyone wants their reality to feel more real, to have consequences. Some people like it."

I look at him. "Some people are sick."

I see it then: a half-grin that he tries to hide, like despite himself he's already starting to forgive me.

"Ready?" he asks. He pulls a holo map out of a box that glows green in the darkness: a 3D virtual model of our current location. "We're here at the National Maritime Museum. The Misfit crew are starting here, by the Cutty Sark. Once you put on your glasses, you'll see the line marking the game areas. This is a turf war. We hide our flag; they hide theirs. The winner is the one who captures the other team's flag first. We get a drone to help us scout, but the operator needs to be within twenty-five metres of the team flag. Meaning when you launch it you run the risk of giving away your own flag's location. The added complication here is that on top of your reality, the game will also project some augmented-reality monsters you need to deal with."

Ruby takes over. "One location rule. You can't go inside the buildings. Only play outside. Got it?"

Suddenly I feel unsure – about the game, about everything.

Ruby spots my hesitation and steps closer. "Asha, it's not going to be like last time. I'll be in your ear with intel. Augie will be beside you. This isn't much different to that virtual running app you had with the zombies." Her voice is a whisper so that only I can hear. She touches my arm. "Look, I know what showing up here cost you. Let's talk afterwards?"

The knot inside my heart eases.

Josh looks at the dark sky and the small pinpricks of stars just visible despite the city lights. "It's time. Let's go."

In spite of Ruby's words, I'm still nervous. I haven't played anything like this since SHACKLE. I pause for a fraction of a second before starting my glasses up.

Now it is Josh by my side. "Before you flick those on, breathe. Let it out. Just focus on what you need to in the game. Leave everything else outside."

His hands adjust a sensor on my glasses. "Remember, it's just a game."

"They always say that, and you know something? Somehow it never is."

My eyes follow the red and yellow dots on the glasses as they calibrate, and then the world around me starts to re-emerge.

I give a soft whistle. Rock have done a good job. This is hyperreality, a layering of VR and augmented reality on top of each other. It's the same place and landscape, but the entire building is now tagged with neon graffiti and gamer tags. Puddles of colour are on the ground. Splashes of lime green, vivid pinks and toxic greens cover the statues and the museum's facade. A giant skull and cross bone motif – steam punk pirates meet neon – painted across the entrance. Augmented reality seamlessly placed on top of physical buildings. The effect is like disappearing down a rabbit hole to another dimension.

Out of the corner of my eye I see a flock of parrots, and

in the distance old-fashioned sailing ships on the Thames. A pirate flag flutters on the top masts of most. I let the wind whip around me, inhaling the smell of the damp leaves, the river in the distance. Then it hits me, that rush of adrenaline that comes from wanting to play. To leave my life behind, even if it's just for a few hours.

I missed this. I missed them.

"Are you seeing what I am seeing?" Ruby's voice is in my ear now.

Josh speaks through the headset. "Next level 'Gamer Land'."

I look over at the dirty square of fabric Ruby holds and it is now glowing neon blue.

"Guess we'd better get going," Ruby says. "See you on the other side."

Josh turns to Augie and Me. "Good luck, matey." He grins. "Don't walk any planks."

"We should leave before he does more pirate puns," Augie says.

I nod. "Higher ground?" I suggest. "Get an overview. Save Ruby from launching the drone too soon and giving our home location away."

Augie nods. "Ruby said we couldn't go *in* the buildings. She never said anything about not going *on top* of them." He points towards the roof of the University of Greenwich. "Think you can make it there? Or are you too out of practice, Kennedy?"

"Are you challenging me?"

I can feel his grin. It feels like before. "You think you can win?"

My voice is certain. "Yeah, I do."

***

We run the length of the campus and the road to Grand Square together. Matching each other's pace and I'm suddenly glad I kept up running on the treadmill in Bill's Gym. The baroque building is lit by neon tags, some of which seem to move when viewed – dozens of different team symbols, a turf war going back years. And I remember it then. The last time I played this game, a lifetime ago, before the tech was cutting edge, must have been with Dark, and for a second the thought of him makes me lose focus. I knock against one of the security padlocks on the exterior doors and it rattles, creating an echoing sound. Too loud.

Augie stops and pulls me into one of the closed doorways, crouching low, our breath becoming one. Close, too close.

"What was that?"

"Sorry." Damn it.

His fingers touch my cheek for a moment and it tingles like an electric shock. "You sure about playing, Asha? You haven't since…"

He doesn't need to finish the sentence. We both remember the last time I played.

I nod. Incapable of more. Suddenly I'm glad that if I'm

playing, it's with him, Josh and Ruby. I don't think I could otherwise.

Augie lets out a sigh then uses a hand signal to move my gaze to the other side of the square, where I can clearly see an orange tag moving in the shape of a lion. The word "Misfits" is underneath. We're getting closer to their territory.

We run again, this time from doorway to doorway, window ledge to window ledge, using the architecture of the building and its shadows to stay hidden. Then we climb up, scaling the structure utilizing the drainpipe, cut stone and ornate rails until we reach the clock tower. My fingers and arms ache from pulling myself up the wall of the building, my back is soaked in sweat. The physical movement means I have no time to think of anything else, and it's a sweet relief. My brain finally stops racing. There's just this.

Beside me, Augie anchors himself against a wall. The training sessions he does mean he's barely out of breath. Games aren't just about your physical skill in the game or your mental ability now. They test your body's resilience. Making you fight on every level. At least in the pro tournaments; for the average player there is always a comfort option. But Augie is a pro and he looks it. I never noticed till now his upper body strength. The ease and grace in the way he moves.

When we get to the clock tower, we pause. The wind is stronger here. Both of us look out at the scene below.

The augmented reality has layered what looks like a pirate market on top of the square. Chests filled with glistening jewels, cannons ready to be fired, food and ale stalls. Skeletons in metal cages dangle from buildings, moving back and forth in the breeze. All eerily quiet. But no sign of the flag or the Misfits.

Then I hear Ruby. "Eye is up and open, scouting the quadrant next to yours." In the distance, our drone hovers low and then starts to move. "Transferring my view to yours." A minimized window opens up in front of me, and in it I catch a tiny flash of orange – the orange of the Misfits' flag. It's hidden on top of the mast of the *Cutty Sark*, an old British sea clipper now on permanent display, with at least two Misfit team members guarding it. I pinpoint where it is below. Mapping a route using our view from the tower to pick the best route. The one that will expose us the least.

"Let's go capture a flag." Augie taps the side of his glasses to close the window. "Ruby, Josh, we are going in."

Night becomes our friend as we pass through the narrow lane between the Grand Square and the green park, heading towards the trees and the building near the *Cutty Sark*. A small circle of water surrounds her, the augmented reality adding sea monsters underneath. Long tentacles stretch out from the water, grasping at anything that flutters nearby. We hide in the trees and watch, looking for a visual on our opponents before we move.

"Asha, are you still OK?"

Augie is blocking the mic in his suit, keeping this between us. I do the same. "No. But I don't think I have a choice."

"We always have a choice. You know that."

I don't think he's talking about the game. "I'm broken, Augie, and I'm not going to ask you to wait and see if that changes."

He gently runs his thumb over my frozen cheek. His expression is crushed but somehow still hopeful. "Asha, I'm here. I know now" – his hand gestures around us – "may not be the right time or our time, but you're not alone. It's weird but I've felt something drawing us together ever since that day outside Zu Tech."

His hand rests on my arm. I move closer to him without thinking, inhaling the scent of coffee and cinnamon, allowing it to anchor me. I'm so tired of feeling cold and empty. Augie has never lied to me. Time seems to slow around us. But then I stop. There's an image in my head. Blue eyes, black hair. The smell of citrus and wood. Dark's been gone forty-eight days. There are four hours left till the DNA results are in. I don't know if he's alive or dead, just that part of me is missing. However much I care about Augie, Gods help me, I love Dark. No matter what happens, Augie deserves something more than a heart already lost to someone else.

I pull away from him and see the flash of hurt on his face. Then we both see a movement: two of the Misfit crew.

The Misfits weren't taking any chances. One is moving

in the shadows of a nearby building. The other remains crouched by the gangway, the only way on to or off the boat that holds their flag.

"Smart."

Augie is all business now, the emotions now locked away and back on his mic. "But where are the third and fourth players, the drone? Ruby, any ideas?"

Ruby sounds out of breath. "I found the drone and operator, but they also found us when the space contracted. Josh is dealing with one player while I try to take out the drone controller." A pause. "Damn it, they found me. They're trying to knock our drone out of the sky. Hang on, guys."

Augie looks at his watch. "We're running out of time. Ten minutes left. The area reduction will be happening again soon. I can keep one of them occupied. Asha, you want to deal with the defence? Try and get on to the ship? If we take the flag, we end this."

I've got this, I think. "Yeah."

"Whatever you do, don't let them see you coming or they'll drop the gangway into the water. If that happens, there's no way to get on board."

Great. I get the plank or water with the sea monsters.

We descend, and as I prepare to go a flash of white light comes from nearby. Augie pulls me down, making me crouch lower. His finger moves to his lips. "Shh."

I hold my breath and watch as the beam of a torch lights up areas around us. Some scaffolding. An old wooden bench, window boxes. And then someone with orange paint splattered on their clothes comes into view.

Augie's voice is calm. "Go."

"On it." I look back as I run to see Augie and the Misfit team player trading gunfire. A stray laser tag bullet passes near my arm, creating a searing heat. Pain response. They always lie when they say it's minor. This one stings like hell.

"Asha, coming round the corner – look out." Ruby's voice in my ear. I look up for a moment, distracted as I watch the two drones crash overhead.

Coming round the corner. But what she said doesn't make sense; we know where all four Misfit players are now. Who's left?

And that's when the tight grip of an arm closes around my neck.

The sniper circle doesn't flicker on my glasses. Is this part of the game? Real? Or not real?

I try to prise the hand from my throat, but its grip only tightens. Fingertips press into my skin, long nails breaking through. Another hand claws at my neck. I'm choking. Panic starts to rise inside me. My eyes well with tears. I struggle to breathe. My throat burns.

Around me I can hear the others in the game. No one seems to realize what's happening. I try to scream but nothing comes out. I use my legs to kick hard against the inner leg of my attacker, once, twice, nothing, and then I connect with their knee. I put my full force into the kick and hear a crunching noise, then a groan. They release their hold for one second. It's all the breathing space I need. Bill's fight training kicks in and I elbow-jab them so hard they stagger, giving me time to turn and face them, fists raised.

A face. Male. Thirties? Almost grey-looking skin, stubble, bruises and a large old angry scar on the right side of his cheek. He lunges and grasps at the chain that holds my locket and the flash drive, but it doesn't break; the necklace instead cuts into the skin around my neck. I throw out a desperate hand, this time connecting with him, nails digging in, ripping material from his shirt. He falls back, just enough for me to scramble up and start to run, choking, gasping for breath.

I keep running. When I eventually look over my shoulder, I see him running into the shadows, his movements jerky.

"One down." Augie's voice is in my ear. "Going for the second player." I can't breathe enough to say anything as I creep towards the ship. Was that part of the game or not? All I know is something feels wrong.

My heart is thumping. On my glasses the countdown clock comes into view. Three minutes left. Ruby's hiding place is now outside the zone area. I can hear her and Josh in my ear, running. They have seconds to find another safe place.

Augie is somewhere close fighting another player. My eyes blur. My throat is raw. I go past the scaffolding we saw earlier and take a piece of light timber, hoping it is long enough. Then I make my way to the ship, the opposite side to where the Misfit guard lies in wait by the gangway. I slide the wood over the water till it gently touches the ship's wooden deck on the other side. I hop on the board. It wobbles, but I am out of time to find another way. I run the plank, praying it doesn't break, then jump to the other side, gun out, shooting the guard in the leg. The pain reaction is instant and again more than minor.

I don't stop. I climb towards the crow's-nest as the guard below recovers and starts to move. They're fast and are at the bottom of the mast seconds after me, shooting with the laser tag guns. I pivot and cling to the rigging. Stretching my hand out, fingertips grasping in the wind, I reach towards the fabric hanging from the crow's-nest.

I miss it. They're gaining on me. So I stretch again, my last chance, and now I grip the flag. As I pull it towards me, a GAME OVER sign floats across my view. I wave the flag, holding it tight as the wind, stronger now, tries to rip it from me.

Almost instantly Ruby starts screaming in my comms. "We did it, Asha!"

Josh is chanting some football victory song.

My head feels like it will explode. Breathing is still hard.

Below, the Misfit chasing me drops back to the deck and I start to descend. I watch them remove their glasses and their baseball cap. Long dark hair whips around them. They're about fifteen, with brown skin covered in sparks of neon paint.

Once I hit the deck, I realize how hurt I am. "You

cheated." My voice is hoarse, rasping, my throat so sore I can barely get the words out.

"What?" They sound defensive, angry.

"That thing that attacked me?" I gasp.

They look at me like I am speaking a different language, raising their hands. "You know, some people are sore losers. You, Asha Kennedy, are a sore winner."

They walk off just as Augie and Ruby come around the corner.

Augie's smile dies on his face as he watches me take off my glasses. "Asha, what happened to your neck?"

Soft rain starts to fall. "Can we get out of here?" I say.

"OK." He looks troubled but follows me. As we move, I open my hand and look at the piece of material I ripped from my attacker's shirt. It's a grey high-tech material – unmistakable. Zu Tech's patented smartwear, and on the reverse a tag:

Zu Tech security, London HQ

I'm still staring at it when a buzzing sound comes from my wrist. The DNA results are in.

10

Confirmed dead.

Forty-nine days after Zu Tech's last tournament, the boy I love has been confirmed dead.

The world falls away when I open the report with the DNA results.

Blood on fragments of debris found in the car are confirmed as the same DNA as that on Dark's toothbrush.

It's like losing Maya all over again. The rock I'd been building my world on, my foundation, is gone.

I'm angry. Angry at myself. For allowing myself to hope, to dream, to want. But dreams and wants aren't for people like me. Growing up in the care homes, I knew that, and yet … Dark is dead. Maya is dead. Annie, the woman Maya loved, is dead. Probably thousands more I never knew too. And Zu Thorp – or whoever was behind Zu Tech – needs to pay.

I don't care any more about the cost of bringing them down. Cold, angry rage fills every hollow corner of me. The words I said before to Jones never seemed truer. I won't stop until everyone involved in this burns.

I don't say anything on the way back to the Tower. I can't. I need to process. The others talk excitedly around me and over me about our win, not realizing anything has changed. Augie looks at me but doesn't push when I shake my head. Perhaps he thinks it's my neck that's bothering me.

I go to my room alone and shut the door when we arrive. Surrounding myself with my murder boards of clues and questions. Maya's face is on one, along with an almost faded Polaroid of Dark. Tears don't come this time. I'm past crying. All that is left is vengeance.

***

It's late when I track the twins and Augie down in one of the games rooms. They're emerging from different pods, having played *League of Legends*. Still Josh's favourite game to play after a win.

Now or never. "Can we talk … please?"

Josh sighs, his smile vanishing. "I know that tone. It's never good when she uses that tone."

Ruby chucks a haptic glove at him. "Shut it. What's up,

Ash? You seemed … different after the game."

We sit on the beanbags on the floor. I'm not sure where to begin, but then Augie sits down beside me and puts his hand on my arm and, somehow, I settle. I owe him this too.

"Augie lied for me when he said I was with him the night of the Zu Tech fire. I asked him to be my alibi." Josh flinches. "I didn't burn it down. But I was there, and I saw what happened. I should have told you at the time, but I thought if I did I'd implicate you, make you an accessory to me breaking in. I made a mistake, and I made things worse. Now I want to tell you everything."

And I do. Like by saying the words out loud they'll lose their power over me. They don't. For me, what happened in the tournament isn't over. I'm still trapped inside. I can't move on, and losing Dark makes me feel like I never will. He was my everything, and maybe I didn't really know that till it was confirmed he is gone. I try to ignore the way Augie flinches.

When I finish, Ruby has tears in her eyes. She doesn't say anything, just reaches over and wraps me in a hug. "Ash, why didn't you talk to me sooner?"

I sigh. "You'd risked so much for me already. I thought if I kept my distance, you'd be safer. I'm toxic, Ruby. Everyone thinks that."

"But we know the truth," Josh says quietly. "After what happened, part of me wanted to believe it was over. That we could all move on, you'd find Dark and go back to normal. But it's not over, is it?"

"No."

"What do you need?"

"I've had an offer from Rock. It's a spot for us in their tournament, aka their publicity drive for Christmas sales. It means I'd have a cover story to go to New York and see what I can find out about why Dark was there and what any of this has to do with Zu's message and the Founders. I won't force you to come with me…"

Josh doesn't even hesitate. "*Capture the City.* We'll go."

"They killed Dark and Maya, maybe more—" I start, but Ruby stops me.

"And you think that they won't hurt us if we stay here and ignore what they're doing?"

"This isn't just your fight, Asha," Augie says. "It never was. They lied to all of us. Hurt all of us."

"Everyone connected with me has officially died. You could sit this out."

Josh laughs. "Seriously? Your cover is an eSports tournament. Who else is going to get you into shape for that? No offence but you need to level up."

I glance at Josh. The guy with so much already on the line. I think of his mum, who still tries to feed me once a week at their flat. Ruby and Dawn, who he wants better lives for and who he would literally die for. Amy, his girlfriend, and how he lights up around her.

Then I look at Ruby, who doesn't hesitate to feel everything, to give everything to her friendships, her family. I think of how she is with Eliza. The way they look when they're together. Eyes always finding each other in a crowd. How they were constantly touching each other when Eliza came to London to see her. Small gestures, a love story. Even if I don't fully trust Eliza, I recognize that.

And Augie, who stayed even when I tried to push him away.

They all have so much to lose, yet they're still here with me.

The tears fall down my face as I blink them away. "OK. Then this is what I was thinking…"

***

The next few days pass in a blur of training with Josh, Ruby and Augie. Augie doesn't try to talk to me about my feelings again. Which is good as I'm not sure I have any left. Only a cold, icy emptiness. He stays by my side as much as he can, not talking, just being there, as do Ruby and Josh. Even with them around me, the anger I feel becomes sharper, until it's almost a solid force.

On my second to last day in London, Unknown texts.

Unknown: Heard you're going to NY.

Me: Where did you hear that? I know who you are by the way, Webber.

Unknown: I knew you would figure it out.

Me: I'm still not sending you anything till I meet you face to face.

Unknown: We'll meet. I'll be in touch.

I look at my trace – the signal as usual has been bounced between six different VPNs. Webber was supposedly sending a message from a VPN in Algeria, Afghanistan, Iraq, Lebanon, Libya or North Korea. If she had added in Somalia and Syria, it would have been the full set of non-extradition countries to the UK. Why is she trying to make it seem like she is hiding where the authorities can't reach her? And where is she really hiding? What does she know?

We'll meet. I realize then. Webber is still in New York.

***

It's late as I start to open other files and searches. Still nothing on Nebulous Arcade, the place in the background of the photo of Zu as a child. I was sure that was a clue, but perhaps not.

I turn again to the company records for Zu Tech. Beth said the Founders were his *early investors.* The interview he gave mentioned Lydia Rock. Was she involved? Could she be one of the Founders or just a close friend like he mentioned to the reporter? It's no surprise that the original documents that might list who they were are somehow "missing" from gov.uk's Companies House. But it didn't take long to track down Zu Tech's first lawyer before they went big. A tiny office run by a nice old man near Cambridge. Bill organized a small break-in yesterday.

Nothing was taken or damaged apart from the hard copy of one file that is now on my desk.

The papers inside list the investors in a brand-new company called Zu Tech. Well, one investor: Pi Investments. The name rings alarm bells. Something Bill said about the company who had been sniffing around wanting to buy Dark's assets. The company that knew too much about Dark and what he did before he went solo. The one that was looking to acquire his holdings. Are they the same firm?

I open up a search on Pi Investments. It's a shell corporation. One of those companies in a tax-free haven that lists a gazillion other companies as operating from a single office. Who actually owns Pi Investments is harder to trace, but I eventually find they own an office block in New York. On the same street where Dark was killed.

It's a slow-dawning realization. The way Dark glanced at the CCTV, making sure his face was caught on camera. He knew I'd search that footage, scan the area, run a search on any businesses.

He was trying to send me a message before he died.

11

If I chase down the truth, then I'll get answers. That's what I want. Isn't it?

I think about it as I have breakfast with Jones. It's just the two of us, early. Jones is flying out before us. Augie, Ruby, Josh and I are flying out tonight. It feels weird leaving this place.

"Here." Jones hands me a small gift bag.

"Thanks? I didn't get you anything," I say as she opens some takeaway containers with pancakes and fruit. Inside the bag is a light silk scarf. Expensive. Not my style.

Jones sighs. "It's for your neck. To hide the bruises till they heal, not a fashion intervention." She pours us both coffees. "No leads on who attacked you when you were playing?"

"No. It was weird, though, the way that guy moved."

Plus the fact that he had a Zu Tech shirt. Could he had been a disgruntled employee?

Jones sighs, her eyes flicking to my necklace. "I don't like it, Asha. Whoever attacked you went for your neck. Why?"

She's right. The man had gone for my necklace, the place where I keep my flash drive, which contains the intel I got from Zu Tech. Only someone who knows me would know that I keep the things that matter most to me there. That I keep them on me. I don't like to think what that might mean. I trust the people around me.

"It must have been a coincidence," I say.

"Perhaps," Jones says. "Still, I don't like it. Promise me you'll make sure I know where you are at all times going forward. No unnecessary risks."

***

Bill is my last stop in my short tour of people to see before the flight. A very short tour – two. Murphy and Bill. I'm sixteen and I can count on my hands the people who I care about and who care about me. Shouldn't there be more than that? But, like Jones once said, business is business, and mine is revenge.

My visit to Murphy is to ensure the police wouldn't object to Ruby leaving the country, given she is a person of interest in the Zu Tech fire. He gives me doughnuts and green tea while he checks and then tries to persuade me not to go.

"Consider staying," he says. "Consider college."

Lack of sleep makes me snap. "You know I can't."

"Why, Asha?"

"Because I got to live. Don't you know what that means? I lived and now I have to fix this because if I don't … then what did Maya die for? What did *he* die for? What was the point?"

Murphy's face goes pale. "The point is you get to live, Asha."

"Without them, it's just existing, Murphy. You've seen life where I come from. Happy ever after, it's not for people like us."

Murphy hand touches my arm and I glance at his bitten fingernails.

"I'm here, OK? The investigation into Zu Tech is ongoing. I'll keep you informed of what we find. Just don't disappear. I worry." He looks almost embarrassed, and I realize he's trying to hide how much he cares behind his hardened *seen it all* police-officer exterior.

I swallow the lump that forms in my throat. "I'll miss you too," I say. "And I'm not about to vanish, I promise."

***

Saying goodbye to Bill is even worse. Along with Jones he's the only link I have left to my life before Maya died. I'd already told him about Dark and the grief is sharp. Raw. Perhaps we were the only ones who ever really knew who he was behind the persona he carefully constructed.

"I'll come with you" is his first reaction when I tell him I'm leaving for New York. His big frame is sunk into one of the leather chairs – where Dark used to sit. "I don't understand, Asha. Why didn't he reach out to one of us?" His voice breaks and I can tell he's on the edge of tears. "If there's anything I can do to help find out what happened, I want to do it."

"You've done so much already, and you need to stay, Bill," I say. "Find out what you can here. There must be a reason he kept this from both of us."

Bill's tattooed body sags a bit. "I don't like you going alone. He wouldn't like it either. Let me send someone."

"No. Jones will have me covered."

Bill looks uneasy. "Don't take risks. Speaking of, what the hell happened to your neck?"

"I'm fine. You gave me boxing and defence lessons, remember? I can handle myself."

"Just because you can doesn't mean you should. Don't forget your training? Sometimes the best defence is to run and fight another day."

"I promise." My brain flashing back to the training he gave me when Dark and I were first becoming friends. When the world wasn't so empty.

"You aren't alone in this, Asha. If you need something, I'm here. I have contacts in New York, old friends who owe me favours and won't ask questions. They can help if needed."

"Thanks."

"No need to thank me." He gives a weak smile. "We're partners now, aren't we?"

Of course. Technically I own half the business according to Dark's will. I still can't wrap my head around what that means – "*tomorrow problems*".

In the car afterwards, I scroll through texts. Jones arranged a courier to pick up the last-minute IDs I need to leave the country and they just dropped them to the Tower. It's my first trip abroad; I never needed a passport before now. Maya, at least, would have liked that. As the car gets closer to the Tower, my phone pings.

Unknown: I'll meet you in NY.

Me: Webber, nice to hear from you. What happened to the others? All of Zu Tech's missing employees?

Unknown: Why?

Webber always seems to answer a question with a question. I pull out the torn cloth from the attack and run my finger across it. The search I did earlier confirmed a name – Mark Patel – a missing former Zu Tech security guard. His photo matches what I can remember of my attacker's face. The scar is identical. His family all live in London. His mum and dad have been posting photos and videos online asking for help finding him.

Patel went to a local mosque, volunteered, had friends he played football with and a fiancée who is desperate to find him. Why would someone like that disappear? Maybe Webber knows. Then again, if she does, would she tell me the truth? I try another angle.

> What do you know about Pi?

A pause. Then:

> It's not safe to discuss this online. They're
> watching you.

I snap my device off. Frustrated. Enough – I need real answers. Hopefully I'll find those in New York.

Back at the Tower, I pack. Everything I own fits inside one small bag.

***

The plane to New York is a private jet sent by Rock. It's just us four. Jones is already in New York.

Tell me you're in a gaming tournament for a company run by one of the world's richest women without telling me. I guess online infamy has its perks. Rock was so keen to have us that they offered us one of their jets. Everything inside the plane has a Rock logo on it, right down to the bottles of water. It's corporate lavishness, and I'm afraid to touch anything, like I will somehow stain the white interior with its gold accents – the soft white leather seats, the white cashmere throws. At the end of the cabin is a polished marble bar and a short corridor to the bathroom and a meeting room.

The cabin is full of photos of Rock events. Launches. Ribbon cutting at new plants and facilities for microprocessors, film studios, resorts and amusement parks. Every Rock representative pictured is immaculately dressed and smiling with bleached white teeth.

The steward nods at me. "Welcome aboard flight N20ZT."

"Is N2 the make of the plane?" I ask.

"No, Ms Kennedy, it's our tail number – it's how private jets are identified. Now, I can take your bag if you like? Get it stored in the hold?"

I shake my head.

"I didn't realize they had planes," I say in a whisper to the others as the steward shows us to our seats while the captain and first officer look on from the cockpit.

It's Ruby who rolls her eyes at me. "What planet do you live on? Rock is massive, Asha. Like, too big to fail. They have everything."

I shiver when she says that. I did research Rock briefly but maybe not enough. Most of my search was focused on Lydia Rock, about whom there is frustratingly little online. I glance up at a portrait of Lydia, CEO of Rock Industries. It's a tasteful back-and-white shot done by some award-winning photographer showing Lydia with elephants in Africa. One of the world's wealthiest people looking like a charity do-gooder. Perfectly highlighted silver hair and a smile that looks warm. Beside it is another framed picture of Lydia, this time on the cover of *Time* magazine. It's a recent issue with a quote: *Don't waste your limited time living someone else's life.*

I strap in. Nerves taking over. First plane ride. I can't help thinking I'd prefer if it had been a bigger plane. Somehow this one seems too small to go over so much ocean.

The twins and Augie adapt instantly. Grabbing eye masks and headphones. Reclining in their seats as soon as we are airborne. I can't. Turns out small planes just make me think of fiery plane crashes. I stay seated when we reach cruising height. They start making cinema salad – popcorn and M&M's – while arguing over which movie to screen first.

I'm too tense to join in, so to distract myself I flick through the diary I found at Zu Tech. It's Zu Thorp's. The last year of his life laid out as series of appointments for various medical consultants, scheduled online team meetings, remote board meetings, award ceremonies where he appeared via video. But scheduled in are a few travel itineraries; despite his illness, Zu took or seemed to take flights to Berlin, New York and Singapore. Why? To meet who? Then towards the back doodles of designs for haptic gloves, smart contact lenses, company growth plans and then random circled dates. All in the same scrawl. Some in different-coloured pens like he had a system of some sort.

But the most striking thing about it all is how mundane and devoid of personal interaction it is. Despite everything Zu had, at the end he was alone.

I start to track the ones written in black that he's underlined.

Draft report on tests due
Presentation to investors / raise concerns?

Then a side note – underlined several times:

Pandora's box

A few weeks later there's another underlined note, one of Zu's last entries: *N19ZT*. What the hell does that mean? And *Pandora's box*?

I go through my notes but can't find a game called Pandora. Was it a project name? It niggles at me, but I can't think why.

Augie comes and sits beside me. He gave up on trying to pick a movie the twins could agree on hours ago and went for a book. "Did you hear the captain? There's going to be some turbulence coming up just before we land, so…"

I look up. "It's going to be a bumpy landing?"

He nods. "Did you sleep?"

"No."

He hands me a bottle of water. "What's that?"

"Zu's diary – Augie, you ever heard of Pandora's box?"

"Let me guess – from the book of ancient myths your sister had?"

"What?"

"Pandora's box –the Greek myth. Let me think… The gods were angry that Prometheus had given mankind the gift of fire, so they created Pandora, the first woman, and gave her a jar or box she was told to keep but never open. She does as they tell her. But then, one day, curiosity gets the better of her and she opens the box – accidentally letting evil into the world."

I sink back into my seat. "What does that even mean?"

Augie shrugs. "It's a warning. *Be careful when you open Pandora's box.* You can never be sure what you will let out."

"Could you all take your seats?" says a crew member. "We're about to begin our descent and it's windy down there."

Great. Augie returns to his pod across the aisle from me and fastens his seat belt. I pack away my stuff and look out of the window and at the lights below as we eventually start to circle New York.

New York. One of the world's most famous cities. This would have been Maya's dream. Travel. Other countries, private planes. She would have been excited. I don't feel anything. I'm numb. Cold. The only thing that keeps me warm now is anger.

I look across at Augie. We're both victims of Zu Tech. It used our grief and fed off it. Maybe that's why we got close. Because, at the end of the day, we both left pieces of ourselves in a game we didn't want to play. He played to pay for medical treatment for his mum, then he lost her anyway. I've been doing this to get justice for Maya, who is never coming back, and now I'm trying to get revenge for the boy I gave my heart to. How does anyone get luck this bad?

The plane closes in on the city. As the lights below us become clearer, something makes me shiver. A feeling of inevitability. That, one way or another, New York will change me and everything I know.

The plane lurches as it bounces off pockets of turbulence. Fear makes my hands sweaty. Augie reaches out his hand across the aisle to me without looking and I grab it. His fingers wrap around mine and calm my nerves. Neither of us let go until the jet touches down and comes to a stop.

***

We land at a private terminal in the airport, where a waiting car takes us to a VIP lounge for immigration and security. Ruby passes through without a hitch and I say a mental 'Thank You' to Murphy for making sure her record was clean after being questioned about the Zu Tech fire. We all pass through without any issues. An assistant from the tournament is waiting to make sure we avoid any crowds as we exit. They lead us to a town car that will take us to the hotel owned by Rock in Midtown Manhattan, where our team will be based.

Once we're in the car on our way, I turn to the others.

"Can we make a detour?"

Augie runs a tattooed hand through his hair. "I figured."

Ruby looks at me. "You sure about this?"

I nod. They know where I want to go. Maybe they've been thinking the same thing. "I have to see where he died."

Josh leans forward to talk to the driver. I sit back in the leather seat, looking at the traffic in the darkness as we enter the Long Island Expressway. The concrete and overpasses gradually give way to a bridge and our first look at the city. Its towering skyline lights up the night. Welcome to New York. The energy of the place pierces me as we slow before the Queens–Midtown Tunnel and then descend into its brightly tiled interior. We exit into Manhattan and a view of a giant billboard screen with overhead lights. The board carries a Rock logo:

Capture the City
Do you dare to play?
Winner takes all at this year's
BIGGEST international gaming event.

The trailer for the game starts as we get stuck in traffic: a heady mix of movement and augmented reality coupled with old-school nostalgia for simpler times. The player in the promo moves like they're doing parkour over well-known New York buildings and then along the shoreline of New Jersey so that the city appears behind them. It cuts to augmented monsters, and zombies that chase them through the subways. The image changes again to an audience watching an eSports event at Arthur Ashe Stadium. A massive crowd of spectators scream at the giant screens before it zooms in on a well-known actor cheering like the rest of the fans. He turns to the camera in his Rock-branded T-shirt. "I'll be there, will you?"

"Subtle" is all Augie says.

Josh, however, grins. "We're back in business, baby!"

But I can't help feeling uneasy. The memories of our last tournament together are too fresh.

All too soon we're at *that* place. The intersection. In my mind's eye I see Dark walking, his glance up at the cameras, before…

When the car pulls in, I jump out first. Then it moves around the corner to wait for us.

There is a smell of burnt street meat, exhaust and vent fumes. The street is quiet, almost empty. The damage has been fixed. The walkway is freshly painted. The blue mailbox is nearby with some stickers on the side – I hadn't noticed those in the footage. Maybe they're new? But no, they're singed – they were just too small for me to see properly. I look around at the other buildings, the bodega across the road and the pharmacy a few metres away. The sources of the secondary CCTV footage. I walk over the subway grates and notice the unsealed NYC sewer cover on the road.

Then I see it: a small section of the pavement where someone has laid a few flowers and candles. A Zu Tech logo with a red line through it is beside the wilting blooms. My heart stutters as I move towards it. A slight breeze moves some rubbish as I get closer.

This is where Dark died.

I sink down in front of the sidewalk memorial. Staring at the photo there. The blurry image of Dark – grabbed and printed from the Zu Tech tournament footage, the only image of him in public. It's just a few flowers, a couple of cheap battery-operated candles that flicker, but it means others cared.

Time passes. I feel the twins and Augie standing behind me. Close but giving me space.

I glance up, and for a second I think I see someone on the other side of the street watching me. Staring straight at me. Long black coat closed against the cold, dark baseball hat. The hairs on the back of my neck seem to stand up. But when I look again, they're gone.

Did I do the right thing in coming? I start to doubt myself. My fingers wrap around Maya's locket. The one that holds digital images of her and now a faded photo of Dark, the only one I had. A small drive beside it with all the information I found to date. The only things I couldn't leave behind in London.

"Asha." Augie's voice is tight. "We need to get back in the car."

"Why?" I look up at him, not understanding till I see that the street behind him is no longer empty. That it's starting to fill with people – a gathering crowd.

His hand reaches down and pulls me up. Josh and Ruby

walk in front of me. As we cross the street, there's a camera flash. "It's her."

"What's going on?"

Josh grabs my hand and starts pulling me back to the car. "What's happening is that the videos from the tournament went viral. Some people knew who he was, Asha – his connection to you, to Zu Tech. I think someone must have spotted you, us, and then posted it."

I should have been more careful to hide my face. Are they haters or fellow mourners? There's no time to find out. We start to move back towards the car, which is parked nearby.

People are staring at us and there's another flash as another phone starts recording. People are shouting, and a voice cuts through the noise and hits me. "Did you kill him, Asha?"

I go still. Stop. "What?"

Augie pushes me gently from behind and Josh drags me along. More voices join in and people start to surround us, some shouting, others saying, "Leave her alone." I only understand fragments.

"Is *Capture the City* safe?"

"Tell the truth. Was SHACKLE safe?"

"What about the ones who went missing?"

The boys and Ruby push their way past another group of onlookers.

But the voices follow me.

"You're a fake, Asha."

"You killed your sister."

"You lied."

Augie bundles me into the town car, which pulls out silently.

"What was that? What do they mean? What the hell happened?"

Ruby looks at her phone screen and then at me. "Rock happened. They posted the list of players for their tournament an hour ago. The event trailer is now live and you're in it. People know we're here. The rumour mill is in overdrive. The boards, threads and theories have been growing since Rock posted. There is no gag order here. The US don't have the same censorship laws as us, Asha."

The car moves into the traffic, and I look out of its tinted windows at the sidewalk. I see the figure again in the distance. The person I thought was looking at me earlier is still there, just metres from where I first noticed them. They never moved. Just a passer-by watching another New York drama unfold.

If this is what it's going to be like every time we go outside, I'm going to need to learn how to be invisible again.

My phone buzzes.

Unknown: Welcome to NYC.

Me: How do you know I arrived?

Me: Are you here, Webber?

Me: Why are you invested in this?

Unknown: Same reason as you. They lied. Tried to take everything from me. I want to end them too.

12

"Wake up."

My eyes don't want to open, but Ruby is refusing to move from my bed. I take a quick peek. It still resembles a bedroom in a hotel. Clinically clean and impersonal. I don't want to engage with it, so I try to go with staying asleep.

"Eliza's here, and you missed the Rock tournament rep. They just left."

I shut my eyes tighter. Eliza still isn't someone I trust. And she's also playing in this tournament. Rivals again.

Ruby's voice goes low. "She brought coffee and doughnuts."

Food and caffeine. "I'm up." My head still feels groggy from the jet lag.

"Asha?"

"Yes?"

"Don't go all interrogation with Eliza."

"What does that mean?"

Ruby looks down at me. "It means you're like a Terminator. I'd rather she didn't find that out just yet."

I stretch. "Why hide the truth? She met me in London. And didn't Josh already do the full interrogation?"

Ruby nods. "He basically asked her what her 'intentions' towards me are. It was a complete train wreck. He morphed into our mum."

"I like your mum. I'll check in with him first, find out what he learnt, and then we can tackle Eliza together."

Ruby shoves a pillow at me. "Do not make me regret waking you up."

But I read the subtext: she doesn't want me asking Eliza any awkward questions. And I wonder... Did Ruby buy Eliza's story at the Zu Tech tournament about overhearing a rumour – a rumour that revealed a traitor in our team – or did she fall so hard for the girl that it didn't matter to her?

***

The tournament has put us in suites in the R Hotel, a nineteen-storey throwback to old New York City. It's one of those buildings from the 1920s built around Grand Central Station. A place that oozes faded glamour.

Cream-coloured walls with grand marble pillars and fireplaces. Thick carpets, gold cloth curtains and velvet pillows, embroidered towels, matched with digital projectors, smart readers, a fully stocked mini-kitchen and a large private sitting room, the central hub of our suite – all with the R logo of Rock Resorts.

Welcome gifts from Rock cover a couple of side tables by the windows that offer a glimpse of Grand Central Station.

I pick a coffee from the ones Eliza brought and hesitate.

Eliza shrugs. "I know we're both competing in this tournament, Asha, but that whole thing about eSports teams putting laxatives in their rivals' food and drink is old."

I ignore her.

She takes a sip of her coffee, and then I take one of mine while she turns her gaze back to the room. "The hotel belongs to Rock, part of their 'resorts' division," she explains.

I look at the doughnuts. "Is there anything they don't own?"

Josh is on the sofa, already on his second coffee and flicking through the website information on the tournament. He's looking through the list of team names and projecting screengrabs on to the flat screen in the room. "Nope, they own pretty much everything in New York. It's where they started, although the technology side is now moving to Singapore. Being in this hotel is weird, though."

"Why?" I ask.

"Cos they've booked it all out. The tournament players, managers, etc. are the only guests in the building."

I blink. "But it's massive." I could tell that when we arrived last night. "Even with press teams and VIPs this place must be half empty."

Josh zooms in on a photo of Thresher, a rival eSports player. I know Thresher a bit from the Zu Tech tournament. The pic is typical of him. Thresher is unsmiling. Tall, straight black hair, dark eyes, pale skin. He's one of the biggest players in the Asian circuit. Last I remember of him he was an ass, a typical player meathead only focused on tournament wins.

Eliza replies to me instead. "The hotel is being closed down – they're turning it into luxury apartments. We're the last guests to stay here. Shame. The R is famous. It has everything, even a rumoured secret tunnel downstairs to the train station used by some president. Art Deco ballroom, twenty-four-hour room service. We should explore. If I could afford it, this is where I would live one day."

"What's on our itinerary?" I ask.

There's always an itinerary with tournaments – we're here to work as well as play.

Josh looks up from checking gameplay footage. "Tonight, there's a welcome party for the players and teams. Tomorrow's Wednesday, right? There's a massive launch in the stadium with the fans and press to hype up the event, which kicks off on Friday. Busy week."

I shudder at the thought of social interaction, but then I get an idea. A crowded welcome party might be a good place to meet Webber, and I could easily duplicate any pass they give me.

Eliza says gently, "You don't have to go tonight if you don't want to. I'm sorry about Dark, Asha."

I swallow. "It's OK. And I could use a night out."

Eliza smiles. "Great. I know you guys didn't have a lot of time to pack so I also brought some clothing options with me." She nods towards a suitcase in the corner.

"Why would you do that?" I ask.

"Asha." Ruby's tone is sharp.

Eliza reaches out and touches Ruby's hand and smiles. "Because I get to go out tonight with my girlfriend for the first time in months. She's an eSports star and I want to show off and kick back before the tournament starts. I need her to love my city so she can finally give me an answer on whether she would move here. And because she … cares about you. So, if bringing a few dresses and trouser suits helps, then I will be your personal stylist."

Ruby smiles at Eliza. "I guess this is us making things publicly official?"

Eliza rolls her eyes. "It's been official for months, as far as I'm concerned. I did a bloody UK tournament so I could hang with you."

Ruby's smile gets even bigger. "What happened to all that *relationships within the industry never work* stuff?"

"I was an idiot. But since you were arrested and I

realized I might not see you again – I've known for sure. I'm in this."

Josh groans as Augie laughs at him. "Can you two just get a room? I mean, there's a few here to choose from. Some of us need breakfast."

Ruby throws a cushion at him. "Like I never had to listen to your relationship dramas with Amy." She grabs a bag from the table. "Hey, Dawn made these for everyone; now seems like a good time." Friendship bracelets made with beads, each with our name in the centre. Very Dawn.

Eliza swallows when Ruby hands her one with her name. "It's perfect."

Ruby's face glows and my chest gets tight. I look away and text Webber the address of the welcome party.

***

The "intimate" welcome party mentioned in Rock's itinerary is in a massive converted warehouse in the garment district. The low-key event has giant lights that project the *Capture the City* text logo like a Batman signal into the night sky. Jones is meeting us there. I've already cloned my pass and left a copy of it in a nearby coffee shop for Webber.

"I can't believe this," I murmur. The driver is beaming with excitement as he tells Josh and Ruby, who are in the front section of the limo, that this is one of the big events of the year and to make sure to post pictures. All of us look through the tinted car windows at the red carpet outside as we pull up. Crowds of people with phones are already lining either side.

Augie raises one eyebrow. "If it helps, people are going to be just as surprised to see you at an actual party." His gaze lingers on me, and I feel myself flushing. I'm wearing the plainest item Eliza had, a simple black dress, but it's much more form-fitting than I'm used to. I tug awkwardly at it. "Asha, you look…"

"Out of my comfort zone? I was trying to blend in."

Ruby looks at me from the other side of the car and gives me a half-smile. "There is no danger of you fading into the background wearing that. You look stunning, Ash."

I turn away so she can't see the heat that's rising on my face. So I don't accidentally tell them that no one has ever told me that before. Expensive dresses like this have never been a big part of my wardrobe. At least Ruby let me keep my runners.

There is a group of photographers and fans outside. Cameras start to click before we even exit and on instinct I turn away from the flashes. A blonde PR person from Rock with a clipboard detaches from another group and waves to Augie, taking us quickly into a small lobby. She kisses him on both cheeks, leaning in close.

"Long time, no call. Good to see you."

Augie smiles, his star persona instantly flicked on. "Isobel."

Isobel beams. "You remembered. I'm impressed, Santos." She nods to Eliza and glances at Ruby and me.

"You keep interesting company."

"They're my team," he says. His voice is pleasant but there's steel in it.

She mutters almost to herself, "So it's true – you are seeing her," before scanning our invites. "By the way, you're late. Your manager is already here and asking for you. Eliza, the rest of your team is inside. This way."

She takes us past three security guards, and I notice the cameras above the door.

"That's a lot of protection for a welcome party, right?"

Isobel gives me a cold smile. "Unconfirmed sources suggest that a special VIP is coming to welcome the players. Hence the extra precautions."

I shiver. I don't like surprises.

"Who?" Augie asks above the noise of the music inside.

Isobel gives an elegant shrug. "Chloe is inside the VIP section with the details. Have fun, but not too much." She takes a small card from her clipboard and holds it against Augie's phone for a second to transfer her details. "Just in case you need me for anything."

She points us towards a corridor and barely looks at me when she leaves. I'm left with the uncomfortable feeling that I have been judged and found wanting.

Hologram projections float in front of us from recent eSports events sponsored by Rock.

I glance at Augie. Black blazer, white T-shirt, jeans. Messy blond/brown hair, tattoo. He looks at home here. And I guess sometimes I forget he is. Augie Santos is an eSports superstar. He's been famous for years. Aspiring players have posters of him in their room.

Ruby elbows me. "This is insane. I guess we know who the number one games studio is, though."

I grin. "Are they a naturally occurring solid mass?"

Ruby looks confused. I sigh. Maya always said my humour was an acquired taste. "I mean because … a naturally occurring solid mass is a … Rock? Never mind," I say.

The music gets louder as we move further inside, the walls vibrating. By the time we reach the main entrance, it's almost deafening. The door swings wide into an internal courtyard with a glass ceiling, open to the night sky crowded with people.

Lights glow over the space like an art installation. The dance floor takes up the central area. Under the arches there are DJ decks and projectors with gamer pods, couches, games tables, classic arcade games and additional screens scattered in between.

"Want to find Jones?" Ruby asks.

The boys are already eyeing the food. I wonder if Webber is already here. "Sure. Let's split up. Text once you find her?" I move before she can say anything else.

As I go into the main club, I feel a growing sense of unease that gets stronger the further away I am from the others. There are too many people here. Too many faces I don't recognize. Worse, I'm to be attracting attention. I let my hair fall in front of my face, using it to hide as I scan the people around me. I take out my phone.

Where are you, Webber?

Nothing. I elbow my way through people, ending up in a different area, further away from the VIP section I was supposed to stay near. Damn it. This is like looking for a needle in a haystack. Security is on every door. Would Webber have been able to get past all that?

I feel an arm on my shoulder that I shrug off.

"Don't I know you?" It's a male voice.

"No, you don't."

"But I bet you want to know me."

Two guys who have consumed way too many drinks. Just my luck. I push past them.

Another male grabs my arm. "He was talking to you – don't be rude."

I stop. Pulling myself up to my full height. The guy has a heavy build. Entitled. I meet his eyes. "I don't want to talk to him or you."

He chuckles because he doesn't care. He is now standing in front of me. His friends watch. Giving him confidence. An audience. "Well, that isn't friendly. It's a party – have a drink with us." He gestures to a nearby bar.

"No." I remember there are cameras. "Thank you."

I go to move but he catches at my shoulder this time. I turn. "I don't want to be touched. I don't owe you my company. And you have two seconds to remove your hand or I will remove it from you." I take a step towards him. "Trust me – you won't like how I do it."

He drops his hand from my shoulder. "No need to be such a…"

I stop him with a look. "I wouldn't finish that sentence." I move towards him and he instinctively takes a step back. "And don't try that again in here." I glance up at a nearby CCTV camera. "Someone is always watching." I move, throwing the words behind me as I go. "Good thing for you or I wouldn't have been so polite and you'd be on the floor."

But one of them follows me. This time I don't hold back. I use my foot and the guy trips over it as he approaches, landing face first full force on to the floor. There's a crunching sound that I expect is his nose.

A person beside me gasps as I move away. "Some people just can't seem to hold their drink," I murmur as I walk on.

"Glad to see you haven't changed, Asha."

I've nearly walked straight into him. Thresher. This place is turning into a haunted house.

"Thresher. What are you…?"

He gives me a slight smile. "Same as Eliza. Playing but on different teams. I saw you and thought I'd say hi."

I look at him. He seems taller, stronger than before. He's wearing a plain short-sleeved T-shirt that shows off his physique. A slight bruise on one of his upper arms. A cut that's bandaged on his hand.

"You box?" I ask.

He looks startled. "No. Tae kwon do. Why?"

I gesture at his arms.

He shrugs. "Asha, I wanted to see you."

Thresher looks down at his hands for a moment before looking up. "I wanted to say I am sorry for what happened in London. You lost a friend. I know how hard that can be."

"How? How do you know what that feels like?" And this time I'm really interested.

"It's not the time or place now, Asha, but, believe me, I know. If you ever need anything … I wanted to make sure you knew there are people who can help."

Curiouser and curiouser. "Thank you." And I don't know what else to say except, "You staying around here for a while?"

"It isn't my scene." He looks past me and frowns. "Interesting company Santos is keeping. Be careful. And I'll see you soon."

When he leaves, I turn to see Augie, Ruby and Josh behind a roped-off section. And they aren't alone.

A small army of bodyguards stands between me and them. Whoever they are with is clearly a celebrity or extremely wealthy or both. Black suits and earpieces in a place like this make a statement. I get closer. One of the guards steps in front of me. His eyes sweep me up and down and I bite back my irritation.

"She's with me." It's Augie. His hand already moving the guard to one side. There is a woman in front of him and she turns. Early fifties. Expensively maintained facial work, platinum-silver hair in a bob, discreet make-up. I recognize the face. Lydia Rock. The head of the world's biggest gaming company, which, as I already know, owns half this city. The woman hiring us for this tournament. Someone I hadn't expected to see here in a place full of gamers and tech heads.

Zu's words float into my head again. *I couldn't have done this without one particular friend – Lydia Rock.*

Augie pulls me towards her. "Ms Rock, this is Asha Kennedy."

Ms Rock smiles – the same warm smile in her photo. Her polished American accent somehow cuts through the noise of the party. "Asha Kennedy. A face that needs no introduction."

I hesitate. I can see Jones just behind her. She shoots me a look that says, *Make nice, Asha.* So I try.

"Ms Rock." I hold out a hand and she ignores it. Weird but not unusual given the recent pandemic. "Thank you for this opportunity."

Rock gives me a polite smile. "It's a pleasure." She lowers her voice. "I can't wait to see you play, Ms Kennedy. I'm sure we're all going to learn so much from watching you. Have you managed to meet everyone you wanted to so far?"

A shiver runs down my spine. Does she know I was looking for someone tonight?

She frowns. "All the event organizers are keen to meet you," she adds.

I'm being paranoid, I think.

"Great," I say. "I'm keen to meet them too."

Jones gives me a faint nod.

A photographer appears just as I wonder how I can bring up Zu Thorp without sounding suspicious.

"Can I take one with you and the team, Ms Rock?" he asks, but she shakes her head.

"Not now." She gestures at a press person with a clipboard. "If you will excuse me, I need to say a few words before it gets too late."

Lydia leaves with her entourage before I can ask her anything.

Eliza comes up beside me. "Weird, right?"

"What is?"

"That she's here. Bothering with a gaming tournament. The woman owns half the planet and she's a STEM grad, electronic engineering, and, well, it's inspiring, how far she's gotten and yet she still has time for a kick-off event."

"Inspiring. Or something."

Lydia Rock steps on to a platform. The music stops and a spotlight comes on as a thousand camera flashes seem to go off in her direction. She … glows in the attention.

"Welcome, players, to the *Capture the City* tournament." Rock's tone is practised and rehearsed. The crowd around us screams and she smiles before continuing. "You eight teams represent the best of the best from around the world. That's why you were chosen. And the winner will walk away with the biggest North American prize pot of the year. Tomorrow you'll meet the fans who will adore you … or hate you, depending on how you play." A ripple of laughter. "Either way, the whole world will be watching as we stream the action from the New York flood zone and Arthur Ashe Stadium. I'm here to say good luck to all of you from all of us. You are the ones that younger generations will look up to, and we're so happy to have you here. Let the games begin."

Applause. She hands the mic to the event organizer and steps offstage with a smile. I zone out and glance around at the eight other teams. Rock wasn't lying about having the "best" in this tournament. I recognize a lot of these players and it seems we are all openly sizing each other up under the guise of listening to Lydia Rock's speech. Thresher may have skipped, but the rest of his team, the Dragons, are all here, and they look not just unhappy but angry, and I wonder why. Eliza stands near us and I can see at least one of the other members of the Phoenix's team that she captains glaring at Ruby. Ru hasn't noticed yet, but I start to feel a prickling sensation. I'm uneasy enough to make me take a step closer to Ruby. Eliza's team don't seem thrilled about having her new girlfriend in the same tournament as them. Or maybe they're wondering if Ruby will eventually be the reason Eliza leaves them.

I scan the rest of the room. It's like a who's who of eSports stars.

"Impressive, isn't it?" It's Eliza, also looking around.

I nod. "It's a lot of pro gamers in one room."

Eliza gives a slight smile. "With all those egos, it's amazing we all fit. Rock owns the circuit now. With no Zu

Tech around, they filled the vacuum for doing big-stadium events. It's now Lydia Rock's way or no way."

"You're impressed by her?"

Eliza's voice drops. "I'm not sure. Don't get me wrong. She is awe-inspiring, and I like having nice things, but could you ever really trust someone with that much power and wealth?"

I glance back to Lydia, who is watching from the wings. Then my attention is distracted by Josh, who has gone towards the fire escape, talking on his phone. I can tell by the tension in his body and his frustrated expression that he's arguing with someone.

Beside me, Eliza follows my gaze and sighs. "I hope he works it out."

"Works what out?"

She shrugs. "What's the thing most people stress over? Money. We all have problems, right?"

Does Josh have issues I don't know about? Something that might make him vulnerable? And if Eliza knows that and not me, what kind of a teammate does that make me?

13

Too much security. Another time.

The message from Unknown comes once the speeches are done. I sigh. Webber isn't showing tonight. Clearly she got spooked.

But the tournament's proper launch for the fans at the stadium tomorrow should be different. It's a bigger space, with regular people attending and more opportunities to sneak in unnoticed. I need to know what she knows. I send her a quick reply.

Last chance, tomorrow, Arthur Ashe Stadium. Text when you're in.

After the speeches, we leave, and the others go to bed. I'm too wired and jet-lagged to sleep. I do some more research into Pi Investments, but I don't get any further – it's a Delaware-registered company name that seems only to link to other companies in the Bahamas and Cayman Islands.

There must be some clue I'm missing as to who owns it. A link between Pi and some names for the mysterious Zu Tech Founders. I need a lead.

I give up on the idea of sleep. I put on some running gear and wander through the empty hotel, avoiding the late-night after-party sounds coming from the ballroom and heading into the street. It's empty around Grand Central Station as I run. The buildings feel different without so many people. Ahead of me, I catch a glimpse of the Chrysler Building, and then I change direction and run towards Bryant Park and the place I know Maya would have wanted to see: the New York Public Library. She'd had images of the lions outside the building as a screen saver since forever. Her ultimate bucket-list destination, and I'm here without her. Without him.

I sit on the steps of the Schwarzman Building, the stone cold under me. I need to find answers for them both or else what was this all for? But then my senses start to prickle. Someone is watching.

I stand and look around. I can't see anyone, but the hairs stand up on the back of my neck. I'm not in the mood for another run-in with haters or drunks, so I head back to the hotel and sleep for a few hours. Tomorrow needs to bring answers.

***

I wake as tired as when I went to bed. It's the day of the launch. I pack the photo I took from Zu Tech and the diary and push them deep into my backpack. I lengthen Maya's locket and wrap it around my wrist a few times before covering it with my shirt. The only necklace I wear around my neck now is a cord one that holds my small pen drive and lies out of sight under my shirt. Old habits.

We travel to the stadium by car. Me, Josh, Ruby, and Augie. Jones is already there. Eliza is heading there with her own team. I zone out in the back seat beside Augie, watching Ruby and Josh in front of us. Their easy back and forth. The way he teases her about Eliza and the smile that comes over her face when he does. Josh looks like he hasn't got a care in the world, but last night he was so upset.

I turn to Augie. "Is Josh OK?" I whisper.

Augie looks surprised. "Yeah, why?"

"Nothing."

Augie thinks for a second. "He said he was worried about Ru; he thinks she's over her head."

"With Eliza? Let me guess, he said, 'If she ever hurts my sister, I'm coming for her'?"

Augie grins. "How did you know?"

I smile. "Maya would have been like that."

There is silence between us until we get interrupted by laughter. Some weird video Ruby and Josh found online.

"Guys, you have to see this," says Ruby, turning back to us. The video turns out to be hilarious, a skit on eSports players. And suddenly, despite everything, two minutes later we are all laughing – until the stadium appears.

Arthur Ashe Stadium is huge. It seats over twenty thousand lucky fans, all of whom will be live casting to millions more. It's also historic. This is where Billie Jean King, the Williams sisters and McEnroe all played tennis. But the building looks different now, with event projections, Rock banners, lights. It seems daunting, vast. The screens outside show gaming clips from past tournaments, with players screaming in triumph or despair and collecting their trophies. There are welcome videos from celebrities and the mayor too, all saying how excited they are to have such a major event here in Queens, New York.

Already we can see fans snaking around the block as we drive through the players' entrance. Security is tight; I just hope the guest pass I left at the hotel coffee shop from our welcome pack will work for Webber.

Inside, none of us has much time to process where we are before we get pressed into the US eSports machine. Passed from room to room to be poked and prodded by stylists and the branding teams from Rock. Augie is the only one of us who is used to it, immediately grabbing a coffee and placing earbuds in so he can zone out. Then zoning back in to give charming smiles to the Rock staff and posing for a selfie before moving on to the next section.

I can't do that. I feel awkward. In the make-up chair, I barely recognize the reflection in the mirror that stares back at me. I'm not the only one feeling weird. I catch Ruby sighing, and not in a good way, at the clothing options picked for us but saying nothing, because isn't this the American dream?

Too many people, too many fake smiles, an army of cameras and groups of fans and bloggers. Hours later there is a thick layer of make-up on my face, and it feels like my skin can't breathe.

When I look in the mirror, I see smooth complexion and subtle eyeshadow, carefully waved hair, glossy smile. I don't see myself but a version of a gamer I don't recognize. I've been changed into a tracksuit smothered with Rock logos. The tags scratch me and, regardless of the price tag for the outfit, none of this feels comfortable; it feels cheap, like a veneer put on top to make me into something I am not.

"Hold it together, Asha," Jones says. She's appeared at my elbow, as immaculate as ever, and guides me backstage. "It's part of the game. Breathe." Her hand gently touches my shoulder.

We wait backstage, one of the last of the eight teams to be presented. The initial excitement and high energy around us fade as time drags on. My feelings of being starstruck lessen with each pro player who passes by and the celebrities who smile vacantly in our direction. They're here to plug new movies and products at the junket. We're on a slick and polished conveyor belt where the same phrases get repeated over and over again: "*Delighted to be here. I love playing in New York. This is a dream come true for me.*" It is like seeing behind the curtain in *The Wizard of Oz* – once you do, you can never unsee the fact that someone is pulling the levers.

Other highlights so far? When we arrived at the stadium, I spotted Thresher and Eliza. He seemed upset, his fist clenching as he spoke; she looked concerned, their heads close together. I didn't realize they knew each other that well.

After Thresher moves off to join his team, I also see an interaction between Ruby and Eliza that makes me wonder.

"Hi," Ruby says, going over to Eliza.

Eliza nods at her. She seems distracted, cooler. "You OK?"

"Are you?"

Eliza shrugs. "Getting my head in the game." She gestures to another backstage area where the rest of the Phoenix team is waiting. She leans towards Ruby and gives her a quick kiss on the side of her cheek. Perfunctory. Her emotions locked away. Her focus already on her team. Eliza's all business now. Ruby, however, seems lost as she walks away.

Josh nudges Ruby. "You can't let a relationship get in

the way of winning," he hisses. "We came here to play, remember? Get it together."

Ruby's voice is a whisper, but I hear it and the edge it carries. The pressure. Something she doesn't normally let show. "You think I forgot why we are here? Why I train as hard as I do?"

"I'm not saying—"

"I never get a break, Josh. All I do is train. When do I get time for me? When do I get my person? You have Amy. Don't you think I deserve someone too?"

Josh looks flustered. "Ruby, that's not what I meant. I—"

She cuts him off. "You still have nightmares about Zu Tech. I know you do. Don't think for one second that you are the only one still having them. Eliza helps me get through; the same way Amy helps you."

"Right, but we're competing against her now," Josh warns her.

"And that terrifies me. Gaming against Eliza. It's my first relationship, Josh – what if I stuff it up?"

I move away before I can hear his reply. I shouldn't be listening. But it's a reminder that everyone has their baggage after Zu Tech.

All this waiting around is making everyone tense. The teams stand together, stiff now, chatting only to their coaches, eyes searching out potential rivals. A Rock production assistant comes by with a reminder that there can be no pictures or phones for the next hour. Lydia Rock will be arriving soon.

My phone buzzes.

Unknown: I'm here.

Me: We're doing this in public.

Unknown: Fine. I'll text where.

I snap my device closed before the assistant comes back to remind me of the press embargo, the phone embargo, the fun embargo. I zone out, while I wait for Webber to text a location.

I realize then that Rock's *Capture the City* is the game we used to dream of when we were kids. The cost of the systems, glasses and haptic gloves meant people like us had to do just that … dream. Later, when the metaverse became mainstream, its accessories got mass-produced, and it became affordable, an exciting prospect for any serious gamer – but limited to virtual reality. Tournament-style games like those from Zu Tech dominated. *Capture the City* though – this new version. Like in London, it hits me – it's something else. A game that delivers on the promise of those tournament games and then brings the experience into the real world. A mix of virtual and augmented reality to create something new. Like old-school *Pokémon Go*, it turns any location into your own personal battleground or playing arena. It's fast-paced, movement-orientated and occasionally violent.

Maya would have loved this, I think. She'd have been amazing at it too, given how fit she was, how sharp her brain was at strategy.

For the tournament, Rock is using an area of the city

that had been marked as a flood zone, a newly abandoned ghost section hidden behind flood barriers. They've layered the space with traps that will release holo monsters, and augmented-reality projections. Cameras will capture our every move as well as tapping into our glasses. Viewers will see what we see. The monsters, the zombies, the ghosts and everything in between. The challenges here won't just be the other teams; it will be the game itself as we compete until there is only one winner.

Ruby comes over. "The Rock rep is here, talking to Josh. We should go and help him out. Ready?"

"No. But let's do this anyway."

She grabs my hand with a smile. "I'm with you."

***

It's too hot. I feel sticky and sweaty. The make-up is sliding from my face under the lights. The effortless blow-dry that took two hours seems to be deflating. An efficient stage manager wearing an earbud and holding a clipboard motions me forward.

Augie moves beside me. He looks completely calm. He grins. "It gets easier."

"I don't think it ever will for me." But I smile anyway. I'm glad he's here. When did that happen? Relying on Augie?

I glance at Ruby and Josh. Smiles on their faces now. Show time. They radiate energy. I cause chaos and pain. Maybe opposites attract.

"We should take a team photo," Augie says. He takes out his phone before anyone can object and sneakily snaps a pic and then goes to send it to our group. "Weird. Wi-Fi must be down."

"It's time, you're the last ones." The stage manager starts to push us onstage, and my mouth goes dry. Lydia Rock still hasn't arrived.

"And now … let's give a huge welcome to … Tower team all the way from Englaaaaaand."

Hands shove us out on to the stage. Nothing, not even the size of the stadium, has prepared me for the sheer volume of people who now sit in the arena in front of us. A vast fully seated stadium. Rows and rows of people. Most are holding devices set to record.

A wall of flashes and cheers throws me off balance as we walk out. I look behind me, but all I can see are the digital projections of us, along with our tournament stats. Mine is blank compared to the others. Before I can breathe, a microphone is thrust in front of me. It's Alan Star, a presenter I recognize from the leading eSports channel. My mouth suddenly feels dry.

"Here she is. Someone who needs no introduction – Asha Kennedy. Probably the most famous female eSports player of all time. We're all so excited to see you play. First time in New York, right? Anything you want to say to the fans out there, Asha?"

All the drilling I've had from the PR person deserts me. My mind blanks. My heart starts to beat too fast. I look at the sea of faces, hoping for inspiration. My hands are clammy. I see signs. Someone at the front of the audience is holding one I can just about read.

Is it safe?

"Is it…?" Without meaning to, I start to read the words out loud.

Alan whips the microphone away and turns to Augie. "Well, you're a familiar face, Santos! Good to have you back at last."

"That's right, and I'm very happy to be back. I'd like to thank Rock for this amazing opportunity…"

I swallow and read the sign again.

Is it safe? Is the game safe?

I have an almost overwhelming desire to be anywhere but here. To run. Everything feels wrong. I scan the crowd. Is Webber here? I look out and think I see her. A dark figure that stands out against the crowd of Rock gamer T-shirts and baseball hats. Someone standing to the side by the furthest exit door. But I'm not sure.

"So happy to be here in New York, Alan, and so excited to play – we all are." Ruby.

"And you, Josh?" Alan is saying. "You must be excited to finally hit the stadium!"

As if on cue, the crowd roars.

They were cheering for Augie, but this is something else. It's deafening. I frown. Augie has more experience. More significant followings, higher game scores. But when the spotlight falls on him, Josh smiles. Easy, relaxed. Handsome. Charming – like he was born to do this and the crowd love it.

Someone starts chanting his name and he glows. It's his time.

My forehead is damp now. Josh, however, looks entirely fresh and in control of the crowd. The heat from the lights feels like it's too much. There's a slight buzzing noise in my ears. Suddenly I know I need to leave, whether I cause a scene or not. I look around for the exit.

Fingers close around my hand then – Josh's hand in mine. He's pulling me back into the spotlight. Closer to the edge of the stage. I want to pull away but I can't.

People are chanting both our names now. "*Josh, Asha.*" There are cheers. Josh lifts the hand holding mine above our heads and the crowd are eating it up. Screaming their support.

This is wrong, I think. *Something is wrong.*

He's holding the mic in his other hand and smiling at me as he leans in.

"We're here to win," he shouts. Then he sees the same sign as I did.

Is it safe?

"And I can tell you it's safe," he says, pointing to the sign. "Asha and I and the whole team are here because we love this game. We go way back with *Capture the City* and always dreamt of this. We're going to show you how it's played." The crowd seems to explode into more noise. A wall of a thousand devices with their flash lights on. Our image is on every giant arena screen, the tournament's signature music swelling in the background. A cameraman starts circling us to capture our expressions. It's a carefully orchestrated moment.

This is all part of the game, I tell myself. *Calm. I just need to stay calm—*

And then the first shot rings out.

14

Josh throws me to the ground. A metallic smell is in the air. For a second, I don't understand what is happening. Then the screaming starts.

As we hit the stage, he yells out two words. "Ruby. Run."

A backstage security team comes towards us. I gesture at them to grab Josh first as I roll to where Augie was seconds before. My shirt gets caught on a nail, ripping it. The lights and music cut out and the screams get louder. An alarm sounds. More security dressed in black run onstage. One of them grabs Alan Star, bundling him towards the exit. The doors are open all around the arena now. An automated voice tells everyone to *keep calm and go to the nearest exit*, but no one listens. Everyone is scrambling. People are running.

I look to the front of the stage. Augie is still there. Frozen.

Why isn't he moving?

The second shot rings out.

And another.

Three shots. I look up, trying to work out where they're coming from. If I had to guess, it's the upper level of the stadium. I crouch, eyeing the distance between me and Augie, who still stands motionless. We need to get out of here. I can't wait. I run towards him.

"Augie!" I scream.

His eyes are glazed. I grab him and drag him down on to the ground.

"Asha." His voice sounds far away. I can hear shouts from Ruby and Josh. They're screaming at us to run. I glance back and Josh is struggling with a security guard to get to us.

I shake Augie. "We have to get out of here," I say.

He doesn't respond; he seems dazed.

I try to snap him out of it. "We have to go now, do you understand?"

I glance down and see blood on my shirt.

Not my blood.

"Augie?" And it's part word, part cry. He's been hit.

I don't think. I drag him up, then off the stage, down the steps into the main part of the stadium, running towards the nearest emergency exit. But he's slow, too slow.

"Augie!" I scream. "Come on! Move."

This time Augie seems to wake up. "Asha?"

Relief floods through me. "Augie, see that exit? Can you run?"

My heart is hammering now. Augie nods. We sprint past the empty seats towards the lower exit door. The entire stadium has emptied out – I glimpse one last figure pausing to watch us, before slipping through a door on the other side. Security is locking the place down.

I cry out, hoping they see us, but the door slams shut.

I fall against the door, hitting it with my shoulder to force it open. An alarm rings. Then the feeling of air and the smell of dust from the concrete stairwell. I pull Augie past me into the weak light. The aroma of old pretzels and popcorn from a concession stand below surrounds us. After we pass through the door, it bangs behind us and I let out a ragged breath.

Augie doesn't say anything. He leans against the concrete block wall, then slides down it.

I see red marks on the floor and the wall. Blood. Lots of blood.

I grab a fire extinguisher from the wall and uses it to jam the exit door we just came through. That shooter could still be in there. "We wait here till the all-clear sounds, OK?"

Augie nods, holding his shoulder.

"Does it hurt?"

"Like. Hell."

I rip the shirt the stylist gave me, making it into a makeshift tourniquet, leaving me in just a vest top. "I need to tie this around your shoulder. It's going to feel uncomfortable."

"More uncomfortable than being shot?"

"Maybe? I don't really know. I just need you to lie down and try not to move until help gets here."

I toss my tournament jacket on the floor and help him lie on it. Then I tie the tourniquet around his shoulder high and tight. He inhales sharply. His face is pale. His skin clammy. Fear starts to rise inside me. I look at the wound. The blood flow is slower now but it hasn't stopped. I wad the rest of the shirt fabric into a pad to apply pressure to the wound.

"I hope you didn't like that shirt too much. Because I know for a fact that blood never really washes out."

I apply pressure to the wound. "Well, your sense of humour is still intact."

"Now what?" he asks.

"We wait."

Both of us are quiet, listening to the sounds around us. People screaming and sirens from the emergency services.

"Asha?"

"Yeah?"

"There's something I want to say to you. Something I've wanted to say for a long time."

"How about you do that after we get out of here and get you fixed up?"

"I got shot. I'm not willing to take the risk that the perfect moment will happen later."

I try to loosen the tension. "You got shot just to force this on me, didn't you?"

He gives me a tight smile. "No. But now that we're here,

I'm not going to pass up the opportunity." He winces in pain. "In case I don't make it..."

My eyes start to tear up. "No. I am not losing you. Got it? You don't get to leave me. You don't get to even talk about doing that. Clear?"

But Augie is ignoring me. His face is serious and he's pale, too pale. His eyes are unfocused, his voice weak. "It's selfish and corny. But I … I care about you. I need you to know that."

I blink back the tears. My hands are still applying pressure to his wound. "Augie, I..."

He gives a small shake of his head. "I know. You're not ready to hear it. Part of you will always love … him."

I choke back a sob. "This is … not a good time," I try to joke.

"When is there a good time for us? We don't know how long we get, Asha. We deserve to be happy. Don't we?"

Damn him.

We hear noises from below. Security on walkie-talkies, checking the stairwell below ours.

I don't move. I don't break eye contact. I keep pressure on his shoulder as my voice trembles. "I care, Augie. I feel something too. But I'm still..."

A shout from the stairwell: "This is security! Is anyone up there?"

I'm still in love with *him*. With a ghost.

I shout out towards the stairwell. "Up here. We need a medic."

***

"What the hell happened?"

I'm in a private hospital room, sitting beside Augie's bed, when I hear Jones outside. An audio soundtrack against the low beeping of his monitor.

Turns out the wound is clean, a through-and-through one. Stitches, cleaning. No fragments. Since they wheeled Augie here from the ER, I haven't left his side. I've been afraid to. I need to see him wake up. I can't leave till he does. The hospital smells and sounds remind me of after I found Maya. When she died. There's a fist around my heart, squeezing it tight. I can't leave in case history repeats itself. I won't lose Augie too.

"I said, what the hell?" Jones sounds angry.

Josh's tone is hard. "I don't know."

A second female voice, gentle: "I can't have you all in here. If you would like to move to the relatives' waiting area..."

Everyone ignores her.

"Why were you and Asha out at the front of the stage?" Jones asks. "I saw the footage. That wasn't part of the plan was it, Josh?"

"What do you mean?" he asks.

"I saw the video clips. You dragged her to the centre of the stage."

"I was told to—"

Ruby interrupts him. "Enough. Augie's stable. Asha is

with him. No one else was injured. Do we know if they caught the shooter?"

"Not sure," Jones says impatiently. "And why would anyone want to take out Santos?"

"Are you sure he was the target?" someone I can't place says.

"ENOUGH." It's Ruby's voice that cuts through. Her tone shows how on edge she is. "Let's stick with what we know. It was a flesh wound. Asha is in there with Augie now. He will come around shortly. When he does, the first thing he hears is not going to be us arguing. Clear?"

"Ms Jones?" An American accent. "We spoke on the phone. Paul Cruz. Public relations for Rock. Now that we know Mr Santos is stable, I was wondering if we could talk – Ms Rock would appreciate it."

"Fine." Jones's voice is crisp, angry.

"Please." That soft voice again. "You can't all stay in the corridor. We can page you in the waiting area if there is any change."

"Someone just shot at my friend." Josh again. "We aren't going anywhere."

A sudden movement by Augie snaps my attention back. His fingers twitch against the bedsheet and I grasp his hand. "Hi."

His eyelids flutter open, and his fingers wrap around mine. The fingers on his injured arm.

I let out a sigh. No nerve damage to his hand or arm then.

"Hola."

"How do you feel?"

"Like I just got shot."

"Remember much?"

Augie squeezes my fingers. "Everything."

Damn him.

"Did you see who shot you?" It's Josh.

He, Ruby and Thresher enter the room. Thresher – it was his voice I heard. What the hell is he doing here?

He sees my look and shrugs. "My team had a car on standby. It was the fastest way to get the others here, so I offered."

"Did you see anything?" Josh asks again.

Augie shakes his head. "Someone cut the lights, remember? I couldn't see anything."

Ruby comes over to the bed. "Do you know why anyone would...?"

Augie shakes his head again.

"Sorry," she says. "How would you know what happened? The important thing is you're all right."

"Thanks to Asha," Augie says.

"Any leads on the shooter? Or why?" I ask. "No one is telling us anything."

Thresher leans against the wall behind the others. "Still searching. Whoever it was knew the building and the emergency response plan. They were gone by the time the police arrived. Forensics are checking out the place and interviewing witnesses, but..."

"But?" I ask.

"I know one of the security guys. Apparently the security logs were wiped clean when the shooter was active. Which implies that there was more than one person involved."

Josh says, "I'm sorry, man."

"You weren't the one shooting at me," replies Augie.

"Yeah, but … I could see you, both of you. Security wouldn't let me go back out to get you."

"I heard you speaking outside," I say. "Jones said there was footage. I need to get hold of it."

"But—"

"Josh. Someone shot at us. They hit Augie. I need to know why."

Ruby looks at me. "You think it's related. The threats against us, what happened to Dark…?"

"You don't? Also, last time we played in London, I got attacked during the game. I didn't say anything then but … yeah, I think it's all related."

There is silence then, and in that pause another person enters the room. A woman wearing a grey suit and an earpiece.

"Tower team?"

We turn to her. "Yes?"

"I'm your security guard."

"Sorry … what?" Ruby.

"I work for Rock Industries. I'm Anika Singh. After the events today, all teams will now be receiving security.

I'll be outside if you have any questions. Your manager has asked you to wait here for now." She leaves and takes up position outside.

Thresher looks at Augie and then at me. "We're getting … minders? That's not strange at all."

Ruby chews her lip. "Maybe it's to reassure us that we are safe? Protection is good, right?"

"Depends," I say slowly.

"On what?" asks Josh.

Thresher answers for me. "On whether it's protection – or a spy."

***

It's later when we finally get answers. The others have gone in search of food, but I'm curled up in a chair in Augie's room while he sleeps. The only visitors so far have been doctors and nurses, including a physio who talked about how "fortunate" Augie was. How "lucky".

Then I see movement outside the door. Someone unexpected.

"Asha. Lydia Rock, we met at the welcome party."

"Everyone knows who you are, Ms Rock."

Rock gives a small grin but then quickly hides it. "I'm so sorry about what happened. I can assure you we're taking your safety very seriously, which is why all teams have been assigned personal security." She takes another step into the room. "I wanted to check on Augie."

I study her. Everything about Lydia screams power and money – and feels slightly cold. It's not just her air of determination. It's the expensive but discreet tailored clothes. The highlights in her well-maintained silver hair, the overly smooth, ageless face. The gold jewellery and tasteful diamond earrings. I can see her security team outside, along with a male assistant on a phone, holding what I presume is Rock's expensive black-leather handbag.

"The doctors say he's well enough to be moved," Lydia goes on.

"Moved?"

"Yes. I've arranged a suite in a more private area of the hospital while he rests overnight – he no longer needs to be so near the emergency department. You can stay with him if you like." Rock flicks through the chart at the foot of Augie's bed. "His vitals are good. The shot was clean. No nerve damage … fortunate. His doctor says he can still play in the tournament."

She's worried about the tournament. That is what this is about. "You're not a doctor."

Lydia puts the file down on a nearby tray table. "I am many things." She turns to Augie, who is stirring. "Hi, Augie, how are you feeling?"

"All right," he says. He sits up gingerly. "Better actually."

"That's good to hear." Suddenly there is someone else in the room – a guy holding a camera. Tanned. Brown hair. Early thirties, cargo pants, jumper, camera bag swung over his shoulder. A model who transitioned to working behind the camera. "I was wondering if we could get a quick shot of you to show that you're recovering well. Alleviate any concerns people might have."

I clench my teeth. Augie puts on a grin. "Of course," he says, as I get swept to the side.

The photographer snaps away.

"There's something else – something I wanted to tell you both in person," Lydia continues. "The police apprehended the person who was behind this. A lone shooter has confessed. The police will come by later to speak to you both and take your statements. It's a relief for all of us – but especially for you. The case is now closed."

I swallow. Something about this doesn't feel right. "Wasn't there more than one person involved?" I ask. "Only I heard the security log was erased."

Rock gives me a smile that doesn't reach her eyes. "Who told you that?"

"I can't remember." The jet lag, the shooting – exhaustion seems to hit me suddenly.

She continues. "The police are satisfied it was a lone individual," she repeats. "Someone looking for their ten minutes of fame. There will be an announcement later."

"What are the charges?" I ask. "Assault with a deadly weapon or…?"

"Oh, didn't I tell you?" Her eyes meet mine. "It's terribly sad. Unfortunately the shooter opened fire during his arrest and was killed by the police. He did, however, leave a detailed confession."

Nothing about this feels right.

"You look tired, Asha," Lydia says. "Why don't we go for a little walk, stretch your legs? We can get a coffee. My security will stay with Santos."

"I think I would rather be here, just in case he needs me."

Augie opens his mouth, but Lydia breaks in. "He won't. Will you, Augie? See, he's fine and needs his rest. Let's go, shall we?" She gestures towards the door.

Augie gives me a small wave.

A whiff of expensive, cloying perfume makes me choke as I follow Lydia Rock. Why am I going with her? I don't want to. But there is something about her, and I'm not the only one who feels it. It's star power, the way people seem to clear a path for her as she moves.

She nods to her security as she passes. "I know where they keep the good coffee here."

"How?" I ask, curious.

"All our hospitals have similar layouts."

Of course. Rock Medical. We're in one of Lydia's own hospitals. I take one last look at Augie and start to walk down the corridor with her.

Lydia fills in the silence. "I am looking forward to seeing you play, Asha."

"I'm not sure if Augie…"

"He'll be fine." Her voice is calm but I catch the steel underneath it. This is a woman who is used to getting exactly what she asks for, and I wonder if anyone has ever said "no" to her. "I want to see you achieve your goals here. Your whole team but particularly you."

"In your tournament?"

"We have invested in you, Asha."

"You invest in a lot of things." I see an opening and run with it. "Lots of different businesses and companies."

She glances at me. Her look is less pleasant. "That's what we do at Rock, Asha. Is there something in particular you want to know?"

We reach a small coffee station, and she pours a cup and hands it to me.

"I was wondering about your connections to Zu Thorp, Ms Rock," I say. "You see, I was in the final tournament. It made me curious about him. Did Rock ever invest in Zu Tech?"

Lydia doesn't say anything for a moment, as if considering something. "We invest in many tech companies. Small amounts when it matters most. Although, given what happened to Zu Tech, if we did, we certainly didn't make money on that endeavour. As for Zu Thorp, probably we crossed paths when he was on the tech circuit, but I can't recall when the last time was." She glances at her phone. "I'm sorry, something has come up. I must leave you here. Let's chat again soon. I must say, you are impressive, Ms Kennedy. It was good to spend some time with you." Her smile never reaches her eyes.

A shiver runs down my back. She just lied. I'm sure of it. She denied knowing Zu Thorp personally, and in his interview, he mentioned her as a friend. I wait till she is out of sight before pouring the cup she gave me down the sink. There is something about that woman.

I turn and go back to Augie's room, entering as another nurse leaves. Inside are Ruby and Eliza, both holding takeaway bags.

"We thought you might need sustenance," Eliza says.

"Thanks," I say.

Eliza starts to unpack the food and Ruby sits on the bed next to Augie. "So, what did I miss?"

"I asked Lydia Rock if she was an investor in Zu Thorp's company. She was vague, too vague, about knowing him."

Eliza looks at me, puzzled. "And?"

I shrug. "I think she's lying. I think she knew him personally. I think maybe she was an early investor."

***

Later in the darkness that night, I dream.

There's a sensation like I'm falling. I see the stage again. The security guards rushing it, dragging the others away. Everyone but Augie and me. I see him get shot. I see blood. We run and, as we do, I see that shadowy figure again, watching us from the back of the arena.

I wake with a jump. I'm in a larger private hospital room. Stretched out on a reclining chair near Augie's bed. The curtains are drawn back to show the lights of the New York skyline. I can hear a TV somewhere tuned to a news channel. The bed Augie lies on is clean, with crisp cotton sheets, vases of flowers on the side table and the window. A monitor and a drip with fluids nearby give a steady beat and provide some light.

It's still night-time. I wonder what woke me and realize it's the pressure on my hand, the fingers wrapped around mine, and I know before I even look down that in this dream they are Dark's. His fingers holding mine. His other hand gently moves the hair away from my face when my eyes open.

"I am so sorry, Asha." His voice is ragged. He's thinner than before, more haunted, and I wonder why I've dreamt of him this way.

Before I can reach the edges of the dream and catch it, it's gone. The darkness is total. The nightmares find me. Only now they end with me being shot too.

15

I wake when the light streams into the room. There's a noise as the curtains retract, which is strange as I thought I fell asleep looking at the skyline. A nurse with a small medicine trolley walks towards Augie's bed.

He's awake and sitting up. "What time is it?"

The nurse starts to check Augie's vitals. Moving around him in a quick efficient manner. "Six a.m."

I groan and Augie laughs. "How long have you been awake for?"

"Since five."

"How are you feeling?"

"Surprisingly good. Whatever they put in that drip is working. You?"

I do a mental check on my body. "I feel like I slept in a reclining chair."

"You didn't need to stay. You could have gone with the others."

I stretch. "We're in this together, Santos."

The nurse gives me a look as she flips through Augie's chart. "Physio will be here shortly to assess his shoulder, but by the looks of it..."

"I was very lucky." Augie finishes her sentence for her.

The nurse moves over to check on the drip. "You are, you know. Not many survive a shooting; you want to be careful who you get mixed up with." Her eyes dart in my direction.

I look at her. She's in her late forties, her white skin framed by the views of New York. "Augie isn't a criminal – just because it's a gunshot doesn't mean he's in a gang." Why is the nurse so hostile?

She ignores my comment and writes on a chart. "One of your friends came by during the night and left you some stuff." She nods to a Rock Games bag on a chair.

"Did they give a name?" I ask.

"John. No, wait – Josh."

I wait for her to leave and close the door. It's a large duffel bag with a drawstring. There is a note inside.

Thought you might need these.

There are jeans, T-shirts and toothbrushes for me and

Augie. He takes his stuff and goes to the bathroom. I offer to help him but he gives me a look that tells me to stop. So I search through the rest of the stuff Josh dropped off. My bag from the dressing room is at the bottom. Josh must have somehow got past security after they locked the building.

The bag was Maya's. When I lift it, I catch the rose scent that Maya used to wear – it's strong. I dig through the other items carefully – the glass rose-perfume bottle has shattered – some pens, a notebook, my wash bag with the broken bottle of perfume inside and, at the bottom, my phone that needs to recharge. I lost track of it yesterday. I put it on a charging pad. Then I take out the photo and diary I took from Zu Tech.

The frame in the photo is now cracked. I run my finger over the break and wince. Then I suck the blood that flows from my fingertip and sigh. I remove the broken glass from the frame and put it in the bin. As I do so, the photo falls to the floor. It lands picture side down, revealing a scrawl across the back.

W42

W42?

On instinct, my fingers reach for my sister's locket, now around my wrist, something I keep doing lately when I'm stressed, and then it hits me. The other necklace, the cord with the drive from around my neck, is missing.

I remember my shirt catching and ripping during the shooting. I must have lost it and the flash drive then – when I got Augie off the stage. I'm still standing there processing that when I hear a knock at the door. Quickly I hide the photo again in the bag.

Jones glides in with a woman carrying papers and a laptop.

"Asha, morning. Where's Augie?"

I nod towards the bathroom as she settles into an armchair.

"Do I want to know who you are?" I ask the woman carrying the paperwork.

"Probably not. I'm damage control. You can call me Cortez. I work for Lydia Rock."

"Damage control?"

Jones says, "The UK police have come into possession of some new CCTV footage near the Zu Tech building in London on the night of the arson attack."

That doesn't make sense, I think. *I made sure to hack all the feeds.*

I sit down beside Jones and Cortez puts a laptop in front of me, then hits play.

It's an extract from a news panel show, the lower third of the screen saying they have "exclusive" footage. ASHA KENNEDY, VICTIM OR VILLAIN?

My blood runs cold. "What is this?"

Jones sighs. "Just watch. It is, unfortunately, great TV viewing."

The panel is three white men in their fifties, the presenter a blonde-haired woman in her twenties. In the background in the upper right-hand corner is a smartly dressed black woman in her thirties holding a microphone from what seems to be a live camera feed from outside the Zu Tech building in London.

The blonde-haired woman is asking her questions. "Thanks for that, Mary-Kate. So police have confirmed that Asha Kennedy is wanted in relation to this recent arson attack on the Zu Tech building?"

"That's right, Portia. It has always been unclear whether Asha Kennedy was the hero or the victim of the Zu Tech tragedy. Now, though, police here in London are looking to question her in relation to malicious fire damage that took place only a week ago. CCTV footage and eyewitness statements, as well as car hire records, indicate that Miss Kennedy was at the Zu Tech building on the night of the fire. This fire has, the police say, made their investigation into the missing Zu Tech employees more difficult, as evidence has been destroyed."

Portia nods, her expression serious, and turns to one of the panel members. "Brian, I am in shock. I was Team Asha and now it seems that she might have been—"

"A dangerous attention-seeking out-of-control teen?" Brian shakes his head. "I know, Portia. It would seem we need to re-examine everything that Asha Kennedy tried to convince us of. Maybe she had a grudge against Zu Tech all along."

"But," one of the other panellists interjects, "we still have to remember that this is a girl who grew up in the care system, whose sister tragically died young."

"Of course," the other panellist agrees. "But while many young people have had to grow up in care, not all of them are allegedly burning down buildings and impeding the work of the police—"

Portia interrupts. "And then there's the recent news from New York, where Asha Kennedy is currently taking part in the launch of Rock's new tournament. She was onstage when her teammate Augie Santos was shot at yesterday. Thankfully no one was seriously injured and the perpetrator was found – but trouble really does seem to follow this young lady around."

Portia turns towards another camera and gives a wide, concerned smile straight down the lens. "Our socials are open – I'm sure you'll all have plenty to say. We'll be back with this story along with an exclusive interview with Dr Sawyer, author of the book *When Teens Go Wrong: Signs to Look For*, and he will be here giving us his thoughts right after this break."

Cortez snaps the laptop closed. "It continues in much the same way after the commercial. This is the main morning show on the biggest US network. Over ten million people here watched this segment with their breakfast."

I'm stunned. I glance at Augie, who is standing in the doorway, now dressed. "It's a lie. I didn't set fire to the Zu Tech building in London."

Jones looks at me wearily. "They have CCTV footage of you in that area on the night of the fire."

I swallow. "Can we chat in private?" I ask Jones.

Cortez gives me a look. "I think it's better that I'm included."

"No offence, but don't you also work for Rock?"

"Yes, and otherwise you couldn't afford me. Right now, I'm your only hope. Damage control only works if there is honesty between us. First up, tell me – *truthfully* – did you set that fire at Zu Tech?"

I meet her eyes and shake my head. "No. I also don't believe there is footage of me in the area on the night of the fire. If there is, it's fake."

"Fine. And you haven't been contacted by the UK police?"

"No."

"In that case, assuming the UK police don't have enough to charge you with, I think we go public. You give an interview."

I gasp. "I am *not* doing an interview."

But Jones is nodding. "Just one," she says, "to a credible news outlet, setting the record straight." She picks up her phone and starts texting. "I'll reach out to Murphy and ask him to help make this go away."

"Ask him to run the footage past one of Bill's experts," I say.

Cortez is typing fast on her device. "If you can arrange for the UK police to give a statement to the effect that Asha is cooperating with their investigation, Rock can say how they have every confidence in Asha or else she wouldn't be here representing them in New York. Then we can run an interview, on the same network." She frowns, thinking. "She'll need to give them something personal, juicy, something to shift public opinion to her side."

I glare at Jones and then Cortez. "I am not going to—"

Jones silences me with a look. "One interview." She looks at Cortez. "We'll think of something."

Cortez nods and puts away her laptop. "OK. Talk to no one outside this room apart from your team. And, Asha, if I find out you lied to me, I'm out. Not even Lydia Rock will be able to get me to stay. Those are my terms."

The door shuts behind her with a bang and I groan.

Meanwhile my phone finishes charging and beeps to life. The first thing I see when I click on messages is the stupid goofy photo from yesterday that Augie took of all of us backstage. A lifetime ago. Then another more recent message from Josh. He's on his way.

"What just happened?" Augie asks.

I stand, putting my phone in my pocket. "Jones can fill you in. Are you OK if I go and Josh stays with you for a bit? There's something I need to check."

Jones glares at me. "I don't think…"

I look at her. "I promise it won't involve anything public. I'll keep a low profile."

Jones shrugs. "That would be a change. Fine, but text me a location. The NYPD want to take a witness statement about the shooting before they close the file. They'll be in touch when they're heading over."

I'm nodding as Augie says. "Asha … you saved my life yesterday."

I grin at him. "It's what I do. I didn't think you'd remember – you were out of it."

He gives me a serious look. "I remember. And I meant what I said."

I feel the heat rise in my face as Jones stares at me. "I've got to go. Are you sure you will be all right?" I mumble.

"They're doing tests, nothing scary. I'll be released later today." A pause. "How are you going to shake off the security person?"

Damn. I hadn't thought of that.

He smiles. "So, I'm going to go back into the bathroom. In around ten seconds I'll start to shout. I am guessing our Rock security person, Anika, will then come running in, then you go. Happy?"

I grin at him. "You know me so well."

He *does* know me well. I also realize that, unlike Dark, Augie has always let me do what I wanted. So why do I feel guilty thinking about him as anything other than a friend?

***

My phone loads with more messages as soon as I clear the hospital.

You need to leave. Now.

Did you get out?

I glance at the timestamp. The second text was sent just after the shooting. The Wi-Fi was down, I remember, in the backstage area. Probably to stop photos being leaked or control who was allowed to stream what. Rock security was extra tight that day.

So, Webber had been there – we'd arranged to meet. Which means that Webber's text would have been sent using a cell phone provider.

I got her.

Cell phone providers and their metadata tags are different from web-based texts sent via a VPN. Text messages I can trace. But I need a base. Leap of faith time.

I call Eliza. "I need a favour from a local."

***

Eliza's apartment turns out to be a small loft in Sutton Place. She is dressed to go out when I arrive and holds up a key. "There's food in the fridge – make yourself at home."

"Thanks."

"And the shower is just in there, along with some clothes."

I realize what I must look like after the shooting and sleeping in a chair last night. "Thanks again. Really."

"It's no trouble." Eliza hesitates. "I think Ru is secretly thrilled you called me for help. And I want to help – you know that, right?"

"Yeah. The thing is, me and Ruby..."

"She's your teammate. I get you want to look out for her."

"You make her happy. But I'm just letting you know. To me she's not just a teammate. She's family. I look out for my family."

Eliza hands me the key. "You British people are so weird."

I watch her go. The truth is, I still don't trust her.

***

Eliza's loft shows her love for the better things in life and her eSports career. Its walls are covered in trophies and pictures of her punching the air after her gaming wins. The interior is modern and minimalistic – high-tech equipment softened by natural materials. A leather couch that could double as a bed is in front of a projector screen. Classic reading chairs, books, vinyl records. Polished wooden floors, exposed brick, and white walls. A walk-in closet that looks like a mini clothing store. A bathroom the size of a single bedroom. A photo of her and Ruby on her desk. More importantly her apartment also contains a high-tech gaming set-up that I can use to trace Webber's IMEI number.

Using a modified version of scanner, I create a physical alert so that the next time it connects to the system I'll have a location. Then I open the software that connects to the tracker I hid on the pen drive that was around my neck. The fake necklace I started wearing after I got attacked in London. The bait. Once someone tries to open it, I'll know where they are.

I can't help wondering if Webber's location and that of the person with my necklace will be the same. But for now, I shower and rest.

The ping comes later. Webber, her phone and my pen drive come up at the same location – Broadway and East Tenth Street.

Time to get some answers. I move fast. When I leave Eliza's, I keep her borrowed hoodie pulled down, my hair tied up, dark clothes.

***

Broadway and East Tenth Street turns out to be a church: Grace Church. It's at least a thirty-minute ride away on the subway. If I take too long, I risk losing her. I take a self-driving taxi, keeping my face down as it heads to Greenwich Village.

The church is closed when I get there, but I notice the keypad to the basement. A few small adjustments and I'm in. The building has no lights on as I walk past storerooms of Christmas decorations, stacked meeting-room chairs and head towards what must have once been a crypt or a cellar of sorts. The air smells of damp and disuse, which matches the shoddy condition of the walls and floors. But someone has been here recently. I see footprints in the dust on the floor. Where are they now?

Light creeps up the cellar steps and a shiver runs down my back. This has all the feels of a horror movie. The part where you know the person who goes into the cellar will end up trapped, dead. Then again, my life already feels like the worst kind of twisted story – and if I want to change that I need to follow the clues. I go down the steps silently.

There's a screen in front of me and a shadowy silhouette behind it. I swallow. Take a step.

The figure turns.

It takes me a second to believe what I'm seeing. It has to be a dream.

"Dark."

16

I can't breathe. His arms are around me and he smells exactly as I remember, like citrus and wood. I breathe in every piece of him that I can.

"You're alive." Tears fall down my face, and that hollow feeling that I've had since the tournament ended shifts. My arms are around him, and he's real, and he kisses my neck, and I hear his voice in my ear. "Asha." And everything, everything, falls away for a moment, and there is just this, this joy.

His lips touch mine and it's all I can think of. There's nothing gentle in our touch, just a terrible need to reassure each other that this is real. That he is somehow alive and with me. His touch feels like it burns me, and I shiver as I move even closer to him. My breath matches his as our kiss deepens, and his hands are on my cheek, fingers threading through my hair. There isn't any space between us now. I can feel his heartbeat, and mine echoes his, thumping too loud.

"Asha." It's barely a whisper, and the way he says it is like a prayer. His arms hold me like he'll never let me go. I feel that pull towards him that's always been there. That need to be with him. That feeling that we've always been inevitable.

I lose all track of time. There is only him and this kiss burning with want and everything words can't say that somehow proves we're both alive.

Then my brain kicks in.

"Wait. You were alive. This whole time, you were alive?"

I pull back so I can see his face, and in that moment of silence I hear it. Slow footsteps on the floor above us. Dark's blue eyes narrow and he raises a finger to his lips before pulling me towards a bookcase. He angles one of the books on the middle shelf, and it slides open, revealing a concrete room lit by an emergency light. He pushes me inside and the door closes.

The wall shows the feeds from three CCTV cameras inside the building, all showing people searching the premises.

I stare at him. *He's alive.* Why let me think he was dead?

We stand apart, cold seeping into the space that is now

between us. My heart is hammering in my ears. Lips swollen from where he kissed me. My body feels alive, the ghost of his touch still there. It's taking everything for me not to step back into his arms.

He runs his hand through his hair. "This place was here from the probation era but got upgraded to a panic room during the riots. It's soundproof. We should be OK."

He let me think he was dead, repeats again in my brain. Anger builds within me. He put me through hell. Augie was right. There's a cost to loving someone like Dark, and I paid it in full.

My hand moves without me even realizing it, striking his cheek. The sound echoes around the room.

He doesn't flinch. "Asha."

"You let me think you were kidnapped and then that you were dead. FOR MONTHS."

A quick look at the monitors reveals the search is still ongoing outside. *Breathe. Think. Answers, that's what I want, right?*

"It looks like we have time. SO START EXPLAINING, Dark." My tone is harsh.

He knows he is losing me. "I'm sorry, I never wanted to—"

"You weren't taken. You faked your death?"

He nods. Eyes never leaving mine.

"I thought you must be alive," I say. "But then the DNA matched… You broke me. You know that, right?" My eyes fill with tears, my voice hitching.

"I had to, Asha. They would have killed you. Don't you get that?" His tone is raw, pleading. "They would have used you to get to me. And you want to know what's funny?"

I look back at him, a challenge on my face.

"Look at the monitors, Asha. They're here. They used you to find me anyway."

I step further away from him. "That's impossible. No one knew where I was or where I was going."

"Didn't they?" His voice is quiet.

I think back. *Eliza.* She knew where I was. She would have told Ruby, Josh if he was with her. I trust the twins. Don't I?

"Tell me everything," I say. "Go back to the beginning, and this time tell me the truth."

He nods, and I see it on his face then. That look which tells me that for once he gets it; if he withholds anything this time, I'll walk.

"You're everything to me, Asha. I never really told you that, but you always have been. Since the factory and those stupid Zu Tech classes when we were competing. You're smart, Asha, and beautiful, and I resented how good you were at first and then when we started to hang out..." He pauses. "When I'm with you, I feel ... I FEEL. It scares me, makes me vulnerable. When I left the system, I wanted to get you out too. I thought we could build something together. But you stayed with Maya. So I tried to protect myself. I went all in with Jones." His eyes are full of pain. This is the truth now. "At first it was good. The money, the perks. Then one time she hired me out. I knew something about it was off; what they were asking me to write code for, it was impossible. I pulled some strings, followed the money and realized I was working for Zu Thorp. I couldn't not reach out, ask to meet him. We … grew close, for a while, till I realized the endgame." He notices my lack of reaction, the way my face doesn't change. "But you already knew that. You figured it out, didn't you?"

"Keep talking. What happened next?"

"At the start Zu was … everything you want your hero to be. He convinced me that SHACKLE would be a code that would help people. That we'd use it to rewire the brain, help people who had brain damage to recover, to create pathways to help those with paralysis, to stop the body from fighting transplants. The possibilities were endless."

"You both thought you could play God?"

"I was arrogant. But yes. I thought we were doing something that would help people. I only saw what he showed me. Remember what we were taught at the care home? That Zu Thorp was a benevolent genius. His company was groundbreaking. I wanted to be a part of that. He made me feel … important. Like a player in something bigger than me, and … I fell for it."

I can understand that. When you have nothing, any bit of praise or recognition is addictive. "Until you didn't?"

"I started to figure out that there was another side to SHACKLE. That the investors who had poured billions into it might want to use it for something less than noble. People noticed I was digging, and I was followed. Jones told me to ignore it. But I couldn't shake the feeling I was getting involved in something very wrong. So, one night I copied everything I worked on, put it on a drive – and deleted all the work I had been a part of from their system. I left. I was so sure they wouldn't be able to recreate my work. I was arrogant. I went out on my own after that and locked it all away. Until..."

"I came to you looking for information about what had happened to my sister," I say quietly.

Dark holds my gaze. "I'm sorry, Asha."

"Did you know then what they'd done?"

"Not at first."

"But you suspected, and you didn't tell me."

"How could I? How could I tell the person I loved that I was responsible for her losing her only family? I wrote part of that code, Asha, the code that killed Maya. I never knew how they would use it, but my fingerprints are on it. I never saw the big picture, just a puzzle that I was asked to fix. I didn't know they would use it to kill people, to control people."

Tears fall down my cheek and I wipe at them with the heel of my hand. "You should have told me."

"I was selfish. I thought you might be finally beginning to feel ... the same way I felt about you. I couldn't risk losing you."

I sink towards the floor, leaning against one of the

concrete walls as he sits across from me. The room is tiny – we are close. Too close. Neither of us saying anything.

Eventually I look up at him. "Go on."

He looks at his hands and then at me. "We destroyed SHACKLE together in that tournament. But I knew that wouldn't stop them. Zu's original investors, the Founders now knew what was possible. They wouldn't stop until they recreated the code they'd spent so much on. To do that, they would need one of two things. A copy of the code..."

"Which we destroyed in the tournament."

"Or..."

"The person who helped create it. You."

"I made a mistake, Asha," he says. "I tried to protect you instead of telling you the truth and asking if you'd fight beside me. I swear if you forgive me, I'll never make that mistake again."

I work through the pieces. "What about Webber?"

"Gone. I used her details to hack the system."

"So those messages ... that was you?"

He looks uneasy. "Yes. I needed to know that you were OK."

"You didn't intercept a game in Greenwich, try to take my necklace?"

"No, Asha, what—"

"You don't get to ask questions, got it?" I sigh. "It happened when we were beta testing Rock's game."

"Asha—"

"The shooting at the stadium. Did you have anything to do with that?"

"Of course not. I wouldn't hurt Augie. Whatever happens between you and him, I wouldn't do that."

There's an edge. Like he's, what … jealous?

"You should have been honest," I say. "Instead of hiding behind Webber."

He glares. "Because that works out so well for us. I was trying to keep you safe. When you found me, they did too, and now you're in danger again. And it's my fault."

"I was in danger anyway," I say, suddenly tired again.

Neither of says anything after that for a while. We watch as the people in the cameras pack up Dark's equipment. Including my decoy pen drive that I used to locate Webber/Dark.

Two people, however, remain behind, searching every square centimetre of the church.

Their strange, jerky movements remind me of the people at the Zu Tech fire. "Why do they look so … odd?"

Dark sighs. "If I had to guess … you're looking at people under the influence of an incomplete SHACKLE code."

I move closer to the monitors. "They look…"

Dark sighs. "Like dying zombies?"

I shiver.

"You didn't answer my question earlier. Who knew where you were going? Because someone alerted the Founders. The group behind Zu Tech and SHACKLE. There's a traitor in your team."

"I trust them. All of them. The only one who betrayed me, Dark, was you."

He says nothing for a moment. I can see the hurt in his eyes, and I almost take a step towards him, but I stop as the pain he put me through floods back. *He let me think he was dead.*

When he speaks again, his voice is steady, logical. "Asha, you asked if I was behind you being attacked in London. I wasn't. But someone who had access to your schedule was – same thing at the arena when they shot at you. They leaked manufactured CCTV footage of you at the scene of the Zu Tech fire – I saw the news. There's been a credibility campaign against you since Zu fell. The people behind this have someone on the inside close to you. You can't trust your team any more. You might not like it" – he steps closer to me – "but if you really want to end this, you need to work with me."

I meet his gaze. "I hate you."

We are close, too close, and I can feel my heart starting to beat fast and I hate that I react this way to him.

"Here's the thing, Asha. I don't think you do."

His hand reaches out to move a strand of hair behind my ear. The touch gentle.

I shiver. Because it's *him.* I don't know what to feel or think any more, but it doesn't stop how my traitorous body reacts to his.

His voice is low as he says, "I think you know I'm right."

17

It's late by the time the church is empty and it's safe to move on. Dark helps me up off the floor where I have been sitting, thinking, putting as much distance as I could between the two of us.

I stumble to my feet. My legs are cramped from being on the cold floor for so long.

"You've been quiet a long time," Dark says.

"I've been thinking."

"Reach any conclusions?" He sounds hesitant, like he's afraid of my answer.

"I don't trust you."

"You should."

"Why?"

"Because … damn it, Asha, I know what I did was wrong. I know you have every right to be angry, but there isn't time for this. Be angry with me later, when we're sure there can be a *later* for both of us. You can trust one thing about me." Dark steps forward, and my breath almost leaves my body. "I will always put you first. You need to know that. Please."

Dark so rarely says "please" it stops me. He's close again now, so close it's like we share the same breath, and my heart is so loud I think he must hear it.

"You want revenge on the people behind this. The Founders. You want to make them burn?" he asks.

I hold my head up high. "Yes." My voice is strong, even.

"So do I."

I look at him. I'm pretty sure I am going to regret this. "Till the end?"

Dark doesn't hesitate. "Till the end."

We step outside the panic room and I feel lighter for the first time in months. Then my phone buzzes.

"Where are you?" Jones says angrily.

I debate telling her but then think better of it. "Long story. I lost track of time…"

Dark snorts beside me.

Jones sighs. "The NYPD are here to get a witness statement. Get a car and meet me at the hotel." She hangs up.

"Got to go." Then I stop. I unwind Maya's silver locket from around my wrist. I hold it tightly for a second. Then release it. I give it to Dark, putting it in the palm of his hand and closing his fingers slowly around it. "I scanned everything I found at Zu's lab that night and put it on a drive inside this. The other drive around my neck had nothing on it apart from a few bogus files hidden behind layers of encryption. It was a tracker device, part of how I found you. The people who searched this place have it now. It's how we'll find them."

Dark holds the drive close. A slight smile. "Impressive as always, Asha."

"Don't. I'm sure you know the hotel I'm staying at. Meet me there. Let's find out where that device ends up."

A worried look passes over his face. "Asha, I meant what I said earlier: you can't trust anyone else with this. We end this together. The two of us."

I hesitate. I shut my team out once and it nearly tore us apart. I won't do that again.

"The two of us and my team, Dark – take it or leave it."

***

Back at the hotel, I find Ruby in our suite. She's curled up on the couch, a screen in front of her that she closes when I enter. She looks on edge, her fingers playing with the bracelet Dawn gave her.

"What did I miss?" I ask.

"The good news: we collected Augie from hospital. He's cleared to play. Jones arranged for her eSports coach,

Rachel, to train him here. Bad news: when we went to collect him – someone broke in."

"What?"

"Yeah. They went through all our stuff, but nothing seems to have been taken apart from the new phones in the Rock gift bags."

"Any of the other teams get targeted?"

"A few. Some of them lost electronics, jewellery, that kind of stuff. It might have been some petty thief."

She looks at me. I look at her. Neither of us believes that.

"Did Eliza go with you and Josh to the hospital?" I ask.

Ruby shrugs. "No. Just me and Josh. Why?"

Part of me longs to tell her what happened today. That Dark is alive here in New York. Ruby is one of the few who could help me make sense of the mess that my head is in now. But Eliza wasn't at the hospital. Did she follow me from her apartment? Or did she turn over our suite? If I tell Ruby about Dark, will she keep secrets from the girl she loves? Can I ask her to do that?

"No reason."

Ruby doesn't buy my reply, but all she says is, "Come on. Jones is in one of the conference rooms downstairs."

***

Jones is with two officers. The police questions are as expected. Focused on where I was standing on the stage when the shots started. Whether anyone odd had spoken to me that day. Whether I'd seen anything unusual. Jones gets more and more impatient as they proceed. At last, she interrupts.

"Asha has had a huge shock. She is also competing tomorrow and has press commitments. You already have the shooter, so if we could wrap this up?"

The police officers share a look. The female officer turns to me, her face sympathetic. "One last question. The Met have released a statement saying you are no longer a person of interest in relation to an arson incident at Zu Tech. It turns out the footage was doctored. A nasty bit of sabotage from one of your haters, they think."

I swallow. How much of that was Murphy pushing them to check the footage was authentic? How much of it was Jones looking out for me, demanding immediate tests by experts to verify it was real? I'm not sure. Either way, I'm grateful to them both.

"However," she continues, "we'd be very obliged to you for any information you can give us about Zu Tech. We have open cases on several of their missing American employees."

I hesitate. She's asking me something she shouldn't, according to the gag order. But then it hits me: the gag order is limited to the UK, isn't it? I could talk; can I trust them?

Jones stands up. "I believe this interview is about a traumatic shooting event, nothing more. Anything further and Asha will need to have a lawyer present. If you will excuse us."

The officer tries again. "I understand, but if we could..."

"Are you charging my client with anything?" Jones's tone is all business.

The officer sighs. "No. We are not."

"Then I'm afraid I need to cut this short. I'm sure you can understand."

"Of course." The male officer closes his notebook.

His colleague looks like she wants to argue but she just looks at me. "Good luck, Asha." And it seems genuine.

"Thanks," I mumble as they leave.

When the door shuts behind them, Jones turns to me. "We need to talk."

"Words no one wants to hear."

"Business is business. Asha, we made a deal when I became your guardian. You wouldn't go MIA. Well, you just did. I'd install a tracker, but I'm pretty sure you'd find it and hack it. So I am going to repeat myself – you can't disappear on me, not again."

"I can look after myself."

"I know that. But guess what? I am not just your manager any more. I'm legally responsible for you now. You're my ward. What you do impacts me. Do you get it?"

I swallow. She's right.

She looks at her watch. "I've set up an interview with WABC and they're going to use some prearranged questions. You have to do the interview."

"Any way we could cancel it?"

She shakes her head. "Trust me, Lydia Rock isn't someone you want to annoy. If she asks you to do this, you need to. It's just one interview. After it's over, you can sit out any other PR bits. Santos and the twins can do the talking."

"OK."

We walk down the corridor to the media area, passing other teams, gamers and endless brand ambassadors doing vlogs.

Jones hands me a lanyard. "You'll need this for the press area."

I take it and slowly put it over my head.

"You want to play in Rock's tournament, you have to play by their rules."

"Who's this interview with anyway?" I ask as I flick through the notes.

Jones looks at her device. "King, Ciara King. She's a news host, but one of the gentler ones. Cortez will meet us in there. Here take this too." She passes me a bottle of fruit-flavoured water, and I raise my eyebrows at her.

"You need to stay hydrated."

***

Augie arrives as I get changed into a Tower team shirt. Hair and make-up left a few minutes before – or, rather, I made them leave. My patience is rapidly running out. I feel more exhausted than before, less sharp. And I am done being someone's idea of what a female gamer is.

"You OK?" I ask.

Augie gently moves his shoulder. "All good. For the match, though, we're doing a switch. I'll take Ruby's god's eyespot with the drone; she'll play healer. You and Josh are on the attack."

"Good."

He studies my face. "Ash, is everything OK?"

I nod, and then I go to him, putting my arms around his neck, holding him close and breathing him in. That faint smell of coffee and cinnamon. Augie would never betray me. I know that. So I whisper into his ear. "Dark's alive. I saw him. We're in trouble. I need you to meet me later. Trust no one."

Augie says nothing. He just stills and then squeezes me tighter, his face buried in my hair.

A cough comes from nearby. A production assistant with a clipboard. "If you're ready, Asha, we are all set up inside."

Augie whispers back in my ear. "I'll see you later." He steps back. A fake smile, eyes worried. "Good luck."

***

The lights in the studio are too hot when I sit down with Ciara King. I can't look up because they shine right into my eyes. We're in the centre of the press area, surrounded by Rock logos, with glass floor-to-ceiling windows overlooking VIPs doing interviews below.

Cortez notices and clicks her fingers loudly. "Soft key light only on my client." I then see her talking to the producer.

Jones comes over and crouches down beside my chair. "OK?" She hands me another bottle of water.

I give her a look as I take a sip. *No, not remotely OK.*

She gives me a faint smile. "I meant, do you need anything before this starts?"

I shake my head.

"You're going to nail this, Asha."

I look away. "I..."

"Is there something you need to tell me?" Jones looks at me, looks through me, and I feel like she can see I am keeping something from her.

I swallow. "Yes. But now isn't the time to get into it."

Jones nods. "After this, we talk. I'm here for you."

"As my guardian or as my manager?" I try to make a joke and it's so lame even I cringe.

Jones shrugs. "How about both? I'm new to this too, Asha, but you're growing on me." She stands. "I wasn't expecting that."

Ciara King sits down opposite me. She's in her mid-thirties. Polished. Dark skin with perfectly applied make-up and styled hair. She wears a conservative navy sleeveless dress with a skinny belt and high heels. Her nail polish is a French manicure, understated but expensive, like her slim gold watch.

"Asha."

"Ms King."

"Call me Ciara. Have you ever done a live interview before?"

"No."

"It will be fine." She starts to flick through her flash cards. "You're a natural. Clearly you know what you're doing. We're just giving the people what they want."

Something about her tone feels off. What exactly do the people want? The lights still feel too hot. There is a dull ache between my eyes and a low-level buzzing nearby. I've been in over my head ever since this started.

I try taking a deep breath and inhale some of King's perfume. The mix of sandalwood and something else catches in the back of my throat.

"I'm not a natural anything," I say. "I'm supposed to be in London, at school, studying for exams. Not here."

King pauses and looks at me. Direct, frank. "So why are you here?"

"Because … after what happened, this is all that I have left."

King doesn't say anything for a second. She studies me, before gesturing to the producer that she is ready. "As I said, a natural."

***

The warm-up questions are easy. King asks about the pandemic in London. How Maya and I lost our parents and ended up in care. All questions Cortez covered in the prep document I had flicked through before. All things I knew were coming.

Then the hard questions start.

"Asha, this is a difficult thing to ask. How did you feel when you found your sister dead?"

What does she think that felt like? I detach and reply, using words like "shock" and "pain", but not letting myself feel them.

Then she gets on to Dark, and my whole body stiffens.

"He went missing after the tournament and died here in New York, the victim of a seemingly random act of violence. So much loss for you in such a short time. Can you tell me about him?" King's tone is gentle. I look out at the studio floor beyond the lights, where Jones nods at me. Deep breath.

"He was my friend." True – he was. Now I'm not sure.

"Just a friend?"

I shiver, flashing back to just a few hours ago, and then my mind goes further back. To the night I kissed him in London, to how he was there for me at Maya's funeral, how he found me after I was attacked in Annie's apartment before the Zu Tech tournament. The way he sacrificed himself for me at the tournament. Before faking his own death and putting me through hell…

"Asha?"

I take another breath and look at King. This is starting to feel like therapy. Except in front of an audience.

"In care you create your own support system," I explain. "The people in your group home become more than just friends. You rely on them like family, even when you leave. And that never stops. With Dark he was more than my friend. We were always complicated."

King nods. "Asha, do you think there's a link between Dark's death and the shooting the other day? Could the person who killed Dark and the person who shot at Augie Santos be one and the same?"

What kind of question is that for an eSports piece? "I don't know who shot at us. The police said he was dead."

King tilts her head. "It seems there's more to the story than they first thought. The shooter made a video before he died."

I go still. I look for Jones but can only see Cortez, having what looks like a furious argument in the control booth.

King moves her head to look directly into another camera. "This is new information, Asha, that I think you need to respond to. We have a clip we can play now."

The screen in front of and behind me changes. The image is of a dark room with a hooded masked figure standing looking at the camera. *What is going on?*

King talks to the camera directly. "This is an exclusive breaking news story: footage reported to be from the shooter at Arthur Ashe Stadium. We are live in the studio with Asha Kennedy for her reaction. Let's play the clip, Sam."

The figure speaks; their voice is distorted like it's been

run through some sort of voice changer. The video's low quality or perhaps made to look like that. The voice is male, cracking with emotion.

"*I have asked for this to be released after the event. Asha Kennedy has been lying. SHACKLE was never anything more than a video game. She has always been the real evil, pretending to be the victim of a grand conspiracy. My father was one of the many who lost everything when Zu Tech collapsed. I couldn't protect him from her lies, and he became so depressed afterwards that he took his own life. His blood is on her hands.*

"*People all over the world lost their jobs, and for what? So a teenage girl gets her ten minutes of fame? Enough. TELL THE TRUTH, Asha Kennedy. You and that criminal Dark – you are both killing people with your lies.*"

Then the screen goes black.

Ciara King gives me her best concerned look. "Would you care to comment, Asha? Is there anything to this statement – and, if so, will you tell people the truth?"

I swallow. We are on live TV. And I just got set up.

18

The lights in the studio are glaring now. I can feel the sweat on my forehead.

"I never lied about SHACKLE."

"There are people out there who claim that you did, Asha. People who are wondering if you can be believed. I can't help but wonder whether, in your grief over the unexpected death of your sister, you created a story that has, in essence, destroyed thousands of lives. What exactly did you think would happen to the workers at Zu Tech when you started this? Did you think about them at all?"

"I didn't *start* any of this. I—"

She presses on. "You haven't been entirely honest, Asha. Your friend Dark, for instance. You neglected to mention that he was a known criminal. Was he working for you?"

"No! No one is working for me..."

"How do you see this crusade of yours against Zu Tech ending, Asha?"

I repeat what I know. "Zu Tech killed my sister, Maya Kennedy, when she tried to expose them. They killed her girlfriend, Annie Queen. SHACKLE was about mind control. I didn't make anything up."

I struggle to breathe; my heart and my anger levels are racing against each other.

"Asha, I can see you're upset, but I have to ask: do you have any *proof* of a conspiracy? Anything at all, beyond rumours and your version of events?"

"I ... I..." But I don't get a chance to finish because my body starts to sway. It's too much, the lights, what King is saying. How could anyone think...?

King notices. "Cut to Screen Two."

The image behind her changes. It's a group of people standing in an office. I see the Zu Tech logo behind them.

"Maybe we should hear from some of Zu Tech's former employees," King says. "Listen to their side of the story."

My vision starts to turn black. There is a ringing sound in my ears. Palms clammy. Dizzy.

The last words I hear are King's. "Surely you have something to say, Asha?"

But I have no words. The world fades away and I pass out.

***

When my eyes open, I'm in the dressing room. I see Cortez's assistant on standby with water, painkillers and an ice pack. Outside I can hear raised voices – Jones, Cortez and the producer.

I glance back at the assistant. "How bad was it?"

His face looks grim. "Pretty bad, but I've seen politicians come back from actually committing murder so..."

The voices get louder.

"We walked into a trap! None of that was what we agreed. If you think you've heard the end of this..."

"Ms King is just trying to get at the truth. She's doing her job."

They go on, each blaming the other.

"I'm getting out of here," I say. "I have to see my team."

He glances again at the door before shrugging his shoulders. "Fine by me. For what it's worth, I believe you aren't the person they keep saying you are."

"Why?"

He shrugs. "Honestly? I've worked a while with Cortez, and I think the stories about being wanted for questioning in the UK for starting the fire were planted."

I'm curious. "What makes you think that?"

"Because this has all the hallmarks of a disinformation campaign. I should know – I've run enough of them. Someone started those stories. They leaked footage of you near the scene on the night in question. They built the narrative, broadcast it, and then the police were forced to act on it. But honestly, I was never sure how real the footage they claimed to have was. No one ever asked you to come in for questioning, did they?"

"No, the police dropped it. What about this statement from the shooter?"

"The statement from beyond the grave? When they guy giving it can't be asked anything? It's … off. I'm saying this to you because I want you to know – if anyone can fix it, Cortez can. Don't hold what happened today against her. If someone set you up, they set her up too."

But I'm not listening to him any more. I'm just thinking, *Dark was right. Someone set me up.*

***

I call Bill. Tell him I need a clean room to work in. He has a contact in New York who finds me somewhere underneath the R Hotel. It breaks my heart not telling him the truth about Dark, and I vow to make Dark come clean tonight.

In the basement I find the old tunnel entrance that leads to Grand Central Station. The door is metal and modern, with a security keypad leading into the clean room.

The first thing I check is the tracker from Dark's workshop. I run the program while opening another window. A long shot. There has to be a reason why the photo and the diary were in the background of Zu's video message. He included them on purpose. They must be a clue.

Lastly I open the file of data Bill sent. Everything he could find out about Pi Investments. Dark was right about another thing – the answer is normally to be found by following the money.

I leave the search running and settle in to read. The answers are here. I just have to find them.

***

It's late by the time I get back at our room in the main R Hotel, and my stomach is growling. The home Maya and I had could fit at least twice inside the hotel suite with its four double bedrooms. It smells of expensive linen and food. In the large sitting-room area, along with couches and armchairs, are several trolleys of room service.

Josh spots me first, turning off the screen he was watching. "We weren't sure what you'd like, and Rock is picking up the tab, so … I angry ordered. What was that interview?!"

We have bigger problems, but I can't help myself – I have to ask. "Did you order one of everything on the menu?"

"I told him it was too much," Ruby says. "Still. Figured you might need some comfort food."

Augie is standing by the window. I take in the awkward way he holds himself. He's not admitting it but, even with all Rock's private healthcare, I can tell he feels sore. Tired. He shouldn't have to face danger again, not so soon after last time.

"We were just going through tactics for tomorrow," he says. "If I'm running the drone, then—" He breaks off at a small knock on the door of our suite.

Ruby glares at Josh. "You can't have ordered more food… There was literally nothing left on the menu."

"He didn't," I say. "There's something I need to tell you… I only found out today."

I leave the room and go to the door to our suite. It opens with an electronic click.

A courier with a delivery box enters. Except he's not a courier.

Dark shuts the door behind him. Face hidden by his helmet, he goes to the first wall socket he sees and plugs a signal jammer from the box he was carrying. Then he takes off his helmet.

His voice is low as he says, "The jammer will block anything getting out, but my guess is that the Founders have bugged your room, so they'll notice soon enough that their signal is scrambled and send someone." He nods towards the main suite area. "You sure about them?"

"Positive. My team would never betray me."

The truth is, I don't have proof. Just a feeling. One that I need to trust.

We step into the sitting room, and everyone falls silent. Staring at Dark.

There's a moment or two where everyone just looks at him. Stillness.

Then the room explodes.

Josh is the first to reach Dark, fist raised. "How could you let anyone go through what she did, thinking you were gone? You lowlife piece of—"

Dark ducks. "I was trying to keep her safe and also…"

Josh pauses, fist still raised. "Also, what?"

I step in between the two of them, my nerves stretched. "Also … we don't have time for this. We're all in danger." I glare at them both until Josh reluctantly backs down.

Ruby's voice is quiet when she speaks. "We deserve answers."

Dark meets her gaze. "Then ask. What do you want to know?"

But Ruby is looking at me. "When did you find out that he was still alive?"

I swallow, sitting down. "Today. Dark wasn't sure you could be…"

"Trusted," Ruby finishes. "He didn't know if he could trust us."

Augie looks at him with anger in his eyes. "What's that supposed to mean? The question all of us should be asking is, can we trust you?"

Josh is frowning. "I saw that car explode."

I sigh. "The explosion was rigged; he entered and then left the car through a pre-cut opening in the floorpan of the car that gave him access to the sewer cover he parked over."

"But the DNA?" says Augie. "It matched. Who was in the car?"

"The bodies were two unclaimed John Does from a morgue upstate," Dark explains. "I planted some of my own blood and hair in the car. I wasn't sure how much intel they – the police, the Founders – might have on me. I needed to make it convincing."

"How could you do that to her?" Augie's voice is strained.

Darks says nothing.

Ruby cuts the tension between them. "*Tell* us why. Start at the beginning."

Dark sits on one of the chairs. "Fine. It goes back to Zu Thorp. I worked with Zu. I was unknowingly one of the original coders on SHACKLE. I didn't know what we were building it for. I thought Zu was one of the good guys. We got to know each other a bit. He told me stuff about his childhood. How he first got into gaming as a small kid in New York. His parents were still together then. His mum was teaching a summer course at NYU. At that stage, rather than argue in front of him, they'd go for a walk, then give him a roll of quarters and send him to an arcade while they hashed out their divorce and yelled at each other on the pier nearby. He never mentioned it in interviews, but he told me the story.

"The arcade is where he fell in love with video games. They were his salvation while the rest of the world crumbled around him. Zu never forgot about that place. He even joked about buying it as a gaming museum. Anyway, that place, that arcade is in New York."

I think of Zu's video. *I collected some insurance, along with the code. Something … that will tie every one of them to SHACKLE. I've left it where it all began.*

As though reading my mind, Dark says, "The arcade is on West Forty-second Street. Very few people would know what that place meant to him. I knew if he had something to hide, it would probably be there."

"Nebulous Arcade," I say, and he nods.

"Would you care to tell us how you ended up such close pals with Zu?" Ruby asks coldly. She's more angry than I've ever seen her.

"Jones hired me out. I was impressed by Zu at first – we all were. But once I realized what SHACKLE could do, I deleted my work and left." He turns to me. "Asha, that photo of Zu as a kid in front of the arcade, could Rock have seen that?"

"Why?" I ask.

"Because I looked at where Rock Industries are staging the tournament final. It's the flood zone around West Forty-second Street and Pier 81. Where Nebulous Arcade was. Someone else knows its significance. I don't believe in coincidences."

I meet his eyes. "Me neither. Two things. I went through Zu's diary. He wrote down a reference number the month before he died – *N19ZT.* I couldn't figure out what it was – turns out it's the tail number of his personal jet. The flight was to New York."

"So Zu flew to New York just before he died?"

"Sounds like it. Also, I traced the drive that was taken from the crypt by whoever followed me there. Care to guess where the signal is?"

Dark leans forward. "Surprise me."

I nod. "Rock Industries corporate offices, a few blocks from here."

Josh has gone pale. "And that could be a really weird coincidence?" he asks in a hopeful tone.

Dark rolls his eyes and I shake my head. "I also went through the data Bill sent on Pi Investments – one of the companies which invested in Zu Tech as a start-up. It turns out that Pi Investments is actually owned by…"

"Rock." Ruby's voice is a whisper.

"Yeah. Rock, or Lydia Rock specifically, is one of the Founders. She wants to get her hands on SHACKLE and she's using us to do it." I sigh. "We got played. They invited us here to either draw Dark out or find out how much I knew." I glance at him, loath to admit it. "You were right about that."

Dark looks at me with a slight smirk. But it quickly fades. "You talked to Bill?"

"Bill hooked me up with a contact – a clean room under the hotel. Turns out the rumour about a secret train station entrance is true. And by the way, Dark, you're telling Bill tonight that you're alive. He's putting himself in danger poking around in Zu Tech's past. He needs to know what could be headed his way so he can prepare and defend himself."

Dark's sigh is heavy. He really thought he could keep Bill out of it. "Fine."

Augie looks at me. "So, to recap?"

I take them through it. "We think that Lydia Rock was an early investor in Zu Thorp, part of the group called the Founders who contracted Zu Tech to make the SHACKLE code. Zu realized the harm it could do and hid a prototype of the code and evidence on the Founders before he died. He gave a clue as to where in the message I found the night of the fire – the code would be hidden *where all this started.*

"That seems to be right here in New York, on the site of the arcade where he used to play when he was a kid. The place it started for him. It was his insurance in case things went wrong."

"But if Rock are staging the tournament final there..." Ruby says slowly.

"Yeah. It means Rock suspect the same thing – they just haven't managed to find anything yet," says Josh. "This tournament is a set-up. They're hoping we'll make it to the final, access the old arcade and find the evidence. They can follow us and we'll lead them straight to it."

"But what choice do we have?" I say. "We need proof to put them away. We can't do nothing. SHACKLE is too dangerous to risk the Founders getting hold of it. The people who set the fire at Zu Tech and who searched Dark's place the other night – something wasn't right about them. They're ex-Zu Tech employees, infected by the game and turned into ... I don't know ... zombies? Puppets? We have to stop them. Otherwise what was all this for?" I look at them all. The twins, Augie. My heart twists. "This information puts all of you in danger. I'd do anything not to involve you."

Ruby's expression is determined. "But we're already in danger. I mean, they shot Augie, right?"

I repeat what Dark said earlier because it's true. "They will come after the people they think are close to us, and they won't care. They killed Maya, Annie..."

I look at Augie, Ruby and Josh. Then the door of the suite clicks as Jones walks in and I jump. Finally. I sent her a message two hours ago.

When Jones sees Dark, she goes completely still. A slow smile spreads over her face. "I knew it. You're like an unkillable cockroach."

Dark shrugs. "I missed you too."

Jones sits in one of the chairs, taking food from a room service tray as she does. "OK. What's the plan?"

I swallow and turn to Ruby. "Before we get into it ... we can't trust anyone outside this room."

She looks hurt, angry. "Meaning what exactly? Don't tell me. You think we can't trust Eliza. Why?"

"Because someone followed me from her loft to where Dark was hiding."

She shakes her head. "You could have been spotted and followed by anyone."

"Yeah, I know. But until we're sure, we can't involve her."

"She wouldn't betray me, Asha. Wait, don't tell me, you think she just got close to me because of you? Come on."

"Asha isn't saying that, Ruby." Josh shoots me a warning look. "She's just saying until we know more..."

Ruby throws up her hands and grits her teeth. She's unhappy – that's the understatement of the century. "Fine." She's not *fine.* I wouldn't be either. "You're wrong about her, Asha. She's on our side. But FINE."

"Maybe, but we can't afford to take the chance. I'm sorry. Now let's talk about the plan. We need to use the tournament to find what Zu hid – before Rock does."

Jones looks at me. "Not to cause issues, but Rock is the largest company on the planet. Lydia Rock has an empire that covers the globe and a good chunk of space exploration as well. She is smart and has endless resources. I believe in you, but at the end of the day we're a UK eSports team that has yet to win a tournament you don't somehow destroy. With Zu Tech, we got lucky in that we got out alive. How the hell are you going to pull that same stunt a second time?"

Augie grins. "David versus Goliath. We go down, we go down fighting."

Jones shakes her head. "The 'go down' part is not reassuring."

I owe Jones, and she's already put so much on the line for me. "Dark and I are the only two who need to go into the building. We just need the rest of you to create the diversion and be careful."

Augie's eyes lock on to mine. "You're not going into that place alone. Also, you mentioned zombies?!"

"They're people infected by an incomplete SHACKLE code. Zu's code was perfect – this one isn't. Worse case, it eventually breaks down." Dark's voice is flat.

"Meaning?" snaps Jones.

"That over time they die – their brain short-circuits; it stops regulating involuntary movements like breathing, their heartbeat. An incomplete code allows you to control someone but only barely. The control is noticeable … and eventually … it kills them."

Augie shivers.

Ruby looks at me directly for the first time since I mentioned Eliza. "No way. We're all in this, and no one is going down. Don't get me wrong" – she glares at Dark – "I am still processing how angry I am at you. And I'm not remotely over what you just implied about my girlfriend, Asha, but … we are a team. Not your support act. Someone comes after one of us – they deal with all of us."

My eyes fill up at her tone, but I blink the tears back. "You and Josh have family, Ruby. You have Dawn, your mum, Josh's girlfriend Amy, Eliza—"

Josh cuts me off. "Yeah, and all those people will still be there when this is over, Asha, because we are doing this for them. We're fighting to protect them. We aren't losing them. Stop trying to be the martyr here. Let's focus on a plan."

After that, we go back and forth on what diversion

we can create, finally agreeing on something just before Jones tells Dark it's time to leave. If the Founders really are bugging our suite, then a black-out this long means it's no longer safe for him to stay. I don't want him to go, not after just getting him back, but something stops me from saying that out loud. Like it might give him some power over me. Instead, I go with him to the door.

He turns to me. "Come with me? This place isn't safe."

"I can't. The second they see me gone, they'll know I suspect." I look into his blue eyes. "Where will you go?"

"I'll contact Bill and then find a place near here. Asha…" He takes a step closer and puts a hand to my cheek.

"What?" It comes out as a whisper, and I hate that he can still do that to me.

"I'll be close. I'm not leaving you again."

I loathe him, and yet I don't. But this isn't the time. I stand up straight. "I can take care of myself."

"I know."

He leans in so his words are a whisper only I can hear. "I never told you before. How much it hurt when we were apart. I'm not taking the chance again. I care about you. I always have. And … I know you feel that too. I saw what you kept in your sister's locket."

I startle and my eyes go to his. I'd forgotten about the photo of him I'd put there. "It doesn't mean anything," I say.

Dark looks at me, serious. "It means everything, and you know it."

***

About ten minutes after Dark leaves, someone saying they're from housekeeping comes by to check on our Wi-Fi. I guess Dark wasn't being paranoid about Rock spying on us. It's one of the many things I think about later as Augie and I sit on a lounger on the balcony outside our suite looking at the lights of New York.

"How do you feel?" he asks.

I look at him. "Shouldn't I be asking you that?"

He flexes his shoulder. "It pays to be in a tournament sponsored by a corporation with access to cutting-edge medical tech. They may be the big bad, but they have awesome doctors." He goes quiet. "You saved my life, Asha. I froze, and you saved me."

We look at the skyline and the people passing by below. I shiver in the cold, which is helping me focus as I try to put my thoughts in order. I feel confused, overloaded, like all I'm doing is reacting in a game someone else is making me play.

"We're so close to this being over, to finding out the truth," I say. "To destroying SHACKLE for ever. But I'm worried the Founders will kill all of us before we can expose them. Without proof no one will believe a word I say. And if we fail, Augie… It's not just about me getting justice any more. Those people at the church, at Zu Tech, more could be infected like them. I'm scared." My voice starts to break and I stop.

Augie's arm is around me. "Fear makes us careful. And I

see how you react to it, Asha. It lights you up inside. Brings your survival instinct out. I think you need to embrace it. Let it help you get through this. Trust your instincts. And … I'm here for you."

"Augie. Don't."

"Because you think you need to be strong for everyone on your own? Or because he's back?"

I look at Augie. At his brown eyes, the hair falling over his face. "I packed all my emotions away. I need to end this. I can't think about anything else till then. And I still don't know how I feel about him."

Augie sighs and moves his arm away. "Yes. You do. I guess I always knew that, Asha. I see the way you look at him, even when you're so angry you want to hit him. But, no matter what your decision is when this is over, you're not in this fight alone. You never have been." He sounds wistful.

He stands and goes inside. His face paler than usual.

I stay looking out into the night. Tomorrow the tournament starts.

19

Semi-finals

To have a chance of finding whatever Zu hid, we need to get past the first round. Only the finals are being held around West Forty-second Street and Pier 81, where Zu Thorp hid his proof. The only way to access it is by playing in that final. The only way forward is through.

As we wait backstage, I look over towards Ruby.

She glances away. She's still upset about Eliza, and I get that.

Josh gives me a nudge. "She doesn't stay mad for long."

"You really think she'll forgive me?"

"It's Ruby. Of course she will. Just … this is her first

time, you know, in a relationship, and she's freaking out that maybe Eliza isn't who she says she is. And it's weird for her being here in competition with her. For what it's worth, it took me a while to warm up to Eliza, but when Ruby got arrested … her reaction felt real. She cares about her, Asha."

Then I remember something else – Josh's angry phone call. Another secret. "Hey, Josh, is everything OK? Apart from all this, I mean?"

I see him almost instantly tense. "Why?"

I meet his gaze. I'm not lying to him; we don't have time. "I saw you arguing on the phone with someone after the kick-off party. Eliza thought it might be money worries."

He thinks back. "Oh, that. Yeah. Wasn't about money, though. Amy wanted me to come home. She's worried that things might get bad. Like at the Zu Tech tournament…"

So Eliza lied. Was she trying to weaken our team by hinting Josh had money problems? Or deflecting attention from herself by suggesting Josh had a weakness others could exploit? Is Eliza our traitor?

After everything that has happened, it feels strange to remember that we're at an eSports event. That this is supposed to be fun. That the players and managers who push past us are just here to put on a show. The lights lower and music pumps up, as a voice echoes out over the sound of stadium cheers. "And now welcome … the teams!"

Images of the first players in the semi-finals start to play on the giant screens dotted around the stadium from where most of the fans and the commentators will watch. Fireworks light up the sky and a band plays.

eSports tournaments don't make money. They're paid for by brands and advertisers looking to connect with an audience that doesn't care about their products and are run by gaming companies who make so much money they could write off the cost as a marketing expense anyway. Stack the annual output of music, film and TV on top of each other and it still doesn't come close to what the main gaming companies make each year. So, the tournaments become bigger, bolder and more spectacular each time, and Rock has gone all out. After the Zu Tech's SHACKLE tournament, the eyes of the world are on this arena, all of them watching, invested. If something happens at this event, the ripple will be felt around the globe and yet for Lydia Rock this is just about getting her hands on SHACKLE's code.

The teams in front of us chat excitedly to each other as they wait in small groups backstage for their turn to go out. Josh is with Ruby. I follow her eyeline and see she's watching Eliza, who's suited up. Her look is glamorous compared to the rest of us. Her nails are painted with gold glitter – a look that's carried through to her eyelids. Her hair is in box braids and pulled back from her face. Standing by her is Thresher. His hand rests on his chin, concealing his face as he talks to Eliza. He glances our way and nods.

"I wonder what his deal is?" I say to Augie.

"Thresher told me something after I got shot," Augie says thoughtfully. "That he was here if we needed him. Said he believed what you said after the tournament in London because of something he saw in one of the Asian tournaments."

I turn to Augie, suddenly interested. "What did he see?"

Augie shrugs. "He never got a chance to say. We got interrupted. Jones came in and he changed the subject, put on the usual Thresher act, pre-tournament trash talk. Probably nothing. Didn't realize he and Eliza were so close, though."

I wonder.

We wait, tense. When each team is announced, they are transported by car to their designated playing area. Today eight teams will eventually become four who will advance to the finals tomorrow. All of us are trying to make it through. In our case, failure isn't an option. The only way to access West Forty-second Street, where Zu's old arcade was, is by getting through to the final.

Then, finally, we're called.

"And here they are, folks, the notorious TOWER TEAM!"

As we walk out I hear some people booing from the audience. I raise my arm higher and smile brighter as we walk towards the microphone. *Never let them see you cry.* The presenter, Alan Star, gives me a concerned look. He isn't used to this type of reaction. He forces his bleached smile wider. Then takes and lifts my hand.

"It's Asha!" he yells. The booing intensifies. "Bit of a divided reaction there, Asha, you worried?"

I swallow. Fake smile in place. "No, not at all, Alan. Just delighted to be here competing with such an amazing team." I wave at the audience before he moves on to Augie. The crowd chant and cheer for him as I step to the side, inhaling the smell of stale popcorn. I need space but there is none here. Just row after row of fans and cameras. I force myself to let out a breath.

The presenter moves further down the line and I edge over to the wings. Last time I was onstage there was a shooting. I'm not staying out here too long.

"So tough, isn't it, Ms Kennedy? Their reaction."

I turn to see Lydia Rock. A shiver runs down my spine. I try to study her face but it's almost impossible to read emotion there given how much work she's had done. Her forehead never moves.

She keeps her back to the stage and head carefully angled so no one can pick up on her moving lips. "Keep smiling, Ms Kennedy. I'm here to make an arrangement with you. One that should help."

I plaster a fake grin across my face. My heart is thumping, my palms sweating. "What kind of deal, Ms Rock?"

"I think its best we're honest with each other, don't you? Then we don't waste time with you pretending you don't know what I am talking about."

I nod, watching as the presenter brings Josh and Ruby to the centre of the stage. Augie is looking around for me, but I'm hidden in the shadows at the side of the stage now.

"You're close to finding something of mine that I want back. I want you to take a quick look at your team, Asha, then think of the people who aren't here but who I know you care about, your friend Bill, Murphy, little Dawn. I am in a position to help you keep them alive – provided you get me what I want. After all, I paid for it."

My heart sinks. "The code for SHACKLE."

She smiles. "Precisely. So glad we understand each other. It does make it easier, and we are both busy women."

I meet her eyes. "If I don't?"

"I don't think you have an option, my dear. Let me guess, you think you're going to find proof and then alert the authorities, reveal my associates and their organizations to the world and be a hero."

Associates. So I was right. This is about more than Rock. The Founders are bigger than one company.

"I didn't say I was going to—"

Rock cuts me off. "You don't have to. I can save you the trouble. I and my fellow investors OWN the authorities. No one is going to believe you. When those videos from Zu Tech went viral, we had to make sure of that. It wasn't hard to discredit you."

I grit my teeth.

"There are more factors at play here than you realize, Asha."

"Why did you create SHACKLE? Can you at least tell me that?"

Lydia Rock considers me. "We aren't monsters. We are a centuries-old collection of business interests. The Founders have always been in the shadows, using our power and influence. But now … the world is falling apart. There is political instability, conflict. Pandemics raging out of control, diminishing resources. SHACKLE is the only way to restore order. It's why we made our original investment in Zu Tech. So that things can continue as they should."

"The way *you* think they should."

"Free will is the most destructive force on earth, Asha. Just look around you. Think about it." She glances past me. "We'll talk again very soon. Make good choices."

She walks away, passing Jones, who is coming towards me. "Best of luck, Tower team," Lydia calls over her shoulder. And then she steps from the wing and on to the stage, waving to the crowd. From the other side of the stage a host of celebrity commentators start to line up behind her.

"Welcome," Lydia says, "to the start of Rock's *Capture the City* tournament, a new type of eSports event that we will be rolling out around the globe next year. Are you ready?" The crowd roars and she beams. "Then let's play."

Glitter falls from above and a giant screen starts playing the film showcasing the gaming space and the team promos. It's time for us to leave. Our team gets bundled into the last of the cars that were waiting outside and it speeds through the darkness before depositing us in one of the flood zone areas of the city, aka Ghost Town, an area of Manhattan regularly claimed by water and abandoned in favour of flood barriers in the more fashionable districts. We're miked up and the camera drones lock on to us to cover our every move.

I'm trapped into playing this game. Somewhere out there in the shadows is Dark. The compromise we came to is that I would stay visible, and he would stay close. After the chaos of the stadium, at least the cold feels fresh. We suit up, adjusting gloves and visors. Augie takes our flag out and starts talking to Ruby about defence.

I go to Josh. "You ready for this?"

He grins back at me before lowering his mask. "Born ready."

I hear a groan behind me and it's Ruby. "Meathead."

"Let's do this," Augie says, and I catch my breath as I look at him. He looks exhausted – more tired than before. Something is going on with him, I can feel it.

I'm distracted by the green fireworks that launch from the boats moored in the river. The signal that marks the official start of the tournament.

Josh is beside me. "Ready? Inhale, exhale."

The smell of garbage and something else musky and earthy catches in my throat. "What is that?"

"Algae from the water. We'll get used to it." Josh leans in and makes a small adjustment to my speaker and microphone. "Tap once and it becomes an isolated channel for the team. Tap twice and it's just me, OK?" I nod. "And here." He slips a small round metal object no bigger than a button into my hand. "Put it in your pocket."

I slip it unseen into one of the suit's small utility pockets. "What is it?" I ask, fingers over the mic.

"Something from your friend in case you need him."

A panic button connected to Dark. Smart. I let out a deep breath. Behind us, the fireworks reach their finale and as the last one explodes over the city waters the world around us changes. New York is still there, but now it has a layer of augmented reality on top of it. Buildings are tagged in neon colours like a dystopian cyber city claimed by various street crews – a sight only visible to those playing with Rock's glasses and the millions now watching via the live feed. To anyone else it looks just as it did before.

"This part never gets old," I whisper.

Josh is the one who replies. "You're right. It never does."

Ruby and Augie take off with their brightly glowing square of blue, our team flag, to the one-time luxury apartment block behind us on West Forty-fourth Street, which overlooks what is left of the now submerged Pier 84, before heading for the penthouse. Once secure and in place, they will use the height of the building to launch the drone and feed us intel on movements around us.

Josh and I run towards a small office building further away, using the doorways of the buildings as cover. Somewhere out there in the darkness are seven other teams, Dark and others too. People from Rock. Those infected by SHACKLE, human zombies, watching us.

I lock away my fear. Right now, we just need to get

through this. We have to find what Zu Thorp hid here. Because if we don't it's clear none of us will walk away. I don't trust Lydia Rock. My gut says that once we have outlived our usefulness, she will tidy us up like loose ends. I haven't had a chance to tell the others what she said yet.

Josh and I start scanning the area from behind an abandoned car, looking for any splash of colour or movement that might show us where the other teams are placed. It's quiet, too quiet. I hear a sudden scream and what sounds like shots in the distance and my blood turns cold. "What was that?"

A message appears in holo text in front of us:

Expect the unexpected, players.

What the hell?

I hear Augie in my ear. "You have to see this."

We crouch as two members of the orange team tear down the street near us. Then we see what they are running from – robot dogs. Their angry mouths are opening and closing as they sprint. Real or not real?

Josh, however, is looking at the direction the dogs and orange team came from. "If I had to guess, I'd say their base and flag must be planted in that direction. Augie, we're going to check it out. See if there are any colour movements over there?"

Augie's voice is clear in our ears. "On it."

We move, using the buildings for cover. All our senses

are heightened now; every sound makes me jump and my heart keeps hammering. *Keep it together, Asha.*

I watch Josh's back as he watches our front. Then I see it, a red dot on Josh's back. I react instantly, pushing him down to the ground with my body while twisting the gaming gun in the direction the laser came from. "Sniper, do you see from where?"

Augie's voice cuts through. "Old bus depot. Recently abandoned. They're on the roof of one of the buses."

We run, Josh just in front of me, crouching low.

"Augie, anything?" I hear Josh ask.

"Negative."

Great, they're hidden now. I pass one of the buses. There are at least fifteen of them parked in a row. "I'm going up top," I whisper.

I use a nearby bin to climb on top of the roof. Its painted bus number is 2777.

"See anything?" Josh asks.

"No." I keep looking. There must be something. I jump across to the roof of the next bus, and that's when I see it. A flash of colour. Neon orange close to the rear window of a school bus parked a few metres away from the bus I am on.

I lie flat and whisper, "We have a flag, orange, inside the school bus."

Augie's voice is next. "Confirmed, it's showing up now."

Ruby's voice breaks in. "There can't be more than two left in your location if the others are being chased by robot dogs."

I see Josh move into position by the wheels of a nearby bus. "We could attack. There are two of us, two of them."

"No, too risky, they could take one of us out in the crossfire. We need to keep the team intact." I glance at the horseshoe-shaped depot. "What if we create a distraction?"

I can hear the smile in Josh's voice as he replies. The guy is a born showman. "What do you have in mind?"

***

Breaking in is easy. It has a standard alarm system that I don't even bother to hack; instead, I find the power box, open the panel, disconnect the backup power supply and then unplug the transformer. I stick to the shadows, passing empty waiting areas and a humming vending machine. It's eerie. Then again, with the floods claiming more and more land, perhaps the city needed fewer buses or there wasn't time to empty this place out. It looks like the bus authority abandoned the place, leaving everything exactly as it was, as if it's just waiting for the people to return and hasn't yet realized they never will.

I check the expiry dates and take a bottle of water and a pack of Twizzlers from the machine, and then I find the depot control room. As I suspected, there is a central control for the electric vehicles along with a stack of key cards and some automated building controls. I start to create a plan. No one said we couldn't use the resources in our zones. The trick will be to see if these things still work – or if all this was left because it had already experienced water damage.

Josh remains on watch outside. Augie's voice is in our ears. "Two figures inside the bus now. One of them seems stationary. The other one is a lookout. The flag seems to be hanging near the back of the bus. It's blocked by the other buses parked in front. No sign of their drone player; they must be one of the ones who ran."

When I finish, I set a timer, sprinting outside with a stack of bus keys, each labelled with a number that matches the numbers painted on top.

I take position, tapping into the team comms. "When the lights go on, the buses will start to move. The orange team should panic and run. When they do, we grab the flag."

Josh gives me a hand signal to confirm. We wait. Did I set the timers right? Then, all of a sudden, the outdoor work lights and floodlights in the old depot flicker on. As soon as they do, I hit start and then the automove button on the keys.

The school bus and three buses around it rumble into life. Interior lights switch on, automated voices start calling out service stops and, as they do, the buses start to move from their parking spaces towards their terminal spots.

I hear shouts from inside the school bus, but no one runs out. Damn it.

We surround the bus. Do we need to go in shooting? Josh and I have raised our laser guns, when a voice calls out from inside. "We surrender. Please, help us."

We're both surprised. I look at Josh and can see him thinking the same thing – this is too easy, a trap?

"Throw your weapons out," I shout.

The door to the school bus opens and two guns clatter to the ground outside. I get to them first and kick them to the side. Josh and I go on board slowly, our weapons raised. A metallic smell hits me almost at once, along with damp, sweat and rotten food. One of the members of the orange team is lying on a seat, blood dripping from their arm. The other kneels beside them. They have shoulder-length rainbow hair, maybe a year or two older than me, but it's the blood on their face that draws my attention. A name comes into my head from the tournament posters.

"Sky."

"Don't shoot. Please. We need your help."

Josh doesn't move for a moment, stunned. "Real or unreal?" he says.

I look at the blood. "Real." We both lower our guns and rush to Sky's side.

"What happened?" Josh asks.

"We were trying to be smart." Sky's words come out in a rush. "When we were getting into position, we hacked the sensor. To make our flag invisible or at least change the neon. We did it before on the beta version. My teammate thought it would give us an edge. But the game knew what we tried to do, and these holo dogs showed up – only they weren't so holo. They were real."

"They did this?" I can't keep the horror from my voice.

There's so much blood; that was the metallic smell that hit me when we entered, and it fills the bus now.

Sky nods. "I thought the game was safe. I've never seen an augment game like this…"

They're spiralling, I can sense it. "Stop, breathe. Your teammate is losing blood, we need to stop the bleeding, and then you need to get out of here, understand? I'm Asha, this is Josh."

Sky rolls their eyes. "I know who you are." They breathe out. "We sent the others to look for help ages ago and they never came back. We tried to signal, send a distress flare, but something seems to be wrong with the broadcast."

That explains the two people we saw being chased by robot dogs earlier.

"Look at me, Sky." I take a Swiss army knife out from my pocket. "Use this to cut one of the seat belts. Josh, once we tie this off, we need to get them out."

Sky cuts the belt while Josh reaches behind me and takes down the orange team's flag. "As soon as we walk out with this, they'll be out of the game. An official will collect them and remove them from the zone. There should be a medic there. Can I take this?" Josh asks Sky, who nods.

"Sky, what's their name?" I put my hands around the wound to try to stop the bleeding. There's so much blood, too much. The bite must have cut an artery. They are conscious, just.

"Spark."

I look at Spark. Their hair, once bright blue, is now

matted in blood that's soaked through their gaming suit. They can't be much older than me. "Spark, listen to me. You're going to be OK. We're going to stop the bleeding and get you out of here. Stay with us."

Spark doesn't respond. Their eyes are barely open.

"We need to move fast," I say as the three of us create a makeshift tourniquet and start to carry Spark off the bus.

When we get them outside, we lay Spark down gently. Sky sits beside them on the ground, looking worried. "Is Spark…?" Their voice breaks.

I don't reply because I'm not sure. Also, what the hell? This is supposed to be a game, not a death match.

"Josh, now." He raises the orange flag into the air. As soon as he does an orange firework spirals up from the nearby boat barge and explodes in the night sky.

Drones start to circle overhead and the voice coming from it is one of the tournament presenters. "Bad luck, orange team, stand by for extraction."

I crouch beside Sky, offering the water I stole earlier from the depot. "We can wait with you if you like?"

She shakes her head as, in the distance, we see headlights approaching. "Better if you get out of here, before the other teams lock on to you." She looks up at me. "They're coming for you, Asha. There's a stupid side bet – some of the other players have a prize pot they all put cash into. Winner is the team that takes you out."

"How much?" Josh asks.

"One hundred K."

Josh looks at me. "I'm insulted, aren't you, Asha?"

I shrug. I miss this. Trash-talking gamer Josh. "I have a feeling we can make them go higher."

We turn to go but Sky grabs my wrist before I can stand, and their voice is a whisper, urgent as they put a hand over their microphone. "Asha, if I had to go out, I'm glad it's against you. I never believed those stories saying you made it up. No one who was at the tournaments does. But everyone is afraid to speak up. Rock controls the circuit now. No one wants to end their career by alienating them. But … be careful. This whole set-up is off. It's like they think they're not answerable to anyone any more."

I give them a small smile. "Let's make them accountable."

Josh looks into the distance. "Incoming. Let's go, Asha."

We only get a few blocks away when I hear static on our comms, then Augie in my ear. "If you can hear me, get back to base…" His voice breaks up for a second but then returns. "I'm not sure how long we can last…"

Then the line goes dead.

20

"Augie, Ruby!"

My comms remains dead. Nothing, not even static now.

Josh tries his. "Ruby? Augie?" But there is no sound. Crucially there are no fireworks either, meaning no one has taken our flag yet.

"It could be a trap designed to draw us out," Josh says.

I match his pace and focus. "Of course it's a trap," I rasp out as we move. "Everything in these games always is."

The abandoned apartment block we had picked as our base comes into view within a few minutes. It's closer to the flood zone with more obvious damage. Our glasses give us an assault of colour, of tags and street names that are painted in over the buildings by the game. The air is arctic now as night swallows us up, running in the shadows of the buildings. Almost there. I dig in and run faster. One crisis and near-death disaster at a time.

Josh's hand falls on my shoulder as we reach the building. He points up and I see the sky around us light up pink as another team is knocked out. He raises five fingers on his hand. There are five teams left.

I nod and then turn back to the building. Augie and Ruby were going to the top floor, the penthouse. Who – or what – found them?

We enter the building through a service entrance on the side. The car park gates are wide open. There are footsteps on the concrete floor from the puddles outside. Recent, judging by how wet they are.

Josh whispers into his comms again, trying to see if it was just a signal distance issue, but the line remains useless. I point upwards and nod to the interior fire exit stairs. He follows me. Both of us are on edge now. The stairwell has emergency lights only, meaning it's dark. The only flashes of colour are the graffiti on its walls that must have happened after it was abandoned. We are tense, nervous. Every footstep sounds too loud, and Augie's last message is still ringing in my ear. *I'm not sure how long we can last…*

We make it up at least seven levels when –

BANG.

Josh and I both freeze. Backs against the walls.

BANG. BANG.

I look up and catch a movement ahead. Someone is trying to break one of the fire escape doors open by pounding on it over and over again.

Josh gestures to the exit door we just passed and we backtrack, opening it quietly and disappearing into what would once have been a brightly lit lobby with an elevator and two apartment doors.

I point towards one of the doors. It has a spring latch, like the one they used to have in the care home where I grew up. I look at Josh and keep my voice low. "Do you have a credit card? Key card?"

He sighs, taking the room card for the hotel from his pocket. "Don't break it."

I give him a look. Seriously? Then I wiggle the card in the gap between the door and the frame near the lock till it clicks and opens.

Whoever lived in 7B left in a hurry. The room is covered in dust sheets over expensive-looking furniture and art.

Josh peeks under one. "Who goes and leaves all this stuff in an area that the city is making into a flood zone? Rich people have more money than sense. That or it's an insurance scam."

"They could have just died?" I offer, fingers trailing over the faded velvet of the couch. "In one of the virus surges or the flooding. I've heard about places being empty when there's no next of kin. New York was hit harder than London."

But Josh isn't listening. He taps the screen by the door. It's dead. "You got a portable power pack?"

Within minutes we have hacked into what remains of the building's security system, which gives us access to the stairwell and the floors above.

Two floors above us, on the ninth floor, a group of people are trying to break down a barricaded exit. Josh takes a holo map from his pocket and puts it in front of us. He points to a red dot. "See here. That's us, Apartment 7B. Then these dots are whoever is trying to break through the fire exit on nine. And this" – he points to a green dot at the top of the building – "this is the penthouse."

"So, another team is trying to get to them, trying to break into the penthouse?"

Josh shakes his head. "Look at the number of dots. There are at least eight people. Each team in the tournament only has four players. Whoever is breaking down that door..."

"They're not part of the game."

Josh looks serious. "We have to get Ruby and Augie out, fast."

We stand there for a moment, looking at the map and the security screens. Finally I say it out loud. "How? They're trapped on the ninth floor. The only way in or out is the fire exit stairwell – which is where they are."

"There is another a way, but you're not going to like it," Josh says. "We'll have to go around them."

He's right: I don't like it.

"Look at the elevator shafts. The ninth floor has regular

lifts but also penthouse access. See here – on the opposite side of the building is a single shaft just for the penthouse through its own private entrance, running from the ground floor to the penthouse roof garden."

"But the lifts aren't working..." Even as I say it, I know what he is going to say next.

Josh nods. "We need to climb up the lift shaft."

***

My fingers are bleeding. Sweat is pouring from me, and everything inside me is screaming, *Don't look down, don't slip.* The lift shaft is dark. It also smells of dust, decay, and things I don't want to think about. Some of the rungs on the ladder at the side of the shaft are covered in slime, others in rust. Every pull-up hurts, and each time I think, *This is it. This is when I lose my grip and fall.*

The panic button Dark gave me practically burns a hole in my jeans as I wonder if I should have used it. But whatever trouble Ruby and Augie are in, I'm not sure Dark could help, and if he did try, he'd be caught. Maybe that's why Rock is making this tournament so hard. To make him come out of hiding. But I'll be damned if I'm letting them get him.

Josh is behind me as we inch forward. I'm almost at the top when my foot hits the rung and it crumbles away underneath me. I hang on to the bar in front of me with both hands while I try to right myself, struggling with the terror that rockets through me. Then I feel Josh's hand on my foot, holding me still, grunting as he pushes my boot up to the next rung.

I breathe deeply. I hate this.

"Don't fall, Asha."

I feel like laughing at that. "Yeah, great idea, avoid crashing to my death."

I hear him chuckle below me. "There's the warm sense of sarcasm I missed."

Josh has saved my life. The rest of my found family, Ruby and Augie, are above us in trouble. I would do anything for them. I dig deeper. We are getting them out.

We keep pulling ourselves up. Counting the numbers on the wall that mark each of the floors. *Six, seven.* We chose to start on a lower floor in case we attracted too much attention. We climb slower, quieter, as we head towards the top, aware there are people on the other side of the shaft trying to break into the ninth floor. Hopefully they haven't figured out the secondary access yet.

Eight. One more floor.

When we reach the ninth floor, I realize my arms won't be strong enough to pull the doors open. Josh slowly climbs in front of me, both of us almost too scared to breathe in case it causes the metal to break or one of us slips. Then we hear another sickening banging sound, this one closer to us. The application of force against a boarded-up shaft.

I look down and see fingers prising apart the doors on Floor Eight. Too close. "Josh."

"I know, give me a second." His voice is strained.

He has a penknife in his hand as he tries to prise open the doors.

I hear a sound below me coming closer and then freeze as fingers grasp at my lower leg. They make contact with my sneakers and start to try and pull me off the ladder.

"Stop! You'll kill us both," I scream.

But the person doesn't stop, and their face comes into view. I know in an instant who this is. It's one of the people who vanished after Zu Tech collapsed. Andy Ryan. One of the missing.

He makes another grab at my leg and I manage to shake him off. He loses his balance and—

Time seems to slow, suspending him in mid-air. I panic and reach down and try to grab at him, but then he falls back and down into the darkness till it swallows him up. For a few seconds there is nothing, then a sickening dull thud as he reaches the bottom of the shaft.

I cover my mouth to mask my scream. That can't have happened. But when I look up at Josh, his reaction confirms it. Whoever tried to grab me is gone. Then I look down and see more faces looking out from where the man came from. All with that same blank expression. More fingers are reaching towards the ladder.

"*Josh, move*," I half scream, half cry.

"I'm trying."

Then Josh gives one final push and the lift doors pull apart enough for him to wedge them open, and freezing-cold air from the roof hits us both.

Josh crawls through the opening, extending his hand to me as soon as he gets on to the other side.

I don't think. I grab his hand as he pulls me through and out, my shoulder slamming to the ground.

21

I can't move. All I can hear is that sickening thud playing in a loop in my mind.

Meanwhile Josh grabs the penknife he used to jam the door, pulling it free so the doors close. No one can follow us for now.

Silence. Then we hear the thumps.

BANG.

BANG.

BANG.

Those people have climbed up and are now trying to get through.

We move. The rooftop is in darkness. It must once have been a spectacular penthouse, complete with a garden and a covered pool that is now a mess of green algae that smells of rot. Broken garden furniture lies around the place, and the wind seems to be hitting the roof from all directions now in icy blasts. I glance at a yellow plastic chute that runs down the side of the building. It's wider than most builders' chutes and must have been added for bulky waste. The interior lights up with various gamer tags, meaning people must have been inside it over the last while.

I find sliding doors that lead into an open-plan kitchen/sitting room of the high-end penthouse. Separate pantry and washroom, central garbage because Americans don't believe in carrying their garbage to the bin, laundry and vacuum robot all lie here covered in dust.

"Ru, Augie? Are you there?"

My voice is low. I head through the penthouse towards the main entrance. I can hear the thump and bang of fists outside. That noise is everywhere.

"Augie, Ruby?"

Nothing, and then: "Asha?"

Ruby steps out from one of the doorways, and I immediately run to her and my arms wrap around her. They're here. We weren't too late.

"Are you OK?" I whisper.

Ruby pulls back and her eyes are bright but focused. "We weren't sure if you got our last message before the signal went. All our comms in the building cut about twenty minutes ago."

I nod. "Augie?"

"Here."

He steps out from the shadows and gives me a weak smile.

"Those people – it's just like you said. They're controlled by SHACKLE. There's something wrong. It's like they're empty husks…" Ruby's voice drifts.

"Dangerous ones," Josh says. "We need to get out of here."

The thumping on the lift doors continues. "How?" Ruby says.

I realize that the plan to get up here was very much dependent on us being able to use that same way down as our escape, and that ship has sailed.

Josh looks around us slightly desperately, his eyes fixing on the yellow builders' chute in the corner. "We could—"

I cut him off before he can even finish the thought.

"No. Apart from everything else, I noticed part of the chute is missing at the end. We would be free-falling at least two floors."

Ruby shrugs. "I got nothing."

"There has to be another way…" Augie says.

I have an idea. I lead the others back into the kitchen and towards the garbage chute. "Josh, throw up the holo map."

We all look at the rotating 3D green projection, twisting it from every angle.

"See here, the penthouse and the apartments below all share a central garbage chute that leads to the basement. If we could fit into that, we could crawl out here." I point to a similar chute three floors down.

"No way," Ruby says.

"Way." My eyes meet hers. "We're desperate, Ru. Come on, we need to look around for something we can tie up here so we have a rope that can absorb the shock if anyone falls. Hurry."

We work fast, creating something that resembles rope from the ends of blinds, dust sheets and items from a toolbox. Enough to get us down two floors, just.

The smell that hits us when we open the chute is almost unbearable.

"You have got to be kidding me," Ruby says, but then the banging becomes louder. She takes a deep breath and lowers herself into the chute, trying not to touch the sides.

Augie looks at Josh. "You go next, then Asha and then me."

Josh gives Augie a quick nod and waits for Ruby's signal, two tugs on the rope to signal she's safe before he climbs in. "This is not what I signed up for," he says.

Augie grins. "Join the club."

Josh nods grimly, his hand grasping Augie's shoulder before he disappears down the chute.

Augie turns to me. "You next, Asha, as soon as Josh gives the signal—"

And then it happens. There's a crash as the door to the penthouse finally gives way.

Augie looks at me. "Go."

"Not without you."

"We won't both fit, Asha."

But I'm already moving, pulling the rope and closing the hatch, screaming down to the others to move. We can't follow the others down – not now. Plan B is over. We need a plan C.

"We can't give them a trail to follow. This way."

We run outside on to the rooftop, closing the sliding doors behind us and triggering the manual switch to bring down the metal security blinds.

"Here," I say, and we run towards the edge of the building. The builders' chute.

"We can't do this," Augie yells. "You said yourself..."

"It's our only choice. There's a dumpster below. There are tags inside the tubes, meaning someone else did it before us."

"Doesn't mean they survived."

I look back towards the penthouse. "We don't have time. We have to do this. Now."

Then Augie is on the ledge beside me. Arms wrapping tight around my body, and we both jump into the tunnel of the yellow plastic chute, falling down.

The chute twists and turns as we fall. We see nothing but darkness and hear only the sound of our bodies as we slide at speed. I can't think; I can only hold Augie with one hand and try to use the other to slow our descent. Then the chute disappears and we plummet through the air. Landing hard in a cloud of cement dust, among the rubbish on top of some old ripped mattresses. Augie's arms are still tightly wrapped around me; he took the brunt of the fall.

My heart is hammering so loud I'm frightened to move. "You OK?" I whisper, and he holds me tighter.

"No, but I am alive. I guess that will have to do for now."

Alive and unbelievably lucky. Everything hurts as we pull ourselves out of the skip and on to the street. Augie jumps first and then raises his hands to help me. I fall into his arms. He holds me for a second as if reassuring himself I'm in one piece and then steps back. We move to the shadows and I scan the darkness for the others.

The sky in front of us explodes as another firework burst overhead. Green. The signal for the end of the game.

Four teams left.

Augie looks at me. "I guess we made it through to the final."

Somehow neither of us feels like celebrating.

22

We find Ruby and Josh outside, around the corner from the skip, towards the front of the building. All of us are looking over our shoulders but the intruders, the people under the control of SHACKLE, or whatever they were, seem to have vanished the second the closing fireworks lit the night sky.

I hug Ruby.

"What happened out there?" she asks. Her voice is a whisper against my cheek.

I let her go but keep my hand on her arm. "Someone got hurt. One of the other teams. The game isn't safe, Ruby, none of us are safe. Lydia Rock knows what we're looking for and she's expecting us to get it and then hand it over to her. I think what happened in the penthouse was her proving she's serious."

Josh kicks at a stone on the ground. "So now what?"

Augie stands beside him. "We get what we came for, then we get the hell away from here. Away from Rock, the Founders, all of them. We don't give them anything. We are done being played."

Ruby pulls away from my arm. "What about Jones? Can she help?"

I shrug. "We can't tell her what happened in here – if we do, she'll pull us out."

Josh looks at me. "Would she?"

The wind whips around us and I shiver. "Yeah, she would. She'd want to protect us."

Ruby looks behind me. "Car."

***

At the stadium Jones is waiting for us. She calmly hands me a note. "One of Rock's people said this was for you."

I wonder what the spectators saw. "Did you see what happened in there?" I whisper.

Her eyes go to mine, confused. "What do you mean?"

"The penthouse?"

Jones shakes her head. "The live feed showed you going to check on Augie and Ruby at the penthouse and then after the last team was eliminated you came here." She puts a hand on my arm. "Did something happen?"

I don't answer. I start to feel shivery, cold. Of course. Rock controls the live feeds. Nothing we do will be seen unless they want it to be seen, especially us being put in danger. Lydia Rock wanted to let us know that she was in charge. And that man who fell…

My stomach lurches. I unfold the heavy paper and read the typed script.

Dear Ms Kennedy,

I hope you enjoyed that sample of what things could be like if you fail to play by the rules. Don't disappoint. Retrieve what we asked, and your friends will live. Remember we are watching, and we are everywhere.

It's unsigned, but only one person would send me that note. My shoulders hunch. Everything feels sore. Augie, Ruby and Josh are behind me. Ruby's eyes go to the giant scoreboard to see who else made it. Thresher's and Eliza's teams are among those going to the final with us. I see her let out a deep breath when she recognizes Eliza's name. My gaze passes over her to Augie, and I see him wince. His arm. Those stitches probably didn't hold up in the chute.

"Cover for us?" I say to Jones. "Please?"

"I know that look, Asha," she says. "You're up to something."

"I have a feeling Augie pulled some stitches and he's trying to hide it. I think Ruby and Josh need time. It was … intense out there."

She scans my face, and whatever she sees makes her nod her head. "OK. I'll cover, but don't disappear, Asha." Her voice drops lower. "But first..."

She takes in the blood splatters on my suit from helping Sky and Spark. The stains on my hands from the lift shaft. She pushes me towards a side corridor. "That'd better be only mud and dirt. Take a shower and then slip out the back. I have a private changing room code: 1929. It's got clean clothes."

"Jones?" My voice cracks.

"Yeah?"

"Whatever happens. I'm ... I'm sorry I brought all this trouble to you."

And I mean it. Since this started, Jones has been my one constant, and I'm not sure she'll ever know how grateful I am for that. For not being stuck back in a care home under the watch of some social worker.

Jones rolls her shoulders. "None of this was your fault, Asha, and I'm sorry too. Now just go."

I catch Josh's arm and slip the note from Lydia and Dark's panic button into his pocket. I don't trust myself with either right now.

"I need a minute," I tell him, and he nods.

I go to Jones's dressing room. I manage to strip down as far as my underwear, and then I give up. I turn on the water and wince as it hits the cuts and bruises that cover my body. It acts like a trigger against whatever was keeping me upright. Washing the blood away won't clear my head of the memories of everything that happened. How did we get here? Fighting for our lives inside another tournament? Always a pawn on someone else's board, expendable, just like that man in the lift shaft. Like Maya was…

My stomach heaves and I'm sick. The adrenaline leaves my body, making me feel worse. When there's nothing left inside me, I sink to the floor of the shower. Hot water hits me as I shake, knees pulled up tight to my body, head bent over. The tears don't stop. I see the man falling down the lift shaft in slow motion. Maya lying dead on the floor of our apartment. Annie Queen in her home, dead, the blood still wet.

I should have been able to save them. Why couldn't I?

I don't know how long I am there until a large warm towel is placed gently over me and I hear the shower being turned off. Arms wrap me in a robe.

I look up and it's Dark. "How?" I whisper.

"Josh. He used the panic button. Said you were shaken up. He and Ruby are taking Augie to get his stitches checked at a private clinic Bill suggested. Right now, we need to get you out before anyone spots us. Someplace safe."

I nod. I can't speak.

He hands me some clean clothes. "Can you get these on?"

He waits in my dressing room till I exit the bathroom and then adds some shades and a pulled-down baseball cap to my head, gently tucking my hair up and into the cap till it's hidden. His touch is light and I almost lean into him but then I remember where we are. How dangerous this is for both of us. He picks up a HD camera and switches it on. "Let's go."

The backstage area is a mass of players and press. Dark wears jeans, a T-shirt, baseball cap pulled down. There's an official lanyard around his neck that says "PRESS", a camera in front of his face, as he navigates the crowd for a few steps, then turns and pulls me towards an exit. A utility tunnel leads to a car park and a car he bundles me into. Two blocks later he dumps the car and we get into another one with a driver and a divider between the front and the passenger section.

He pulls me against him in the back seat. My head is on his shoulder as he gently rubs my back in small soothing circles. "It's going to be OK."

"It's not," I say, because how can it be? We still need to go back into the tournament tomorrow in order to search the arcade. And even if we find what Zu Thorp hid, Lydia Rock is expecting us to hand it over or die.

"It will be, Asha, I promise you." His voice is low, half whisper, half growl.

I breathe him in. That smell of citrus and wood, home, and then I break.

I don't know how long I cry for, just that Dark never lets me go. Not as we drive or as he bundles me afterwards into an empty loft apartment where I lie against his chest on an oversized couch, looking at the lights of New York outside the window. I never knew I had so many tears inside, but eventually they slow and I start instead to listen to the steady thump of his heart. To remember to breathe.

"Can you eat?" he asks after a while.

"No."

"How bad was it?" he asks

"They're turning me into something I hate," I say. "I did something terrible."

"Asha." His arms are tight around mine. "Josh told me what happened. That man attacked you and you still tried to save him. You're not the villain here. What happened isn't your fault. It's theirs. The Founders did this."

My only answer is more tears and not just for the person who must have died but for all of us. Rock controls everything. The tournaments, the live feeds, hell, even the media, because they own percentages of most of the networks and studios. We never had a chance. Not against them. Not against them and their associates.

"Ash, please listen to me..." And I know the next words out of Dark's mouth will be designed to try to fix me, make this better. But I also know that I feel cold and empty inside, and I'm so tired of that feeling. If this is all the time we have left...

I pull myself up and I don't wait. I kiss him.

At first, Dark doesn't react, he's too stunned, and then his lips are on mine, kissing me back as he pulls me closer, tighter to him. His hands are in my hair. He's kissing me as if his life depended on it, and maybe mine does too because I need to feel something other than pain and fear.

I push against him and kiss him with a kind of desperation as the world fades away. My body burns against him. His touch feels like a jolt of electricity and all that is left is us, this moment, and the lights of the city outside. I want it to last for ever. To memorize every second because he always makes me feel this way. Alive. That kiss becomes everything, something neither of us can pull away from. Like a flame out of control.

I lose track of time until, somehow, he does it. He pulls away from me. My lips tingle from kissing him; the sky outside is darker. "Asha," he says, and the way he says it makes my pulse speed. Part of me only ever wants to hear him say my name that way, with a mixture of wonder and raw want. But then his tone changes. "We have to talk."

I reach for him and kiss him again. "No we don't." My hand drifts to his chest.

He reaches into his pocket and pulls out a small velvet pouch and my heart goes still for a second. I know what it is. My necklace, the locket Maya gave me, the one that has a drive in it, photos of her, and a small tracker I added in case I ever lost it, along with my one physical photo of Dark. The one he found when he opened it.

"I should have returned it, but it felt … like having a part of you close to me. Sorry."

His fingers open the bag and he goes to clasp it around my neck, but I shake my head. "Don't." Instead, I take it and put it around his, hiding the locket part under his shirt. "Promise me you won't take it off, that you'll keep it safe for me till this is over? So I can always find my way back to you."

He nods. His hands cup my cheek. His eyes are focused on my lips as I lean in and kiss him. This time it's gentle, slow. He's torn when he pulls back, and when he speaks his voice is rough. "I'm trying to do the right thing. But I need your help. Please."

The "please" stops me. I bite my lower lip and he literally groans.

"Asha."

And the idea that I have any sort of power over him makes me grin, the first in a long time. "What? I stopped."

He moves slightly away from me and I feel his absence. The space between us. "I want to spend for ever with you, but..."

I sigh. "But ... you're going to make us talk instead?"

"You need time to process all this, Asha, to deal with everything. To work out how you feel about me when we're not being hunted. But we only have now, no more than a few hours. And we need to make a plan for what happens once we go outside these doors. Because I am not losing you again."

I shake my head.

His hand takes mine. "There will be a next time, Asha. We're in this together."

I remember what he said at the church. "Till the end?"

He nods. A small kiss to my forehead. "I don't deserve you, but I'm selfish. I'm not letting you go if you decide to stay."

I feel the warmth of his words. This thing between us, this invisible thread pulled tight. Something inevitable.

"OK. Let's talk about tomorrow."

And we do.

***

It doesn't hit me till later how much I changed after that kiss. Somehow Dark managed to put the pieces of me back together. I start to feel that most dangerous and fragile thing of all. Hope. Hope that there will be a tomorrow for us all.

***

I meet the others at the hospital later. Augie's still having tests. One look at Ruby says she is close to where I was earlier. Breaking.

I nod to Josh. "Get her out of here."

Josh scans my face. "You OK now?"

"I will be. Go, and thanks." I take a seat and wait.

The receptionist glares at me, and I wonder why till I see the tabloid website she's on. It's one of the ones that says I'm a self-destructive teen. The new evil to warn your kids against. I zone out. Looking, thinking, but not seeing anything till I notice a small girl aged around seven or maybe eight with her mum staring at me. They sit in the row of chairs across from mine. The mum looks tired, harassed. The kid has a handkerchief over her head. She reminds me a little of Dawn, Ruby's sister. That same cheeky grin. While her mum goes to check something with the receptionist, she turns to me, whispering.

"You're her, aren't you?"

"If by 'her' you mean an eSports player, then yes."

The kid smiles and digs around in her bag for a home-made rag doll. The doll has long brown wool hair, honey-coloured fabric skin and brown button eyes. She wears a hand-stitched blue Tower team shirt with black trousers. The name on the front of her shirt has a lightning bolt near it in glitter: ASHA.

She shows it to me while keeping hold of the doll's arms. "I asked my mom to make her for me. I'm sick, so she couldn't say no," she whispers.

"It's beautiful," I say.

She smiles. "It's you."

I choke a little. The recent press obviously hasn't caught up with this kid yet. I look at her happy face. "Why?"

The girl smooths the doll's wool hair and starts to plait it into pigtails. "Cos you saved us. We used to go to the Rock hospital to do treatments, and they can take hours, so all the kids there play. Sometimes, when you don't feel great, it's the best way to forget, and to chat with the people you knew before without them feeling weird. When we game, they don't see how we look now. We're like we used to be."

I look away for a second, struggling to keep my voice even. Upbeat. "I bet you're good, when you play."

She nods, her expression serious. "I am. I can beat my brothers. On my good days, when I'm not feeling sick."

I change topic. "What's your favourite game?"

"I like *Animal Crossing.* We used to like all the ones Zu Tech sent to us for pre-release testing because we got them before anyone else. Once my friend Jason, he got an advanced download of SHACKLE. He played it all day using an adapted VR headset. But the next day the game was gone. Someone had taken it off the system."

Something about how she says it means I ask the next question even though I'm not sure I want to know the answer.

"And Jason?"

"My mom says Jason is in a better place now. She says the two weren't related. Him playing the game and then going to see Heaven. But after that we changed hospitals." The girl pauses, her voice turning into a whisper. "So I know. It was that game."

She leans back into her seat, and her legs start to swing back and forth. "That's why I think it was a good idea what you and your friends did, no matter what anyone else says."

Her mum returns with a smile and a ticket. "Sorry, sweetie, they need some scans before we see the doctor, OK?"

The little girl nods. "Bye."

I smile at her, and then notice I'm still wearing the friendship bracelet Dawn made me. I take it off. "Here this is for you, for good luck, OK?"

The girl's face bursts into a smile. "Can I keep it, Mommy?"

Her mum looks at me, perhaps realizing who I am for the first time.

"It's just a bracelet, nothing else," I say.

She nods. "Say thank you, Louise."

"Thank you."

And then they go, and I'm left alone once again with my thoughts, and this time they are full of rage. SHACKLE claimed more victims than I realized. Zu Tech didn't just mess with my life but with so many others.

"Asha?" It's Augie, emerging from the consulting room. He looks paler than before. Something is wrong.

I'm beside him in seconds. I wrap my arms around him. "What happened?"

"The consultant, they… I can't tell you here."

"There's a small park across from the hospital?"

He nods.

***

It's nearly morning outside and freezing cold.

I go to hold Augie's hand, but he steps away. "Asha, I…"

His eyes are wide. I can feel his panic. "What did they tell you?" I ask, steeling myself.

"The doctor asked me if I'd experienced any unusual symptoms recently. I told him about the nightmares, how sometimes I can't sleep. He ran another scan."

I nod, confused. "We've all had nightmares – ever since—"

"Right. We were all exposed to SHACKLE in the Zu Tech tournament… We were all in contact with the code. But … I also played the beta version of that game too. You remember my manager, Carlos? That guy hired out my skills to test new games for Zu Tech."

My breath goes still. My mind goes to the little girl's story. Inside my head I start to scream. It can't be…

He swallows. "They saw the start of changes to my brain chemistry. It's like a poison inside my head slowly spreading. It started with a slight tremor in my left hand after the shooting, but it will grow until … either I'm dead or I become like those people."

Dead like Jason. "No. We will stop this."

His expression is tender. "You can't, Ash."

"We have to. There has to be a way."

"How?" There's a resignation in his voice that I can't bear. He's given up.

I start thinking out loud. "You were used as a beta tester for the early version of SHACKLE. It's a long shot, but if we had the code to the game, maybe we could figure out a way to stop what's happening and fix it. Reverse it."

That original code is somewhere at the old arcade, where we will play in the final tomorrow. If we can find it, instead of destroying it we could use it. The problem: Lydia Rock wants it too – badly.

"Asha, forget about me. There's a chance, a big one, that

SHACKLE might have also affected you, Dark, Ruby and Josh. That's why I'm telling you. Trust me, if I could keep this a secret, I would."

"Why? Why would you keep this a secret from me?"

"Because I saw you after Annie was killed. When you thought Dark was dead. I would never let you put yourself through that for me. I've been around dying people before, Asha. My mum. I don't want you to spend time with me because you feel sorry for me. I want you to live. I'm telling you so you have a chance to figure out a solution for yourself and the others." He pauses. Letting out a deep breath. "I'm not going to make it. Dying is one thing. Dying and leaving someone behind … making you watch me slowly go in front of you. I won't do that."

"No. We are not accepting that." My voice grows firm. "You are letting me try. We fix this."

"Asha."

"How long Augie?" I ask.

He swallows. "A few months at most."

I don't let him say anything else. My arms wrap around him again, my head resting against his shoulder so he can't see my tears.

I won't let them take anyone else away.

23

Finals

I grab a few hours' sleep back at the hotel. I tell the others about Augie in the morning. We were all exposed; if there is a chance they might also be infected, they deserve to know. I don't tell them, however, that Augie said his symptoms started with a slight tremor in his hand when he was tired. A tremor that I have, too.

This whole thing ends later today, but the odds are against us. Augie is dying. I told the others that we need access to a full version of the SHACKLE code to even have a hope of saving him, but, even then, it's not a guarantee. What I do know – I will face the same diagnosis as Augie sooner rather than later. All I can do is hope Dark, Josh and Ruby are somehow OK. But we all played in that tournament.

SHACKLE is like an ancient hydra; every time we cut off one head, like when we brought down Zu Tech, another appears. And if we try to bring Rock to justice, would anyone believe us? Rock, the Founders, they have all the power – what do we have?

I change, staring into the mirror in my bathroom. "Maya, if you're there, if some part of you isn't at rest yet and is watching, I'm begging you to help us one last time. I promise after this I will let you go. Please. I can't lose anyone else, Maya. Help me."

I find the others in the kitchen area. Ruby's eyes are red from crying, but she puts on a fake smile. Jones has yet to come by.

Josh has a small Nintendo in his hand. His fingers move lightly as he plays, but from the in-game crashing effects, it's not going well. "Stress relief. Shall I call room service? Last meal of the condemned?"

"I'm not touching their food," Ruby says. "Let's go somewhere else."

Augie enters. I note with a sinking feeling that his eyes don't meet mine, the distance he is already trying to put between us. He's pulling away. "Somewhere else sounds good, Ruby."

We find a classic diner a few blocks away. Noisy, busy, smelling of coffee, pancakes and grease. One with a booth in the back and a few arcade machines. Augie gets spotted by a group of young kids and signs some napkins and does photos while we take over the booth. No one comes near us.

I smile. "This place is perfect."

The *last meal* feeling takes hold as we order stacks of food and then get change for the jukebox in the corner. I don't want this moment to end. We get loud as we make jokes, trash talk about games we've played. We start to trade embarrassing stories.

"Did Josh ever tell you about how he and Amy got together?" Ruby says.

He groans. "Stop, Ruby."

Augie looks up. "Now you have to tell us."

Her face lights up. "Little Josh had placed in his first regional tournament and he handed over his prize money to our mum. It wasn't a lot but even so she wouldn't take all of it. Said we needed to spend some of it on something nice for ourselves."

Josh smiles. "Ruby, of course, went shopping."

"Totally true. But not Josh. He had his eye on some stupid retro game… Remember Retro Mike's shop?"

Josh sinks lower in his seat. "Ru, literally no one wants to hear this."

Augie gives a small smile. "No, I think we're all invested now. Let me guess, something badass? Sega, Atari?"

Ruby grins. "Try a Tamagotchi."

"No." I can't believe it. "An original? They're so super cute. Also … no offence, so not you."

Ruby nods at me. "He met Amy outside Retro Mike's place and got chatting…"

Josh smiles. "Amy had a thing about not dating tournament heads. She thought we were all irresponsible. I convinced her that if we bought a Tamagotchi together, co-parented and looked after a digital pet, like really made sure that little pixel alien didn't die, then after three weeks, she'd go out with me."

Even Augie leans forward. "And?"

Josh looks down. "We co-parented that Kawaii, and I fell in love with her while we did; we've been together ever since. Best money I ever spent."

And the look on his face is everything, so much so we all make an "ahh" sound that makes people look over. I even hear an older person talk about "kids being too loud" as he walks past us. I sigh. Apart from in the old factory with Dark – did we ever really get to be kids? And after this ends, will we be able to be again?

***

The rest of the day is a blur until eventually we're in our gaming suits and Jones reappears. Time.

We're silent in the car and quiet as we enter the stadium for our last pre-game interviews. The noise of the crowd, the lights, all of it feels unreal now. It takes facing death to realize life isn't something I should ever have been afraid to live.

This time I take the microphone when it's passed to me. I don't fidget or project my fears. Instead I smile a real smile at my team. I think of the little girl I met in the hospital – Louise. I ask players to always trust in themselves, in their instincts and not the hype. To have hope that David can take down Goliath.

Augie talks about the privilege of playing on Tower team. Ruby about having found true friends and how playing has changed her life. Josh about what comes next, dreams that aren't about fame or glory but about his girlfriend Amy, spending more time with his sister Dawn and his mum. All of us are feeling it. This is the end of something. The start of something else.

When the fireworks start, we are in a different section of the flood zone near West Forty-second Street and East Pier 81. Augie, as planned, makes a big deal of handing the drone to me as Ruby and I scatter. He and Josh go to play offensive. Ruby nods to a building up ahead, and inside I find a second suit, courtesy of Jones. Also, a camera and a terminal just out of camera range. I hack into the nearby CCTV and create a loop of myself operating the drone before whoever is doing the feeds gets suspicious. Then I change. It feels easy, too easy, and the hairs on the back of my neck tingle.

When I'm done, Ruby looks at me. "Ready?"

I nod and she hugs me off-camera, mic muffled. "Go. We'll cover for you here."

"Ru … I—"

"Asha, I still don't believe that Eliza was a spy. She wouldn't betray me. I know that. I think the Founders' surveillance was just good. I don't blame you for being cautious – you did what you had to do. But after this is over you're going to see you were wrong, and, yeah, I am totally going to enjoy saying, '*I told you so.*' But, no matter what happens, we are good, understand? That doesn't change."

My eyes well up. I don't deserve her as a friend.

She looks at the timer on her wrist. "Go."

***

The meeting point is inside the shopping mall near the arcade. I can't risk being picked up on the street cams so I use the side entrance. The place is dark, smelling of damp and dust. I hear rats scurrying. Everything inside is boarded up, a ghost town bearing the marks of cycles of flooding. Covered in graffiti art and neon street tags. Definitely an end-of-days vibe, perfect for what might be the zombie apocalypse.

I stop when I hear voices and footsteps ahead, leaning in to one of the abandoned shop doors and opening it.

I close it and wait as another team starts to walk towards the shop's exterior. There are at least three of them, one more than I can take. I melt further into the shadows of the disused clothing store with its rails and water-damaged goods scattered over the floor. A rat running past makes me yelp and I put my hand over my mouth.

Their voices outside carry to my hiding place as the team passes.

"I'm just saying something seems wrong." Eliza.

"Look, we're in the finals. You're just spooked because of what happened at the last tournament you did."

"That was different."

"Yeah, and so is this. The Tower team are the ones to beat, the ones that will give us credibility going into the next events. So I say we find them. And, yeah, I know your girlfriend is on that team, but—"

"Ruby's got nothing to do with it. We follow my orders here, not yours. I say we search another sector and take out the flag of whoever we find."

"What about the bounty?"

Eliza's voice is sharp now. "What bounty?"

"Haven't you heard...?"

They walk further away, out of hearing range.

My gut twists. Eliza isn't acting like a traitor. Maybe I was wrong about her.

But I don't have time to think about that.

I wait another few minutes before moving, wanting to make sure Eliza's team have moved on. My meeting point with Dark is an abandoned coffee shop on the second floor. The shutters are pulled down here too, so I crank them up just enough to slide underneath and then close them behind me. It's pitch black, with old plastic chairs stacked on top of tables, faded signs above the counter and a rusting coffee machine in the corner.

As soon as I'm in, a door behind the counter opens, allowing a small sliver of light in. Dark stands there. "You're late." He sounds worried.

"I ran into some complications."

I can't help smiling. I have fallen so hard for this boy, slowly and then all in a rush. Then I think about Augie. I need to tell Dark about how sick he is – later, when this is done.

Dark closes the door behind him. His lips land on mine, causing every thought to empty from my head. Then he pulls away, digs into his pocket and hands me a watch. "In exchange for your locket, seeing as Josh still has your panic button."

It's a smartwatch, the back engraved. "*To find lost things.*" I grin – he found the tracker in the locket then. Dark helps me with the strap.

His eyes stall on my lips for a second before he turns and pulls up a holo map, the image floating in front of us. "I give you Nebulous Arcade – or what's left of it. The front was boarded up and someone went to a great deal of trouble about a decade ago to remove the online references to its existence. Whatever Zu hid is here. My guess? Rock tried to retrieve whatever is inside but couldn't. Hopefully, thanks to the loop you've fitted to the feed, they think you're playing in the tournament now while we slip in and take whatever he left. It's our one shot. We'll never get a distraction like this again. Ready?"

I'm not.

"Till the end?" I hold my hand out, and he takes it.

"Till the end."

Dark and I head towards the alley at the back of the mall. It's full of dumpsters and bordered with wire fences, random bits of paper and, here again, marks on the walls show how much the rising water hit this part of New York during flood season. Across the street we see a team running past, so we wait in the shadows as a firework explodes over the water. Purple. We hold still, waiting for the extraction unit for the other team.

When the van arrives, we move on.

The door to the arcade has minimal security, which immediately makes me feel nervous.

The arcade has its emergency lights still running, giving it a dim glow. "Secondary power source?" I take a deep breath. "What should we be looking for?"

"I'm not sure."

We split up, looking for some raised surface. Some hidden safe. But all I see are old pinball games, unplugged air hockey tables and claw machines with soft toys that are disintegrating. Parts of the floor are sticky. There's a faint smell of bleach in other areas. Nothing out of the ordinary. What are we missing? Better question: where is the power coming from?

I glance over to Dark who has stopped. "Over there," he whispers.

Dark points to an old arcade zombie shooter. Dark wood, stickers on the outside. The console fully intact. He uses his hand to wipe a layer of dust from the top to reveal the name. *House of the Dead.* "This is it. It has to be." He starts to check on the floor for a cable.

"What makes you sure?"

Dark finds a plug. He blows dust from it and then hunts for a power point. "*House of the Dead* was Zu's favourite arcade game. He used to talk about it all the time: how much it meant to him, how he first discovered it in New York. He didn't mention it in public because he didn't like talking about his parents' break-up, which happened around the same time. But this game was his first love. When he was angry at his parents, he'd take a roll of quarters and kill every zombie in the game. If Zu Thorp was going to hide something, it would be linked to this."

"Zu Thorp was a zombie apocalypse shooter fan?" It seems horrifying given what he created.

Dark shoves the plug into the wall and there is a swooshing sound as the machine lights up, making a whining start-up noise.

"Where are the speakers?" I ask.

"In the cab – on the top, just above the monitor. Why?"

The monitor at the front starts to load the game's logo and manufacturer name. "Because as soon as it starts, so will the sound…"

Dark takes a tool from his pocket and starts rapidly unscrewing the control panel at the front. He removes the panel and I use his penknife to cut the cord to the speakers, just as the screen loads with the game's backstory.

December 18th, 1998...

The sound cuts and the images keep playing with their text. An echo from a tragic past...

But then something changes. A line of text appears on the screen.

You must know me well to follow
in my footsteps and fly in. ZT

Five dashes follow.

Dark mumbles under his breath. "What the hell?"

I look at the dashes. "Any ideas? Do we need to fill in the blanks?"

"If Zu set this up himself, he almost certainly included traps, something that would erase or destroy whatever you were looking for if you don't use the right code."

I think back and take out the diary I swiped from the ideas factory what feels like a lifetime ago. I look back at the line of text. You must know me well to follow in my footsteps and fly in. "Fly in. I have an idea. The last flight he took to New York, the number he wrote in his diary. It's three letters, two numbers..."

"You think...?"

"You got a better idea?"

Beeping. A text from Ruby on one of the devices Jones left for us.

Down to the last two. Once someone wins, we all have to leave.

It's now or never.

Dark starts to insert Zu's private jet's tail number. "Nothing to lose."

We hold our breath as he pushes the controller and types the code over the dashes: *N19ZT.*

For a moment, nothing happens, and I wonder if I could have been wrong. But then text starts to scroll across the screen.

ENTER

The arcade machine rolls forward, revealing a small door that opens with a click.

"Time to see what's on the other side of the magic door," Dark says.

I don't smile. I am hoping and praying that what is on the other side is an answer, a way to end this and not another question.

Dark grabs my hand. "Whatever happens we're in this together, right?"

I nod. I lost him once already. I am never going through that again.

We squeeze one at a time through the narrow doorway and into a small dark room which has pockets of blue light.

Oversized steps on one side serve as seats in front of a small screen. As we enter, the door behind us closes.

"Good thing I'm not claustrophobic," I mutter as words appear on the screen.

Take your seat. The show is about to start.

"What. The. Hell?"

I don't like this. Not even a tiny bit. I want answers, but I feel exactly like the character who just went to check out that strange noise in the basement at the start of a horror film.

We sit and Dark's hand finds mine again. The light dims to almost pitch black as a panel behind us lowers. A hologram projection unit.

"Not another..." I don't finish because directly in front of us is a hologram of a man. Iconic black shirt, jeans, glasses. This is the Zu Thorp from the early days. He holds a small data drive. I shiver. He seems to look directly at us, and his voice fills the room.

"*If you're here, then something has gone very wrong and we're all in trouble.*"

I turn and see Dark's face lit by the blue light and the projection. "It's him," he says. "It's Zu."

"*The Beths have decided you were worthy of this. I need your help to fix a terrible mistake I should never have made.*"

The hologram's face looks pained. "*I let my ego get the better of me. I knew right from the early days of Zu Tech that I was dying – the only question was when. At first, I tried to cheat the odds, but I discovered you can't cheat death. Then I became obsessed with doing something for humanity that would outlive me. I thought I was a tech god, infallible. I know now I'm just another stupid human.*"

He pauses for a second while Dark and I sit, almost not breathing.

"*The Founders get you first by offering you the one thing you need. In my case money to crack an unsolvable problem. What if we had the technology to hijack our own brain? To tell it to rewire itself after severe trauma. To get it to create new pathways that could overcome paralysis. To tell the brain to control the cells fighting an organ transplant, or, in my case*" – he gives a wry look – "*to slow down a terminal disease. That was the problem I was invested in solving. My investors offered me the money and resources to create such a code. A code that could hijack the brain. But they didn't want to do good. They wanted control.*"

Dark's eyes are so bright now. Angry.

"*I've made the decision to destroy the code, but if you're here, then I've failed. I don't know who I can trust, and whoever I do will be in danger.*" The hologram projection stops and wipes his eyes. The despair, the way he looks over his shoulder as if worried someone was watching him. The slim drive glints in his hand and it all feels like it's happening now, right in front of us as opposed to in the past. "*This is my backup that I hope never needs to be found. A drive with a full copy of everything, the code, the details of my early investors, our correspondence. What I think it will take to stop them. My dying declaration, if you will. I'm sorry, whoever you are. That you've had to come here for this. I hope you use this evidence for good. Take it. I'll do my best to help and make sure it's linked only to you.*

"*I'm pretty sure the Founders will kill me before my disease does. And if I've failed and the Beths fail, and the person watching this is, in fact, Lydia Rock… I trusted you, Lydia. I hope you and your associates rot in hell. I promise eventually you will. Turns out you can't cheat death, Lydia. I'm your proof of that. Someday you will be held to account.*"

In front of us, the screen rises up to reveal a shelf holding the same hard drive the hologram is holding.

The voice continues. "*This is everything. Make better choices than I did.*"

The hologram switches off. We sit for a moment before I jump up and grab the drive. As I do, I feel something prick me. There must have been a splinter on the shelf. I look at my hand and a drop of blood falls on to the drive, which feels warm, like the shelf was some sort of charging pad.

"Ouch." I suck my finger.

Dark still hasn't moved.

I hold the drive out to him. It's a smooth silver rectangle no bigger than a credit card. When I turn it over, I see a small pad glow in the centre and underneath it an engraving: PANDORA.

Pandora's box. Thoughts crowd my head. I can't look

away from it. Afraid it might disappear. I want to run and run fast.

"We destroy it, now," Dark says.

"No!" Then the words pour out: "We need what's on it. I didn't get a chance to tell you. Augie. We need to use the code to save him first. We can—"

"What do you mean, *save Augie*?"

I should have told him before this.

His voice becomes tight. "What haven't you said?"

"There was no time. I found out last night. Augie is dying; it's the effects of the SHACKLE code on his system."

A look of pure devastation crosses Dark's face. "Asha." His expression changes. "You were exposed too. You played till the end in that tournament."

This wasn't how I wanted to tell him. Not here.

"We were all exposed. All of us played in that tournament; you did too. The code can alter brain chemistry in some people. Augie's symptoms are further along because he was exposed to the early beta version, but eventually it could..." I don't need to finish.

"Not you. I should never... This is my fault."

"You didn't do this; they did. The Founders." I look at the drive, thinking of the kid in the hospital, the boy who died, the others who played the game. "We need to use this code to help people who have already been exposed – we need the proof Zu left to end this."

"Yes." Dark is standing now, fingers taking the drive

from my hand. "You're right. We keep it. We use it. None of this matters if you're dead." His eyes are bright.

I want to live. I want Augie to live. I blink back my tears. That damn kiss made me want to hope, to believe it will all work out. "Let's go."

We walk to the door we came through. Dark puts the drive inside his pocket and secures it. I touch the wall, fingers going to my comms to tell the others to prepare to leave. A small bubble of lightness floats inside me. We have proof. This is our way to save ourselves, to stop Rock. They don't know that we have it – not yet. But we did it. We are going to be OK.

We enter the arcade again.

The only problem is, we're not alone.

24

The lights come on, and at first I only see her face so I don't register the danger.

"Jones, what are you doing here?" I start to move towards her.

I feel Dark's hand on my arm. The warning in his voice. "Asha."

I look down and see the gun in her hand. Pointed at me. "Jones?" This doesn't make sense.

My eyes adjust to the light and I see armed men behind her, all wearing the Rock Industries logo. I take a step closer to her and hear the click of the safety on her semi-automatic being released.

"Stay where you are."

"Jones? What are you doing?"

I look at Dark. He was always faster at processing things than me. "Don't do this, Jones," he says. "Whatever she has on you..."

"Business is business. I told you that from the start." Her tone is heavy, resigned.

"Then take me!" he yells. "Just let her go."

"What," I whisper, "is going on?"

Jones looks at me, and for a moment I see a twinge of regret that quickly passes and is replaced by something else, something hard. "You left me no choice. I told you I believe in surviving, not causes that get you killed."

It hits me then. "*You.* You were the traitor. You betrayed me ... all of us. You were working with Rock from the start. I trusted you. You're my guardian."

"Asha, you're not strong enough to take on the Lydia Rocks of this world and win. Deep down you know that. Long-term I'm doing you a favour. You're ill. Augie too. It's better this ends quickly. This way one of us gets to be on the winning side. Give the drive to me now."

But I'm not listening to her. Instead, I'm processing all the tiny pieces that have started to slowly fall together. "You offered to be my guardian to keep me out of the system so I could lure Dark out. You suspected he was alive."

"I guess I owe you something," she says. "Fine. I didn't lie to you when I said the events of Zu's tournament stayed with me. It made me realize that money wasn't enough, that I needed access to real protection. Real power. They don't come much more powerful than Rock."

"You made sure you were close to me," I said, thinking. "You had access to my training schedule, the shooting. That was to bring Dark out, wasn't it?"

"I knew if he was still alive and thought you were in danger … and if he was dead, you were still the best shot at finding that drive."

"The TV interview – you kept making sure I drank water beforehand. Was it drugged?"

"Rock wanted you to seem unreliable. We didn't want you too alert. You have a dangerous habit of going off script and becoming viral, believable."

"You had me followed when I went to see Dark…"

"Yes, but I also tried to help you, Asha. I told you to let this go. To walk away. That night in the garden … do you remember what you said?"

"I said I wasn't my sister," I say slowly. "That Maya was the nice one. That I wanted my revenge…"

"Exactly. You said you would burn everyone involved. Well, guess what, I was also involved. I couldn't let that happen. You gave me no choice. Now give me the drive."

Dark doesn't move, and neither do I.

"The. Drive."

"No," I say, looking at Dark, who stays silent.

"It wasn't a request." She points the gun at me and

Dark swallows. Then, before I can stop him, he hands her the drive.

No. I should have listened to him and destroyed it while we had the chance.

Dark looks to Jones. "If it's money you want, I'll give you…"

She gives him a fake smile. "More money? Rock offered me a place at the table. Look around you, Dark. It's done. Rock owns everything – and what Rock doesn't own, the other Founders do. Even if you got out of here, where could you go? The Founders are too big to fail. You're already dying; you just don't know it yet."

Dark doesn't move. "What's the plan, Jones?"

"Rock wants you and the original source code. I convinced them to take her as well, to keep you in line. As long as you behave, she lives."

Of all the possibilities for tonight, this isn't one I saw coming. Dark's expression is pure rage.

"I trusted you." My knees feel weak.

"Get up." Jones's voice is cold. "If it helps, I liked you. But I warned you, and you were never going to let this go. You were never going to let your sister go. It's a shame. I liked all of you."

"What does that mean, you *liked all of us*?"

Jones gestures to a guard who brings in Augie, Ruby and Josh, their hands bound, followed by another two guards who walk behind them.

"Asha." Augie's eyes go to mine and my heart twists.

"What have you done, Jones?" I say.

"No loose ends." Her voice is low. Almost a whisper.

Jones lowers her gun and puts the safety back on as two more guards grab me and Dark.

"They need you alive to control Dark. But they don't need anyone else. They're already dying, Asha; you know that. At least this way, it's quick."

The full horror of what she is saying hits me. I struggle against my captors who bind my hands in front of me with cable ties. "You can't. Please. Jones."

She looks at me. Her immaculate suit, perfect nails, high heels. Phone already in her hand. "You're right – *I* can't. But they can. The Founders require some data from them on the code's effects, but after that it will be painless. I made them promise me that." She gestures to the guards. "If you will excuse me. I don't want to be here for this part. I need a public alibi, just in case."

Anger bubbles inside me. That hug after the court case, our chat in the garden. She tricked me and I let her. I was so naïve. I yell at her, "You're sick."

"I'm a survivor, Asha."

The guards start to lift me, one on either side as I struggle, blocking Jones from leaving.

"No." Ruby is crying as a guard moves towards her. "No, please—"

One guard raises his gun. The other guard pushes at

Ruby. "Move." He must have hit her because I see Josh lunge at him. Augie does too, but the guard closest to him pushes him back easily, hitting his wounded shoulder, and I see him wince. Josh struggles with the guard who hit Ruby and then a single shot rings out. Echoing around us.

I freeze. *Just a warning shot*, I think. Then I see Ruby's face and I think she must have been hit. But it's not her who falls.

One moment Josh is standing. The next his head is tilting back and his body follows as blood splatters over Ruby and Augie. Time seems to slow down. Then a scream tears the air as Ruby tries to scramble over to her brother, pulling free of the third guard who had restrained her. I watch as she crawls over the floor to him, lifting him into her arms with her bound hands. Blood drips over her and on to his face.

I look at Dark in shock. This can't be real. *He'll be OK once we get him to a hospital, won't he?* I stare at Josh's chest but it doesn't move.

Ruby is moaning now. "Get up, Josh. Wake up. I need you; we need you." Her hands are covered in her brother's blood. Josh's head falls to one side and the angle is unnatural, his eyes unmoving.

I can't look away. I keep saying one word over and over again under my breath. "*No.*"

Josh is dead. Gone.

25

Jones looks at the security guards in disgust. "Nothing was to happen till I was clear; did you not understand? You have orders. Wait till the tournament is over and the area clear, then take those two and the body to the Madison facility." She jerks her head at me and Dark. "These other two, get them on the plane." She nods to us. "Nothing personal. We may even meet again."

As Jones walks away, Ruby shouts after her. "You'd better pray, Jones, because even if I'm dead, I'll find you."

Jones doesn't look back.

The guards drag me and Dark out of the room and into one of two waiting vans. As they shove me inside, I manage to sink my teeth into one of the guard's hands. Without hesitation he hits me on the side of my head. Blood runs down my temple.

Dark growls at the man. "You touch her again, and you'll die."

The man ignores him and hits me again. This blow is hard enough to make me see stars, and he uses that moment to pull the cable ties tighter on my wrists so they bite into my skin.

A voice comes from outside the van. Flat, emotionless. "Careful, they want these two alive. Let's get the others."

"Why can't we just kill the others here? River's nearby; no one would notice. Less work."

"You heard the orders – not till they've been tested, whatever that means. They pay. We provide. Let's go."

The door slams shut.

"Asha?" Dark's voice is a whisper.

"They killed..."

"I know. Asha, this is our only chance. Once they get us someplace secure, we won't get another."

"They killed..."

"Asha, we want to save the others, right?"

"Yes."

"Then we need to get out of here. Can you do that with me?"

I sniffle and force the tears to stop, to block the image of Josh's face from my mind. I think of Ruby and Augie. Dark's right. This is our only chance. "How?"

"Stand up. They didn't search me. In the front pocket of

my jeans, there's a Swiss army knife. We need to cut these ties off first."

I use both hands to remove the knife, then awkwardly saw at his ties. A few seconds later there is a snap and Dark flexes his wrists.

"Arms in front."

I raise my wrists and he cuts my cable ties. Blood encircles each wrist now, my hands almost purple from the plastic cutting off the blood supply. Dark rubs my wrists to try to get my circulation going again. Then sticks the knife back in my pocket. "Keep an eye on the door and keep the ties on you. We need to convince them we're still bound."

I keep watch from the back tinted window of the van as Dark gets to work on the door. I see a body bag being loaded into the other van, followed by Augie and Ruby. She's so broken I barely recognize her. Dark is pulling at the panel underneath the door mechanism. "Got to love cheap criminals; if they had gone for a more expensive newer model, we couldn't do this. Tell me when we're clear."

I watch as they load the van. Then: "Dammit." My breath catches. "They're coming back. Move."

We sit back further in the van. Shoulder to shoulder, wrists out, cables around them. The guard opens the door, takes a look at us, then turns back to talk to his companion.

Dark's voice is a whisper against my ear. "We let them drive off. Once we're moving, you go for the guard. I'm going to use the door pin under the panel to open the back of the van. We jump and roll. Then we run. You got it?"

I nod.

One of the armed guards gets in. He rubs his hand and I notice the bite marks. His look is pure hatred. He holds his gun loosely in his hands. He looks at Dark. "If you try anything, she gets it. And this time I'll make sure it really hurts."

His companion closes the door of the van and goes to the driver's seat. A metal grill separates him from us. We pull out as fireworks explode in the distance.

The tournament is over.

Rock has won.

The van jolts, pulling me back from that thought. I look at Dark. He hasn't given up. We can't give up. Josh would never have wanted that. We need to make a break for it.

Dark nods and I start to count in my head. Once I reach three hundred, I pounce on the guard holding the gun. Surprise works to my advantage, but I'm not quick enough, not brutal enough. He wrestles me to the floor, and I feel sick at being so close to him and his smell of stale beer. One hand goes around my neck. The other hand raises the gun as my heart beats out of control. Trapped.

I manage to get one word out. "Dark."

Then the guard's gun hand is grabbed from behind and Dark drags the man off me, yelling, "Go."

I run to the door as they struggle behind me. I hear the crack of the gun and then Dark is beside me, gripping my hand. "Now!"

We roll out of the back of the van in front of a car that skids to a halt, but we can't stop. The van is also braking, the driver door already opening. The other guard is shouting.

We jump up and run, looking quickly for the nearest escape route. The subway. We're running past people who stare and shout. Jumping over the turnstiles, trying to put as much distance as we can between us and whoever is chasing.

"This way." I ignore the subway and aim for the maintenance tunnels at the end of the platform, the ones that have fewer cameras. We run past a subway clerk on the platform, who calls after us. The guard is running too, gun raised – and, as I turn back, I see the subway clerk spot him and lift his walkie-talkie.

An announcement blares out, telling people to evacuate. I hear screams. We run on to the tracks and across them. A moment later, a train whips past, blocking the guard.

Dark pulls me to the side, into the tunnel and towards a maintenance hatch. He closes the door behind us.

We hide in the shadows. Hearts pounding, sweat dripping. Neither of us saying anything. I try to control my breath. We hear footsteps running on gravel near us, then past us. Another train in the distance.

"If we wait another minute..." I turn to Dark in the glow of the red emergency lighting. He's leaning heavily against the wall. I put my hand out to steady him. It feels wet. I draw my hand back and look at it. Blood. "You're shot..."

"Asha, it's not my blood."

I realize what that means. The other guard who was in the back of the van, the one who hit me, is definitely dead.

"It was him or you." And there is nothing in Dark's tone that shows any remorse.

It says everything about what I've become that I don't feel anything when he says it either, just relief that the blood's not his. I think about the man in the lift. He never had a choice. The guard with the gun did.

"We need to find somewhere safe."

"Dark, we need to get Ruby and Augie before..."

His face is serious. "I know, but we need a plan to get them out. If we rush in, we'll end up back in the same position as before. I know a place we can have till they arrive in Madison – the facility Jones mentioned, right? Trust me?"

I nod.

This time I do.

***

We move towards the emergency exit, joining the crowds leaving the subway station, avoiding the police and the cars now converging on it. We don't make eye contact with anyone, sticking to the shadows to prevent people from noticing the blood and bruises that cover us. Dark never lets go of my hand.

We walk a few streets and then Dark stops outside an empty Chinese restaurant that looks like it just closed for the evening. The bell on the door tinkles as he pushes it open. A woman who looks like a waitress and a young man are the only people inside.

The man comes towards us; he seems only slightly older than me. "I'm sorry, we're closed…" Then his eyes widen. "Asha? You're Asha," he says. He pulls us inside and then locks the door and hits the button for the window blinds.

Dark looks at him. "Yìzé?"

Yìzé nods his head. "You're with her?"

Dark nods. "We have a mutual acquaintance from London, Bill."

Yìzé gives Dark a look of recognition. "I was told someone might drop by." He goes away and comes back with a first-aid kit and a phone. The woman comes too, carrying a laptop.

"I'll get some food for you. I'm Yìzé's sister, Ling; we're both fans, Asha." She assesses the blood that covers us. "I'll see what we have clothes wise."

"We'll be in the back," Yìzé says to Dark. "I presume you'll need a car?"

Dark nods in answer.

"How do you know them?" I ask when they've gone.

Dark opens the first-aid kit. "Bill used to box in New York in his day. They're his contacts. They won't ask questions. I told Bill everything before the semi-finals, so he could be ready." He starts to clean some of the cuts on my face. I try to distract myself from the sting of the antiseptic by looking at the laptop and the sticker on it – the Zu Tech logo with a red line through it.

For a while we don't say anything. We fix our cuts and bruises, wash up in the bathroom and change into the jeans and dark zippy tops Yìzé finds. Once we've eaten something and had some water, I feel OK enough to ask the question I've been thinking.

"How do we do this? It won't be long before..."

He sighs. "I had an exit plan lined up. But that involved all of us leaving at the same time and London as a final destination."

"We can never go back now, can we? Jones's network is too big. So is Rock's. If we went to London, they'd come after Bill. We'd never be able to hide from her there." I hold his hand, hoping that, in the gesture, he can feel what I am trying to tell him without words. That for me at least, *home* is wherever he is. We have so little time. Focus, I need to focus. "That's a *tomorrow problem.* Tonight, we need Augie and Ruby back."

"Our transport leaves in two hours. After that we need a plan B. If you're thinking of getting them off that van, we'll need more people. Ones we can trust, who are local."

I set my watch. Two hours. "I know someone." I hand him the waitress's laptop and pick up the mobile they left. "I'll make a call for reinforcements. Can you confirm the transport and arrange some cash, warn Bill just in case?" In case we don't make it.

Who to contact to help us has been on my mind since the subway. It turns out Ruby was always right.

I leave a message for Eliza and then go back to Dark, who's moved to the chef's office in the kitchen, closer to the routers. I watch him work. Trying to distract myself from thinking about other things by looking at the posters and ticket stubs for old gamer events and boxing matches that are on the wall behind him. The waitress and her co-workers are gamers, but Yìzé's father, it seems, was the boxer. Those posters are older. One shows a younger-looking Bill covered in slightly fewer tattoos. They are good people, the kind, it seems, who don't ask questions. It's the first time my fame and Dark's connections have been remotely helpful.

Dark finishes and I notice him flinch. His ribs. "The car's on its way."

"How long?" I ask.

Dark looks up. "Five minutes till the car arrives. One hour forty-five minutes left."

I take some bandages from the first-aid kit and help him take off his zippy and then the borrowed T-shirt with the ridiculously cuddly panda that's underneath.

"Cute," I say.

"When I imagined you taking off my shirt, this wasn't what I had in mind." The words are teasing but Dark's voice is heavy. "I almost lost you."

I gently kiss his lips and then pull away. "I'm here."

"Asha, about…"

"Don't. If we go too many steps ahead, we won't get Ruby and Augie back."

"You're sure about this? It's not too late to run. The car is two minutes out. Jones was a lot of things but she was usually right. Rock are big."

"Everyone has a weakness, Dark. So does Rock. And when they fall, they're never getting up again. I need to believe that right now. OK?"

"OK. We'll do this your way."

I hear a knock on the restaurant door. Voices.

No turning back.

The swing door to the kitchen opens, and it's Eliza who stands there. Worry is all over her face. Her eyes are red, mascara smudged. Behind her is Thresher, who I hadn't expected. He does a double take when he sees Dark but says nothing.

Eliza moves towards me, ignoring Dark. "Where. The. Hell. Is. My. Girlfriend. Asha. I've been calling her for hours. Jones has vanished. What happened? And what was that phone message you left?"

"Ruby's in danger. We need your help."

The waitress walks back in, this time carrying a bag of takeaway food. Dark thanks her. My voice becomes a whisper. "Not here. We can tell you on the way. Please?"

Thresher looks at me and then at Eliza. They have no reason to trust or believe us. But we need them. He gives Eliza a look I can't read.

Eliza nods. "Ruby trusts you. But I'm not her, Asha. I

don't care about your drama right now. Just her. Got it?"

"She's my family, Eliza, her and Augie."

Dark coughs and nods towards the now open restaurant door. "Car's outside. If we don't move now, it will be too late." He looks at Thresher and Eliza. "In or out?"

"In." Thresher answers for them both as he moves towards the door, and we leave.

***

The car is an electric SUV with tinted windows. Dark takes the wheel, and I take the passenger seat. I load the details of the panic button Dark gave me into the GPS; with luck it should still be where I last saw it. In Josh's pocket.

"Paracetamol and water are in the middle compartment," Dark says to Thresher and Eliza. "Just in case. There's a sports bag at your feet with some other … toys we might need."

Eliza glares at me from the back seat as we drive off. "Start talking."

I swallow – there's no easy way to convey what I have to say. "Ruby and Augie have been kidnapped. We can't go to the cops. There's a tracker in the back of the van they're in. A panic button J— someone was holding on to for me. We need to get them back and then disappear – Dark has transport. We have under two hours."

Eliza sucks in a breath. Thresher doesn't move a muscle. The car keeps speeding through the New York streets.

Eliza leans forward. "Who took her? Why and where are they taking her?"

"People who work for Lydia Rock. They plan on killing them because they know too much. At the moment they're taking them in a van to a facility they own."

Eliza goes silent and sinks back.

Thresher looks at me in the rear-view mirror. "Where's Josh, Asha?" he says quietly. "You mentioned Ruby and Augie but not him."

I swallow. "He's… They shot him."

I hear a sob from the back seat. Eliza. Thresher clenches his jaw.

Dark glances at the map on the device I'm holding and the moving red dot. "They're still travelling. Roughly thirty-five minutes ahead of us."

"They're heading towards New Jersey." I enlarge the map to look at the surrounding area.

Thresher looks at me. "Then they're definitely on their way to Rock's place outside Madison."

He's right. But how did Thresher instantly know that? Unease stirs again.

"The plan is to intercept," Dark explains. "I have a way to get us there faster. We get in position, hack the vehicle, stop it, get them out and run."

"You said they shot Josh," Thresher says. "That means guns?"

Dark answers. "Yeah."

"And we have…?"

"The element of surprise," I reply.

"No offence, but your plan sucks," Thresher growls.

I see Eliza reach a hand out to touch Thresher's arm. "We work with what we got. Hey, dead guy in the front? What's in the *bag of toys*?"

Dark gives a tight smile. "So glad you asked."

***

We make it to a helipad in Lower Manhattan in under ten minutes. We're running on adrenaline when Dark dumps the car, grabs the bag and we sprint. I don't know why Eliza brought Thresher or if we can trust him, but all our options are gone at this point. We are relying on two things: luck and them not expecting us. So far, we've had limited experiences of both. Every step of the way, Rock has been ahead of us, thanks to Jones.

The helicopter is ready. I stand on the rooftop. The lights of New York are below. The helicopter blades start as Eliza and Thresher run for the passenger seats. For a second, I freeze; the world is spinning too fast around me.

Dark's touch on my arm is my anchor. "We're OK, Asha."

It's a lie; we aren't OK, but if we can just pretend for a little bit longer, get through the next hour and a half…

I nod. "First time in one of these." I tell myself that's why my stomach is in knots. Then he grabs my hand and takes the bag from the car and we board.

Dark sits beside the pilot to keep an eye on the route. In the back of the helicopter Eliza glares at me. We're all wearing headphones.

"If anything happens to Ruby, Asha—" Eliza starts.

Dark's voice is cold, emotionless. "I wouldn't finish that sentence if I were you."

Thresher squeezes Eliza's hand. "We're on the same side, remember?"

Eliza doesn't say anything.

Thirteen minutes later, we land outside Madison, New Jersey. According to the tracker, the van with Augie and Ruby hit traffic. We're now around ten minutes ahead of the moving red dot.

The pilot lands the helicopter in a field and isn't too happy about it, but whatever Dark promises her seems to work. She agrees to wait. We walk towards an intersection. A road sign says we're eight miles from Madison. This is the only way to Rock's facility. It's rural, isolated. And it's now freezing cold. We take up position. Two on either side by the suspended traffic light. Earpieces in while we wait. This has to work.

Eliza and Dark are slightly behind Thresher and me. Dark works on establishing a link first with the van's Wi-Fi and then with its ECUs, bypassing most of them. He's looking for just two – the electronic control unit for the locks and the engine.

Thresher insisted Dark and I split up. Trust is a big issue for all of us. I set up a laptop and radio transmitter, which should be all I need to control the signal. I do a test to make sure it's working. Turns out UK and US systems are similar. The van is four minutes out.

"Set?" Thresher asks as a small breeze whips around us.

I nod and hit the earpiece. "Done. Dark?"

"Good. Thresher, if anything happens to her..."

Thresher rolls his eyes. "Same. Eliza?"

"I'm watching him."

I shiver.

"All right?" Thresher asks me.

"Yeah. Just, you know..."

"I know."

"Thresher." My voice is low as we crouch in the shadows beside the road. Surrounded by the smell of grass and hickory trees, it feels almost peaceful here. The stars larger in the sky without the city lights drowning them. I take a breath to concentrate, but I can't help it, I need to know. "Why are you here? How come you know so much about Rock?"

He closes his eyes for a second. "You should have come to me before this, Asha. SHACKLE has always been bigger than one tournament. They tried to release it before London. The Founders had people other than Zu working on it. You're not the only ones who lost people, who are looking for a way to take them down." He looks determined. "There are more of us. I don't think you've really grasped how far this goes, how big it is. What the risks are."

He looks down and sees my hand in the pocket of the jeans I changed into at the restaurant. A smile ghosts his pale skin, and his dark eyes glitter. "Swiss army knife? You don't need to worry about using it on me. Just keep it handy for when we free your friends. We're on the same side. At least I hope we are."

Pieces start to move inside my head. "That note you and Eliza gave me at the Zu Tech tournament, saying there was a traitor on our team … it wasn't just a rumour you heard. You were there to investigate Zu Tech."

"I'll answer your questions, Dark's too. I'll also expect both of you to answer mine. But only afterwards."

Thresher has secrets. Is the enemy of my enemy really my friend? I think that's why I ask, "Do you have a place that's safe? For after this? We can't go back to London, not any more."

Thresher nods. "I have somewhere. Provided we survive."

Then Dark's voice is in our ears. "They're coming." And every other thought leaves my head.

26

There's almost no other traffic apart from the van. It speeds up, taking advantage of the empty road to make up time.

"Ready?" I ask Dark.

"Yeah."

I change the traffic lights to red and the van starts to slow. The two guards are both in the front. Looks like no one wanted to travel in the back with Josh's body and their prisoners. *His body.* The anger builds inside me as I think what that must have been like for Ruby.

The van's engine starts to stutter and then it coasts a few more metres towards the intersection until it comes to a complete stop. From where we are crouching I can see the driver panicking inside. He pushes the ignition button again and again, but it's dead. He starts yelling at the other guard, who takes out his gun. Crap.

There's a click as the doors in the cab lock shut. They both start pulling at the door handle. We have seconds at most until they shoot out the lock or the windows.

I run with Thresher towards the back of the van, still hidden by the shadows. We abandon the gear. Dark is at the back door of the van. Eliza is on the other side of him, counting. "One, two—"

Please let them be there. Please let them be alive.

On three they swing the doors open. The first person I see is Augie standing in front of Ruby, fists raised. Ruby's been beaten up. One of her hands lies protectively over a body bag. Josh. The other is swollen and covered in blood and red marks, bruises? The strips of their cable ties are on the floor.

"Let's go," I say. Augie takes a step towards us, but Ruby doesn't move or look at me.

Dark looks at me, worried. We only have seconds and we both know it.

"Ruby," he says softly, "we can't take him."

Ruby ignores him as Eliza moves forward, her voice gentle. "Ru, I'm here. Josh would want you to live, Ru. You can't stay with him."

Ruby blinks back a tear, then unzips the body bag. Josh's eyes are closed now. Apart from the blood he looks like he could be sleeping. She gently unclasps the gold chain around his neck, then she kisses his cheek, her tears flowing silently now as she takes Eliza's hand. Thresher reaches up a hand to help Augie down.

Then we run.

Ruby and Augie are slower, after having been tied up for so long, as we melt into the darkness of the field where the helicopter is. I hear shots – the guards shooting out the lock on the van. The sound feels louder than it should be in the quiet countryside. Then I hear them swearing. Running after us.

Dark is beside me, finger on his earpiece, giving instructions to the pilot as the helicopter blades start to rotate. I look back to make sure the others are with us, and dirt flies up as a bullet hits the ground. The guards are shooting at us.

I stagger and Dark grips my arm, pulling me forward as another shot sounds out.

"Keep moving." Dark's expression is grim.

Behind us, Augie stumbles in the long grass. My heart lurches but then Thresher reaches him. His thick arms go around Augie and they half limp, half run towards our only means of escape.

The pilot is spooked, her face pale, headphones on. Dark hauls us inside. Eliza and Ruby are just behind us, Thresher and Augie catching up to them but still some distance away.

The pilot glares at Dark. "This isn't what we agreed. No one said anything about guns."

"Finn, wait for them. I'll double the fee."

Finn swears. "Money doesn't help when you're dead." But she stays.

The others are seconds behind us. Ruby clings to Eliza like someone who is drowning, and I recognize her overwhelming grief and loss. Dark and I haul them inside. Thresher and Augie are last to board. Augie limps as Thresher pulls and shoves, somehow getting him up, and then the door closes.

The pilot doesn't wait for the door to lock. She ascends, the sound of the blades drowning out the noise of the gunshots. Red warning lights flicker from the controls.

"They hit the fuel line, so wherever your next destination is it'd better be close." Finn's voice is tight as the helicopter lurches.

"Fine. Just get us out of here," Dark says.

"Working on it."

I'm shaking, pressing my hands together to hide the tremor. Praying that it's dark enough that whoever is on the ground doesn't take note of the tail number, that the smell of kerosene doesn't mean disaster. But then we're up, climbing, moving.

The lights of the intersection and the abandoned van, the guards below, are all getting smaller.

I look at Ruby sobbing in Eliza's arms, at Augie slumped against Thresher. Finally I look at Dark. We have them – for now we have them. Everyone but Josh.

Josh.

It doesn't feel real. I think of his mum, his sister, Amy. Oh my God, what do we tell them? I feel Dark's hand reaching back for mine.

"Breathe, Asha."

***

At the private airstrip near Newark we get out and walk towards a jet. The smell of burnt fuel fills our lungs. The plane is similar to Rock's but less pristine, older, and somehow that makes me feel better. Eliza helps Ruby on board. She's still not speaking or looking at me, her eyes bloodshot. Augie follows, still limping.

They sink into the seats inside the main cabin. Time is everything now. There are no guarantees that the helicopter's tail number wasn't traced, that Rock doesn't already have people on their way here. Eliza is holding tight to Ruby. In the light of the cabin her face looks numb, streaked with tears. Augie keeps looking over at her like he's afraid she'll vanish. What the hell happened in that van?

Thresher, Dark and I stand by the cockpit. The pilot, Andrew, is doing pre-flight checks. According to the manifest, this will be listed as an empty flight to collect cargo, but they need a location before take-off.

Dark looks at me. "We need a destination."

I turn to Thresher. "You said you had a place we could go."

He nods. "It takes at least three days to get there. We can answer each other's questions on the way."

"Where?" Dark says.

Thresher looks reluctant to tell us. I can see him weighing up the pros and cons in his mind but we don't have time for that.

I grasp his hand. "Thresher. We need to trust each other. My gut tells me to trust you. You need to do the same with us."

Thresher looks conflicted but then nods. "I told you. This was always bigger than Zu Tech. OK, Karimun, off the coast of Singapore. Start by flying to Ireland, Shannon Airport. We can switch planes there and create a false trail."

"Singapore." Dark's voice is low. The way he says it suggests he's remembering something. "Why?"

"Because that's where the rest of us are. It is also near the Founders' main base. It's where they're planning to spread SHACKLE from. I'm presuming whatever you found in New York is now with them."

"Yeah," Dark says bitterly. "Jones took everything."

But I'm thinking. I look down at my hands, at the mark on my finger, the least of all my injuries, and I finally realize something. We've had one piece of good luck or not good luck – Zu looking out for us. I glance at Thresher and then Dark. "They won't be able to launch SHACKLE, not yet. If they try and access the drive, it's going to wipe clean."

Dark stares at me as I hold up my finger, the one I cut

inside Zu's arcade. "It was driving me crazy, that part of Zu's message. *Take it. I'll do my best to help and make sure it's linked only to you.* And then I figured it out. Zu was paranoid. He had one last fail-safe in place for Pandora, just in case. To make sure that *only* the person to whom Beth gave the message could open it. A biometric lock. Whoever removed Pandora gave a sample of their blood and their fingerprint when they took it off the shelf. The device needs the same blood and print for it to open."

I look at Dark. He doesn't speak but reaches for my hand, threading his fingers through mine. I look directly at Thresher.

"The lock buys us time. We need to destroy them: Lydia Rock and the Founders. Before they figure out a way around the lock." I glance at Ruby and Augie and then back to Dark, my voice colder now. "I don't care how any more, just that we end this."

"Whatever it takes?" Dark asks.

I shiver. Because I know what he means. But I'm tired, hurt, angry. I think rage is the only thing keeping me going. They took Maya from me. Josh. How many others have they hurt? Killed?

Jones. I trusted her, and she sold all of us out.

Ruby, Augie. They were going to kill them. Even now Augie is dying, and Ruby – I know exactly what she is going through because I was there before.

I tried to bring down SHACKLE using the authorities, looking to expose them, to bring them into the light. I wanted to find justice through the system. But there is never equality for people like us. Our enemy never played by the rules. The odds were always stacked against us. It's time to level the field.

Till the end. That's what Dark said. I look into his eyes, and for a moment there is only the two of us.

"We go to Singapore. We end this, or we die."

And it's the truth. It's not even a dramatic statement. There is no other way. If we don't succeed in pulling off the biggest David-versus-Goliath rematch in history, we die. The code lodged inside our heads will eventually take us all, one way or another. If Lydia Rock and the Founders win, the world as we know it will change. Into a world where no one has free choice and everyone is under their control. We have one shot, limited time and partners we have never worked with before. And we're all grieving.

Maya. Josh.

Dark tightens his grip. "Forget the *die* bit. I'm not losing you, Asha."

The look he gives me is everything neither of us can put into words.

I squeeze his hand back. "Same. So I guess we end them." I turn to look at Thresher. "Until then we can't get caught."

ACKNOWLEDGEMENTS

If you are reading this, then it's (hopefully) because you liked the book. If that is the case – and you'd like some sneak peeks for book three, bonus chapters, hints on writing, or the chance to enter the occasional giveaway – then please consider signing up for my newsletter at www.trionacampbell.com (I promise I won't spam you).

Second – I'm a new author, so if you read this and liked it enough to want more, I would be ETERNALLY grateful if you could consider leaving a review on Amazon, Goodreads or any of the online book-retailer sites (even if you bought it from your super-awesome local bookshop or checked it out from a brilliant local library). Honestly, a nice review is the best gift you can give any writer.

Now for the fun part – saying "*Thank You*". It really takes a village.

Special endless thanks to two people without whom there would be no books featuring Asha and Co.

First: Lauren Fortune from Scholastic UK – thank you for your faith in this story and for giving me your AMAZING notes while we worked on this. I have loved every second (and can't wait to do book three with you).

Second: Marianne Gunn O Connor, my dream agent. Thank you.

On the personal side… My kids – Martin, Sofia and João – for putting up with the constant sound of *click, click, click* from the mechanical keyboard in my room. Plus, the repeated line of "*Mummy has a deadline*" (which I said *a lot* this last year). I love you more than I can ever put into words. I am beyond proud of the people you are and are growing up to be.

Thanks (far too inadequate a word) to my husband, Nuno, to whom I dedicated this book. Getting snowed into that hotel in Luxembourg with you and the rest of the crew from EAVE eighteen years ago (where did the time go?) changed my life (and I've been pinching myself ever since). I also wanted to thank my extended family for their support too – especially my brother Eoin Campbell and his family (Dee, Aisling, Tom and Rory), along with Liliana Bernardo and Pedro Nunes (and my adorable nephews: Simão, Pedro, Francisco) – love you all.

Special thanks also to the women who always have

my back (good times and bad): Roisin Kearney, Eibhlin Curley, Helen Ennis, Anna Patterson, Joanne Hayden, Hélène McDermott and Caroline Grace Cassidy. I adore you; you inspire me constantly, and I can't wait to celebrate the launch of this book with you.

I am also hugely grateful to everyone at Team Scholastic UK. Especially Genevieve Herr, Penelope Daukes, Wendy Shakespeare, Jennie Roman, Jessica White, Olivia Towers, Ellen Thompson, Eleanor Thomas and, of course, Jamie Gregory for the book's cover design. Second books are notoriously tricky, and I appreciate everything you did to make this easier for me.

I'm grateful too for all the support from fellow filmmakers, creatives and producers (Damien Donnelly, Paul Tyler and the entire Gamer Mode crew). Finally – I learned so much about storytelling while working in TV, and I wanted to thank Serena Cullen, Anthony Root, and Enrico Tessarin for EVERYTHING while working with you in London.

Writing heroes – I am lucky to have had advice and help from phenomenal writers I genuinely admire. In my experience, writers are a super-supportive tribe (and all the UKYA and Irish YA writers I have met have been INCREDIBLE). I'm especially including here Louise O'Neill, Sarah Webb, Sam Blake, O. R. Melling, Cynthia Murphy, Ellen Ryan, Kimberly Engebrigtsen, Olivia Hope, Jenny Ireland, Francesca McDonnell Capossela, Alison Weatherby, Sinead O'Hart, Eoin Colfer, Kathryn Foxfield,

Joseph F. Murray, Polly Crosby, Shelly Mack, Brianna Bourne, Eve Mc Donnell, Adam Connors, Lizzy Dent and Virginia L. Evans. Also, all the team at #DiscoverIrishYa (especially Lori Moriarty and Aislinn O Loughlin); and from my Trinity creative writing time – Eoin McNamee, Carlo Gébler, Claire Keegan, Kevin Power (and all the rest of the M.Phil. crew at the Oscar Wilde Centre).

In addition, thank you to all the other writers I met at the writing group run by Simone Schuemmelfeder at the Irish Writers Centre for the positive encouragement when I was starting out. (Kind words, early on, make all the difference, and there really is magic in creative writing groups.)

My thanks to all at team Gill Hess. Particularly Declan Heeney – I have loved meeting the fantastic booksellers you introduced me to. Also, I've met some brilliant librarians, school librarians, event organizers, booksellers and journalists this past year. Plus, super bloggers and influencers who've become like virtual best friends during this process (including @all.books.and.some.tea, @BotsBookShelf, @here.andbackagain, @stleoscollegelibrary and the @triedmammiesbookclub – I can't wait to hear what you make of this instalment). I am so grateful to ALL of you for being part of this journey. I would also like to thank the team at Eason's Ireland (for supporting my first book and hosting the launch) and Waterstones, Halfway Up The Stairs and Chapters bookstores (for generally being awesome).

Also … a few people who reviewed my first book, *A Game Of Life or Death*, talked about how the book (among other things) didn't shy away from grief. Those comments, which were heartfelt and lovely, made me think more about life beyond the story world. Those of you who know me, know that loss and I are very well acquainted; in fact, we are far too familiar with each other. No one's life is perfect. How we choose to deal with that is different for everyone. For me, I write to make sense of the world around me and how I feel. For others, it can be something else, but – regardless of which path you take – talking can help. If you need help processing, please consider talking to a friend or someone you trust (or reaching out to a helpline). You're not in this alone. At some point or another, all of us have felt like outsiders looking in, unable to see the path ahead. One person can make a difference.

Finally, to you, dear reader: "thank you" isn't a strong enough phrase for how indebted I am. For those of you who also posted, dressed up as characters from, and sent me comments about the world of Asha, Dark, Augie, Ruby and Josh. I can't put into words how much that meant. I appreciate your support and am so thankful to you for being part of this amazing, crazy, exciting publication journey. It's been the most insane roller coaster and the steepest learning curve of my life. And there is more to come, so let's be friends?

You can find me on Instagram @Triona_Campbell